G000055620

Amanda Boulter is a lecturer in English at a Higher Education College. She lives with her partner and their two sons in Dorset.

Back Around the Houses follows the lives and loves of the inhabitants of Madrigal Close and the Cosmic Café introduced in her first novel, *Around the Houses*, published by Serpent's Tail in 2002.

Also by Amanda Boulter and published by Serpent's Tail

Around the Houses

'Amanda Boulter has written a funny, telling urban tale about a neighbourhood where different identities, sexualities and communities generate conflict, humour and wacky situations in equal measure. But this absorbing first novel is a hymn to freedom. And you believe in the humour and the energy because Boulter doesn't shirk the realities of prejudice and violence. These are tales of the city to make you shake, weep and giggle out loud. I'm already looking forward to the next one' Patricia Duncker

'*Around the Houses* is packed with unforgettable characters, chaotic incidents and a delightfully wicked revenge scene as a climax. *Around the Houses* is a delicious urban fable *de nos jours*' Attitude

'A compulsive read' *Time Out*

'A promising taste of what is to come, and we can look forward to a series of further adventures on the Close' *Diva*

'A funny, light-hearted novel' *Leeds Guide*

'Amanda Boulter serves up a straightforward sitcom in which almost all the expected archetypes appear and interact with a suitable degree of mischief and mayhem. A light-hearted romp through modern urban life' *Gay Times*

Back Around the Houses

Amanda Boulter

Library of Congress Catalog Card Number: 2003105258

A complete catalogue record for this book can be
obtained from the British Library on request

The right of Amanda Boulter to be identified as the
author of this work has been asserted by her in
accordance with the Copyright, Designs and Patents Act 1988

Copyright © 2003 by Amanda Boulter

First published in 2003 by Serpent's Tail,
4 Blackstock Mews, London N4 2BT
website: www.serpentstail.com

Printed by Mackays of Chatham, plc
10 9 8 7 6 5 4 3 2 1

For Ruth, Isaac and Sam – once again

ACKNOWLEDGEMENTS

I'd like to thank Andy Melrose for his advice on the final manuscript and Ruth Gilbert for being an inspiration from the beginning.

Chapter 1

The Retreat

Naked and shivering in the early morning light, Gordon Gates knelt awkwardly on the damp grass. He was not used to prostrating himself in fields. And despite the urgings of his counsellor, he had no desire to 'get close and personal' with Nature. He knew from experience that Nature, like himself, looked distinctly better when dressed and viewed from a distance. And it did not surprise him that the pastoral idyll he had glimpsed through the window of Keith Smedley's Rover when they arrived at The Mountain Retreat last week, had turned out, on closer and bare-footed inspection, to be twitching with invertebrate life.

On either side of him, men his own age in similar states of undress and mid-life crisis were bending forward, backsides in the air, kissing the grass. It was one of the ugliest sights Gordon had ever witnessed. And being forced to watch the flabby embarrassment of his fellow men did nothing to alleviate his own self-consciousness. He searched the sodden vegetation in front of him for slugs, cupped his dangling penis in one hand and lowered his face to the ground. Only Keith could have persuaded him to make such an arse of himself. Or not even Keith as such, but the guilt that flashed through Gordon's mind every time he looked at him. Keith Smedley, golfing legend of Frinley-on-Sea, was his closest friend. But Gordon was closer still to Pam, Keith's wife. Their clandestine adultery had lasted for more than fifteen years and, even after Gordon's wife Pearl had found out about the affair, he still revelled in the gutters of Pam's desire. When Pearl discovered the real foreplay on his golfing weekends, she had walked out. She hadn't said a word, not even to Keith. He was still totally unaware that his wife was the nineteenth hole. Gordon stared at his friend's bald white backside with the infinite pity he normally reserved for himself.

The irony of the whole affair was that the dowagers of Frinley were firmly of the opinion that Gordon was the injured party in the Gates's marital demise. If he so much as strolled down the High Street he was showered with sympathy. They all knew about his mouthy and menopausal wife who had finally lost her mind, abandoned husband and daughter, and gone to live in a dippy-hippy, wacky-backy commune in London. Gordon dug his fingers into the mud remembering the indignity of Pearl's defection to the Cosmic Café. She had left him with the golfing crowd, the life in Frinley. She didn't even tell their daughter Shirley about his affair with Pam. And he was still reeling from the shock. Pearl was someone else now, a stranger, a bohemian. And while he hated her and her new life and the humiliation she'd steeped upon him, Gordon found himself loving Pearl again for the first time in years.

Keith had tried to persuade Gordon that The Mountain Retreat would help him through the emotional aftermath of marital breakdown. Gordon, of course, had scoffed in derision. But Keith persisted. He faxed the brochure to Gordon's office. Gordon responded, as any man would, by faxing back por-nography to Keith's accountancy firm. But Keith was desperate. He quoted letters from satisfied customers. 'My world was as grey as my suit,' he announced when Gordon was putting a tricky ball on the seventh green, 'but your course made it a rainbow.' It was this action, this riding roughshod over the protocols of the great game, that finally alerted Gordon to the facts of the matter. Keith wanted to go.

Gordon had two choices. He could pretend not to have realised the true nature of the situation or he could have a laugh about it with the boys in the clubhouse. The third possibility, that he could talk to Keith, was not one that occurred to Gordon. Even when Keith, teeing off at the thirteenth, admitted that he was using Gordon as a cover to stop Pam asking questions, Gordon still felt no urge to discuss it. Keith didn't say why he wanted to go. Gordon didn't ask. It was as simple as that. Gordon loved Keith like a brother. He thought of him as subbing for his older brother Charles, whom he had loved and lost ten years before. But a level of restraint was necessary if a friendship was to last, as theirs had, for more than thirty years. Even more so when for fifteen of them Gordon had been bedding Keith's wife.

Ultimately it was the thought of his adultery with Pam that spurred Gordon to Samaritan action. He could have been churlish, an attitude he had perfected during his married life, but how could he refuse his cuckold friend? And so here he was on the retreat, lips kissing the ground, bottom bouncing in the air, target practice for any passing pigeon.

'Good morning gentlemen!'

A man in his mid-forties was standing stark naked and hairy in front of them. It was Neil, the group's counsellor. He'd been working with them for the past week: sitting around campfires with his guitar, singing songs from the past, hiking though the forest, camping on the beach. Gordon had found the first few days quite exhilarating, despite the discomfort of the dig-your-own toilet. Almost boy-scoutish.

It was the endless talking he objected to. Grown men sitting around in shorts whittering on about their mothers. Neckless Norman from Bromley crying about the bully at school. Roger the Todger from Nottingham still trying to find the father who had walked out fifty years before. It seemed that Gordon was the only one with the sense to tell Roger that the man was probably dead. But then yesterday, to his eternal shame, Gordon had found himself weeping in Neil's swimming pool therapy session on loss and bereavement.

He'd had no intention of confessing his feelings. Every time the talking stick came his way he simply kicked up spray and passed it on. But Neil kept floating the damned thing back to him. Eventually he was forced to dredge up some story just to keep them all happy. He considered telling them that he missed his brother Charles, that he'd admired him when they were young, and been shattered by the events of ten years before. But he didn't want to go into that. So he told them, in the blandest fashion, that his wife Pearl had left him, that he still loved her and his daughter, and he wanted his family back. Then he found that his eyes were filling with tears, his throat was contracting, and he was unable to speak.

Of course they'd all been very good about it. Lapped it up in fact. Especially Neil. Granite Gordon had finally cracked and Neil's relief was palpable. He'd been the only survivor, clutching to the jetsam of decency. And now, Gordon thought, like the rest of them, he had sunk into the sea of self-indulgence.

Gordon judged the group's nakedness that final morning to be wholly apt, a sign of their communal loss of self-respect throughout the week. With his privates snug and protected in his palm, he balanced on one elbow and raised his head to glance at Neil. Their leader was standing legs akimbo and hung like a donkey in front of them. It was another weighty nail in the coffin of Gordon's self-esteem. He squinted, trying to cheer himself up by making Neil's excessive chest and arm hair blur into a fake fur coat. Neil spotted him staring, watery-eyed, and smiled supportively. Gordon looked away. He had played truant from Neil's one-on-one deep learning session the night before.

'Well gentlemen, it's our last morning together and we are truly back to basics!'

Neil was trying to look natural. Attempting the kind of affable casualness that made Gordon think of the vicar having Sunday lunch in his local. He smiled down at them, shifting his naked weight from foot to foot. His hand wiggled aimlessly by his thigh as if jangling change in an invisible trouser pocket.

'I know you men find this hard. No camouflage, no clothes for disguise. It *is* hard. Damned hard. But,' he paused for emphasis, 'we must bare ourselves, if—' another pause, more emphasis, 'if we are to know ourselves as men.' He surveyed them with admiration, arms outstretched. 'We are here, this band of brothers, warriors in the modern world.'

Gordon looked at the motley backsides of the warriors crouched in front of him. He didn't rate their chances.

'Warriors with the animal souls of men. The mortgage won't feed that soul. Credit cards won't feed that soul. Our animal souls are caged in offices, cars, factories. That's not living. You men must leave here and live.

Love is living.
Need is living.
Pain is living.

Shopping is not living.
Watching TV is not living.
Driving in the rush hour is not living.

Accept your pain.
Accept your needs.
Accept your love.
And live.'

There was a round of applause from the newly living among them. Gordon, bowing to peer pressure, clapped weakly.

Then Neil beckoned to Keith, who got up from his knees, skirted around Roger's tight pink torso, and stood beside Neil at the front. Neil put his fatherly arm around Keith's older shoulders. 'You might have fifty years to live or, like Keith here, you might have only fifty days. It's not the time you live, it's how you live your time. This is the message. Okay, Keith.'

Together Keith and Neil recited the group's liturgy.

'*Feel your animal soul.*
Feed your animal soul.
Free your animal soul.'

Neil clasped Keith to him in a bear hug before holding him out at arms' length and smiling at him proudly. Keith was nodding vigorously, tears rolling down his haggard face. The other men were brushing grass off their knees, heaving themselves up and gathering around Keith. They shook him by the hand and slapped him on the back. Only Gordon stayed where he was, the words 'fifty days' still rattling in his mind. The naked truth was there in front of him. Keith was dying. His best friend had fifty days to live. As the words sank in Gordon gradually realised what they meant. In fifty days Pam, Keith's wife, would become a widow. A widow with twelve-year-old twins and a set of demands. A widow who was no longer fun on the fairway.

Gordon was in trouble. If he was going to save his marriage and get Pearl back, he had fifty days to do it. Before the shit really hit the fan.

Chapter 2

Impractical Parenting

'Are you the one?'

Andy Costello opened his eyes. He thought he could hear a voice, but as he was lying face down on a sun bed, wearing nothing but his Paul Smith swimmers, he ignored it.

'Are you him?' It was the same rasping whisper. He lifted his head and glanced around the garden, squinting in the August sunlight. Nobody. The garden was a narrow strip of weed-filled crazy paving and unkempt lawn squeezed into the gap between houses. It was empty. Anna and Cass had just gone into the house; Anna changing baby Florrie, Cass making more drinks. He reached under the sun bed for the Ambre Solaire and sat up, easing one leg into the air to adjust the elastic round his crotch and have a quick check on his tan line. Then he saw her. A pale and craggy face staring at him through a bald patch in the hedge. He snapped his elastic, dropped the sun oil and swore as a stain the size of Wales spread across his new black swimmers. Ida Prestwick, Anna and Cass's strange and sinister neighbour, was watching him through the hedge, scrutinising his every move. She forced her hand through the privet leaves and pointed a finger at him.

'Are you anything to do with that baby of Anna's?'

'What!' Andy swung his legs off the sun bed and wrapped a towel around his greasy patch.

'You heard me.'

'Of course I heard you, you silly woman. You half scared me to death.' He stood up, backing away from the hedge towards the house. 'What are you doing staring at people like that?'

'I know you're the one. You need to do something about her.'

'I don't know what you're talking about,' he said, glancing at Cass as she came out of the house with a tray of Pimms. He scurried behind her, flapping his arms toward the hedge and hissing in her ear. 'It's the mad woman.'

Cass strolled across the crazy paving and looked through the leafless hole in the privet. 'Ida, will you please get your face out of our hedge and stop harassing our friends.' Ida harrumphed and grudgingly disappeared into her own garden. Andy tiptoed back across the patio and perched on the very edge of his sun bed, avoiding the oil spill. Cass gave him a glass.

'Oh my God, Cass, I swear that woman gets more creepy by the day. Look at the state of my swimmers.' He pointed to his pelvis to show her the stain.

'That scared, eh?'

'I didn't pee myself.'

Cass raised her eyebrows. 'I see. I didn't realise Ida was your type.'

'Less of it, funny girl. It's oil. I only bought these yesterday and now they're ruined.' He fished out the mint and cucumber floating on the top of his glass and dropped it in a soggy heap on the patio. 'Look at me, my hands are still shaking.'

'We don't call her Doris Karloff for nothing,' said Cass, laughing.

'But doesn't she give you the creeps? I mean, first she's barbecuing your bin bags, now she's spying through the hedge.' Andy drained his glass and stood up. 'I don't know how you can live here with her next door.'

'That's not the worst of it,' said Cass, kicking pink flip-flops off her brown feet. 'Doris has got it into her head that Anna should give baby Florrie away to a deserving home.'

'You're joking!'

'I'm not.' She eased herself down onto her sun bed. 'She thinks this is the wrong house for a baby. She told Anna to take Florrie to live across the road with Greg.'

'What is that woman on? I hope Anna told her to fuck off.'

'You know Anna, she's polite to the death.' Cass sipped at her drink. 'She's just hoping Doris will die soon.'

Andy placed his towel over the greasy bit of the sun bed. 'What about the husband?' '

'Boris? Weird and pervy. We want him to die too, but not as much.' She laid out flat and closed her eyes.

'If the Karloffs died I could move in next door.'

'That'd be fab! Let's kill them tonight.'

Andy lowered himself onto the towel. 'Which do you want? Candlestick or lead piping?'

'Revolver. I wouldn't want to get too close.'

'Good point.' He lay down, sinking into the saggy fabric of the old sun bed as it pulled tight around his weight. 'And we could bury them in these things. This material's so slack my bum's scraping the concrete.'

'Enjoy it while you can.'

'Sweetie, I'm so wedged in I've lost the movement of my arms. This isn't a sun bed, it's a canvas coffin.'

'I thought you liked retro.'

'There's retro, Cass, and then there's just plain hideous. Look at me, I'm trying for sun-kissed god and you put me on pink paisley. I feel like a lobster on a bed of prawns.'

Cass laughed, 'You said it!' She was trying to take off her skinny T-shirt without sitting up. She'd pulled it over her head, but it had got caught on one of her many earrings, and she was struggling to wrestle it free. When she eventually got it off, her cropped pink hair was sticking up in sweaty spikes around her ears.

'Ah, the grace and glamour of topless bathing,' said Andy, leaning up on his elbow and watching her. 'We could be on the French Riviera.' Cass flung her arm out to hit him.

'What a lovely family scene!' said Anna, coming out of the house with baby Florrie. 'Nudity, camp fantasy and domestic violence.'

Cass smiled, holding her arms out. 'Come and give Mama Cass a kiss, sweetheart!' Anna plonked the baby down on Cass's belly and she doubled up. 'Ugh! She's all cold and slimy! How much sun cream did you put on her?'

'It's supposed to be thick.'

'Thick?' Andy held out his hands to take the baby. 'It looks like you've dipped the poor child in mayonnaise.'

'Listen, you two, if you're such bloody experts you can do it next time.'

'We're only teasing,' said Cass, wiping her hands on Andy's towel and patting the sun bed next to her. 'Come on, have a drink and show us your stretch marks.'

Florrie giggled, wriggling and kicking in the air above Andy's head. He ducked away from her feet. 'Is all this energy normal at six months or are you two teaching this child martial arts?'

'I think Cass is giving her lessons,' said Anna sitting on the sun bed and reaching out to smooth Cass's wayward hair.

'Yeah, she's practising *tae kwon do* on her Tony doll.'

'Cass!' Anna slapped her head.

Andy smiled coldly. 'I happen to love that man, Cass.'

'It was a joke!' Cass raised her arms in exasperation. 'God, you two are so touchy. Anyway, Andy, why isn't Tony here?'

'Is he welcome when babies are being trained to attack him?'

Cass laughed, lying back down. 'Do you think Florrie would give him a kicking?'

Anna stared sharply at Cass. 'Of course Tony's welcome, Andy. He's part of our family.'

'He is, isn't he!' said Andy. 'Almost another parent.' He looked to Cass for reassurance but she had her eyes closed.

The front doorbell rang through the house and Anna pushed Cass's leg with her foot. 'You can get that since you're in such a mood.'

Cass pulled her T-shirt on, grumbling. 'It was a joke! Can't I even make a joke?'

'Maybe that's Tony now, Andy,' said Anna.

Andy shook his head. 'He's working at the restaurant.' He glanced at the hedge. 'What if it's Doris?'

'It won't be her, you camp chicken!' said Cass. 'She never comes round the front now she's cut herself a porthole in the hedge. It's probably Ruby; she said she might pop round.'

As soon as Cass had gone Ida Prestwick's face reappeared in the gap in the hedge. 'Anna! That baby shouldn't be in this garden.'

Anna groaned to Andy. 'Here we go again! At home with the Karloffs.'

'Did you hear me, Anna? That baby shouldn't be out here.'

Andy hid behind Florrie, who was sitting on his chest, and Anna sat up.

'She's fine, Ida.'

'Who's he?' Ida nodded in Andy's direction. 'Is he the father?'

'Yes, he is.'

'Thought so! I've seen him here before. I suppose he'll be moving in then.'

Andy muttered behind Florrie. 'Not bloody likely with you next door!'

'What?'

'He says he's not moving in.'

'Humph! They'll be moving in across the road. All those students again.'

'That won't be for a month or so.'

'Humph!' Ida stood there with just her face visible through the hedge, looking them up and down. 'They're like you. They don't know about Madrigal Close.'

'No. Bye then, Ida, we'd like to sunbathe now, please.' Anna lay down, but Ida didn't move.

'Is the other girl leaving? I'm surprised she's stopped here so long with someone else's baby.'

There was a muffled shuffling inside the house and Cass struggled out of the backdoor carrying an inflated plastic paddling pool. She leant it against the wall.

'If you're talking about me, Ida, you should know that Florrie is my baby too.'

'What? What d'you mean by that?'

Behind Ida, Anna was shaking her head, trying to stop Cass from outing them as lesbian parents. Cass paused, watching her plead. She hated the way Anna forced their family into the closet. 'I mean I love her like a daughter,' she said grimly. 'And now, Ida, if you don't mind, we're entertaining guests. Goodbye.' Ida grunted but didn't move.

Andy was still hiding behind Florrie. 'Where did that come from?' he asked, pointing her at the paddling pool.

'Ruby got it for Florrie. And she's got us a hose to fill it up.'

'It's fantastic. So where is she?'

'I told her we were having a spot of hedge trouble and she said she'd sort it. She's gone across the road to hers for something, wouldn't tell me what. She's coming now.'

They could all hear scraping and muttered obscenities as Ruby tried to get something big through the front door and down the narrow hallway. Then she emerged onto the patio, beaming, in a beaded sarong. She was carrying the embroidered silk screen from her bedroom.

'Ruby, what are you doing with that?'

'Hi, darlings! Cass said you were being Karloffed.' Ruby walked over to the bald patch in the hedge and stared through.

'Sorry, Ida, I heard there was an ugly view through here, so I've brought something nicer for us to look at. Bye, bye!'

'Ruby!' Anna choked on her drink and Ruby took her glass. 'What?' She took a swig.

'Anna thinks you're mean,' Cass said, as she went inside to get Ruby a drink.

'Mean? Mean be buggered.' Ruby gave Anna her glass back. 'Old Doris Karloff doesn't mind. She can still listen to every word through that screen, and now she's got something extra to bitch about with Boris. They can chew me over in bed tonight. Give them something to do.' She took the drink Cass was offering her. 'I just hope some bloody pigeon doesn't shit on it. Anyway, where's my little Flo?' She put her glass down. 'Come here, sweetheart, it's Auntie Ruby, your soon-to-be-Goddess-Mother.' She kissed Florence once and gave her straight back to Andy. 'And now I need a cigarette.'

'Goddess-Mother, I like it,' said Cass, picking up the paddling pool.

'Thought you would. Greg suggested it last night. He thinks we should be Goddess-Parents. You know how he goes for all that eco-clap-trap. It's not really me, though. I was more of a God-forsaken mother when I woke up this morning.' She lit up and sat down feebly on the edge of Cass's sun bed.

Cass edged past her with the paddling pool and laid it on the grass. 'So come on then, Ruby, dish the dirt while I fill this up. What was it like having dinner with the students?'

Ruby shrugged. 'Who knows? I was so wasted the whole evening's a blur.'

'You must have some gossip.'

'Who was there?' asked Anna.

Ruby waved her cigarette. 'Me and Johnnie, Greg with little Shirley, and the other two. Oh, yes, that's what happened. They all want to move out. All four of them.'

'That's news to me,' said Andy. He was the letting agent for the house. 'I've only had notice from two. I thought Johnnie and Shirley were staying on.'

'Oh, Ruby,' said Anna, 'you've not split up with Johnnie again, have you?'

'Ruby!' said Cass, as she came out of the kitchen, pulling the dripping hose across the patio.

'Calm down, girls! It's nothing like that. A few things got said last night, that's all, and I might have been a bit . . . well—' she traced the Paisley pattern of Andy's sun bed with her finger, 'indiscreet.' She glanced at Anna. 'Don't look at me like that. Somebody had to keep the bloody conversation going.'

'What have you done?'

Ruby slipped off her sandals and walked over to the paddling pool, stepping into it. 'Nothing, Anna. I simply asked little Shirley something about her father, the Grey Gordon.'

'Which was?'

'Which was well and truly bloody coming to her. She kept moaning on about him, going on and on about "Dad being so brave about the divorce" and "Dad going away for therapy".' Ruby dragged on her cigarette.

'What did you say, Ruby?' asked Cass, filling the pool.

'It was nothing. I was just making conversation!'

'Ruby!' Cass sprayed her with the hose.

'All right!' Ruby dropped her sodden cigarette and scrambled out of the pool. 'I just asked if darling Daddy was still fucking Mummy's friends.'

Andy laughed. 'Oh, is that all?'

'You didn't!' Anna was appalled.

'I couldn't help it. The way she was going on. It's time that girl knew the truth. Her mother should have told her ages ago.'

Cass nodded. 'I agree. I don't know why Pearl keeps protecting the wanker.'

'That's not the point, Cass. Pearl didn't want Shirley to know.' Anna turned on Ruby. 'Even Greg's kept his mouth shut on this, and he's been *sleeping* with Shirley.'

Ruby shrugged. 'He's probably forgotten. You know what Greg's like. He can only keep nice things in his head.'

'Unlike your sewer brain!' said Cass, picking Ruby's cigarette out of the water. 'So what did Shirley say?'

'Not a lot. She ran off.' Ruby suppressed a smile. 'Crying.'

Anna was exasperated. 'Oh, Ruby!'

Ruby laughed. 'Don't get all righteous on me. I think I've done them all a favour. Johnnie says Shirley's moving in with her mum now.'

'That doesn't mean you were right to interfere.'

'Yeah, yeah!' Ruby walked back to the patio for her bag. 'I have got more news, but if you're all so bloody sensitive, I won't bother.'

Anna took Florrie from Andy. 'Go on.'

'Well, it's not really news.' Ruby pulled out her cigarettes and lit a fresh one. 'More of a dilemma.'

'About?'

'Johnnie. He wants to move in with me.'

'Oh sweetie, that's wonderful.' Andy raised his empty glass.

'Is it?' Ruby strolled back to the paddling pool and Anna followed, sitting on the grass. She held Florrie in the air, then dipped her feet in the water and kissed her on the belly. 'Of course it is. It'll be good for you.'

'What do you mean "good for you"?' Ruby stepped into the water.

'To live with someone else.'

'Are you implying that I'm selfish?'

'No,' Anna turned to the others for support. 'I just think you might be a bit set in your ways.'

Ruby laughed. 'Of course I'm set in my ways; I'm a selfish cow and I enjoy it. I've worked on it for years.'

'You're not, Ruby, don't say—'

Ruby interrupted, 'I don't know why he's so set on the idea.' She paced back to the patio leaving dark footprints on the multi-coloured slabs. 'Andy, do you think he's a masochist – or maybe even a sadist?'

'Could be, sweetie. Does he do exotic things with cutlery?'

'He wants to be with you, Ruby,' said Anna. 'What's wrong with that?'

Ruby raised her eyebrows. 'Have you read any Freud?'

'Surely you're not worried about his age? So what if you're old enough to be his mother?'

Ruby sat back on a sun bed and closed her eyes. 'Thank you, Anna, your profound words are a great comfort.'

'I mean what matters is that he loves you. And you love him.'

'Do I? I wonder if I'm capable.'

'Of course you are! Cass, Andy, doesn't Ruby love Johnnie?'

'Anna,' said Ruby, without opening her eyes. 'You don't need to resolve my love life by committee. I know my limitations.'

Anna persisted. 'But everyone can see that you're perfect together.'

Ruby sat up, and lifted her sunglasses. 'Anna, you know how much I love you, so don't take this the wrong way. But your backside is so firmly wedged in the closet door that you, of all people, must know that what everyone can see is what we choose to show them.'

Chapter 3

The New Cosmic Café

Cass weaved her bike through the stagnant traffic inching its way up Balham High Street and swung onto the pavement, pulling down her mask to breathe the morning air. There was something about the smell of hot London streets that got her every time. It was a particular kind of grime, rotten mangoes trodden into fruit market cobbles, petrol fumes plastered onto buildings and faces, the reek of perfumed sweat and pigeon shit. She stood on one pedal and wheeled up to the café, skidding around a muttering old man in a trilby hat and a group of teenage girls giggling into their mobiles.

The New Cosmic Café, with its brightly-coloured windows, sat between the bland facades of the hardware shop and the newsagent's on either side like a flamboyant relative no one had invited. Cass peered through a gap in the mess of purple clouds and supernovae painted on the glass. The café was busy. Buzz and Jasbinder were behind the counter looking hot and hassled. They made an odd team, Buzz in his forties, stubbled, pale and wiry with a newly-grown greying mohican, and Jasbinder not much taller than his elbows, in her early twenties, with deep brown skin and straight black hair cut sharply into her neck.

Beyond the queues at the counter, three steps led down to clusters of people sitting on mismatched chairs, drinking coffee and eating off second-hand tables. The café was a throw-back. An old-fashioned cooperative with a shabby integrity. It had started in the late-1980s when a group of political marginals had combined their overdrafts and found a near-derelict building with a twenty-five-year lease. In the twelve or so years that the café had been going, those original people had moved on and Cass was the only one who remembered them now. But the café was still a collective, run on the principles of shared work, shared profit and endless meetings. And the walls were still orange, and the purple ceiling was still painted with stars. Even more surprisingly, business was booming. The very earnestness of a cooperatively-run café, the naff nostalgia of its name, The Cosmic, had become sort of retro-style statements. People who would have laughed at it a year ago were flocking through the doors.

Cass stuck her tongue out at the designer shirts and smiled at her reflection. She was wearing a black crop top and combats and her latest piercing gleamed in her mouth. She was late for work, but the sun was shining, her tongue had stopped throb-bing, and she was happy. Time to go inside. She free-wheeled her bike around the building, kicked open the narrow gate that led to the back of the café and locked her bike to the bars over the basement window. Two storeys above her, Dee leant out of the open kitchen window, her breasts filling most of the frame. 'I thought I heard those bins banging.' She pushed a loose braid of black hair back into the scarlet band on her head. 'You're late.'

Cass grinned. 'Don't have a go at me. I've got something to show you.' She stood back and stuck her tongue out as far as it would go.

Dee was unimpressed. 'Why you showing me your tongue?'

'Can't you see?' Cass stuck it out again. 'I've had it pierced.'

'You expect me to see that nonsense from here?' She tutted, shaking her head.

Cass smiled defiantly. 'Great, isn't it?'

'Riveting.' Dee looked behind her into the kitchen, then, smiling, leaned out further. 'I got some news for you too. Pearl's got her lady friend here again.'

Cass moaned. 'Oh, not bloody Charlene.'

'Uh huh.'

Two weeks ago Charlene had wandered into the café in a full-length red leather coat and fishnets looking like Bette Midler on steroids. Buzz was on counter duty and had refused to serve her. So Pearl had intervened and given Buzz a right talking to. She had told him that even though she and him had never seen eye-to-eye (an unfortunate choice of words considering one of Buzz's eyes wandered in all directions, a result of being hit by a brick in his more revolutionary days), she never expected him to be prejudiced. And then she had told anyone within earshot that it took more than seeing a man in a dress to shock her. But Pearl had got it wrong. Buzz had refused service, not because Charlene was very obviously a man in stilettos, but because of the coat. Buzz was a fully canvas-shod, string-belted vegan and to him full-length red leather with fur cuffs was the sartorial equivalent of goose-stepping through the door and shouting 'Zieg Heil'.

In fact, in spite of her proclamations to the contrary, Pearl was the only member of the collective who really was shocked by Charlene. Jasbinder, who dedicated herself to rescuing monkeys with electrodes in their heads, agreed with Buzz: she was more interested in the coat. Dee's worldview on the other hand was so steeped in irony that Charlene's ethical ineptness and gender incongruity complemented it perfectly. And Cass wasn't so much shocked by Charlene as outraged. She'd seen what she considered to be his particular brand of transvestite misogyny before and she hated him on sight. To her, he was a sexist who thought women were painted puppets. And the only difference she could see between him and any other chauvinist was that he walked around like a pathetic parody of his own sexist fantasy. She had no sympathy.

Cass stared up at Dee, sheltering her eyes from the shaft of sunlight cutting through the Victorian buildings surrounding her. 'I didn't see them in the café.'

Dee pointed a finger meaningfully towards the sky.

It took Cass a second to grasp what she meant. 'They're upstairs? What, in the flat?' Cass stepped back and looked up to Pearl's window. The curtains were closed and the light was on but Cass was sure she could make out Charlene's silhouette against the drapes. 'What d'you think's going on up there, Dee? Must be something if the curtains are closed.' She looked back to the kitchen window but Dee had already disappeared.

Cass let herself in through the back door. It opened into the stairwell behind the café, and before Cass went up to the kitchen, she opened the café door to see who was in. No one she knew. She waved at Buzz behind the counter. He was playing the new CD by the Tooting Hottentots. The Tots were mates of his, and their abrasive home-produced CD was one of his local promotions. She stepped back, pulling the door, and Buzz held up an empty salad bowl. She nodded, noticing that most of the dishes had been rubbed off the psychedelic menu-boards on the walls above his head. Then she ran up the wooden stairs two at a time, pausing at the kitchen, but tempted to go on up to Pearl's flat. Before Pearl had moved in, the top floor had been empty, used for people passing through who needed somewhere to crash. Now, after having left her husband Gordon, Pearl was busy converting the rooms into a flat, bringing a touch of suburban chic to squattersville.

In the kitchen, Dee was standing at the hob with her back to the door. She was wearing a dingy apron over a bright purple caftan and stirring a mammoth pot of chilli. Cass grabbed a tray of lettuces from the storeroom and tipped them into an empty sink. 'Buzz needs more salad.'

Dee stopped stirring. 'Again? Don't these rich people eat nothing else? We should put the price up.'

Cass turned the tap on and grabbed herself an apron. 'That would only encourage them.'

'Put it down then. Put them all down. Too many damned people coming here anyway. I ain't working here to look after them.' Dee came over to the other sink and Cass smiled at her belligerence. 'So if I said I wanted to go off for five minutes to look in on Pearl you'd say—'

'No fucking way!'

'Thought so.' They worked next to each other in silence, Cass washing lollo rosso, Dee rinsing brown rice for the chilli. The kitchen was a high-ceilinged square room with bare white walls and a chequerboard floor. A large, metal-topped counter stood in the middle.

'Pearl said she's giving Charlene the natural look,' said Dee swilling the rice, grinning.

Cass glanced up from the lettuce at the copper-coloured engraving of an eighteenth-century pig hanging above the sinks. When Pearl had joined the collective six months before she had added several such homely touches which for some inexplicable reason no one had taken down.

'Why's she bothering with him? I'm worried about her, Dee. I mean think about it, until last week, had you ever set eyes on this Charlene character?'

'Nope.'

'That's what I mean. A six-foot transvestite in a red leather coat. Even I'd notice him in Woolworths.' Dee started singing 'He's the lady in red' but Cass wasn't listening. 'I mean he just turns up out of nowhere and bang he's in Pearl's bedroom.' She drowned another lettuce. 'Pearl's vulnerable, Dee. For all we know, this Charlene bloke could be a fucking psycho. We could be standing here washing lettuce while he's cutting Pearl's head off!'

Dee bellowed with laughter.

'It's not funny, Dee. You know what I'm saying. I just want to check upstairs to make sure she's okay.'

Dee wiped her eyes. 'Will it shut you up?'

'I won't say another word all day.'

'Don't be no longer than five minutes.' Cass had dried her hands and was already out of the door. Dee shouted after her. 'Or I'm coming up.'

Cass dashed up stairs and knocked on the new plywood door at the top. She could hear Carole King's *Tapestry* playing inside but Pearl didn't answer the door. She knocked again, wondering whether 'You've Got a Friend' could trigger a psychotic episode. She was about to run down the stairs for Dee when she heard Pearl giggle behind the door. She opened it just enough to poke her head out, but Cass could see she was half undressed.

'Cass, what are you doing up here?' said Pearl. 'Has something happened in the café?'

Cass shook her head. 'No, it's fine. I mean, I just . . . I wanted to make sure you were all right.'

Pearl looked nonplussed. 'Me? Why, what's wrong with me?'

'Nothing,' Cass tried to look past Pearl into the flat. 'I just wondered if Charlene was with you?'

'Why? Do you want her?'

'No.' Cass gestured to Pearl's state of undress. 'It's just you didn't look like you had company.'

'Oh, I know,' said Pearl, hiding herself more effectively behind the door. 'We're like two teenage girls, aren't we, running around in bras and panties?'

'Well, you might be,' said Cass. 'But Charlene's got a way to go.'

'Meaning?'

'Oh, come on, Pearl. Charlene's a bloke'

'I see. So that's what this is all about.' Pearl glanced behind her into the flat and slipped out onto the landing. She pulled the door almost closed behind her and stood there in her bra and petticoat, whispering fiercely. 'I'm surprised at you, Cass, what with your lesbianity and everything, I would have thought you might have a bit of sympathy.'

Cass whispered back. 'What with? Some guy who dresses

up like a porno fantasy? Come on, Pearl, he's a complete stranger with a fetish for leather. And now he's got you alone in that flat. Doesn't that seem dodgy to you? For all you know he might be some kind of psycho.'

'Honestly, Cass, does Charlene look like a psycho to you?' Pearl pushed the door wide open. Cass could see Charlene perched on the edge of Pearl's leather sofa in a blond wig and pink candlewick dressing gown. He wiggled his fingers at her and smiled shyly. Cass pulled the door closed. There was something about Charlene that disturbed her, something familiar that she couldn't quite put her finger on. 'You think psychos don't wear dressing gowns? Be serious, Pearl. You don't know him from Adam.'

'Ah well, that's where you're wrong, Cass. I do know Charlene from Adam. Or should I say Eve?' She smiled and went back into the flat. 'Come on, I want to introduce you two properly.' Cass followed warily as Pearl led her into the living room. Charlene was fussing in a mock feminine voice, smoothing the lap of his dressing gown.

'Oh, look at the state of me. You'll have to excuse us, darling, Pearl was helping me with my make-up.'

'Yeah. The natural look. I heard.'

'Oh no, darling, that's not my style at all.'

Pearl had disappeared into her bedroom. Now she came out wearing a kimono and sat next to Charlene on the sofa. 'Cass thinks you're a danger to me.'

'Really?' Charlene raised her eyebrows. 'If only, darling.'

They both giggled and Pearl held Charlene's hand as she spoke. 'You're right, Cass. I have only just met Charlene. But she's no stranger. In fact, I've known about her for years.' She turned to Charlene and smiled. 'You see, Cass, Charlene, or Charles as we call him in a suit, is Gordon's brother.'

Charlene took off the long blond wig and Cass saw the resemblance immediately. Without the hair Charlene was the spitting image of Pearl's ex-husband.

'Fucking hell.' Cass laughed. She couldn't help it.

'Don't worry, dear,' said Charles, 'I've heard worse. I was so pleased when Pearl wrote to me after all those years, and invited Charlene here. We've had a lot of catching up to do.' He winked at Pearl. 'I always knew Gordon had got himself a good woman.'

Pearl blushed. 'And a good brother.'

'It was the sister he couldn't handle,' said Charles, laughing.

'So Gordon knows about Charlene?' asked Cass.

Charles nodded. Without his wig on, his manner had changed. His voice was slower and lower. He even sounded like his brother. 'He met her once in rather unfortunate circumstances. I've told Pearl about it now, of course. It happened when they were staying in Manchester with our late father. I still live there, you see. Anyway, Gordon made a rather unfortunate proposition to the back of Charlene's head one night when she was waiting for a taxi in a rather notorious part of town. Gordon and I haven't seen or spoken to each other since.'

Pearl was nodding sympathetically, still holding his hand. 'Anyway, I blame myself,' he said. 'If only I'd talked to Pearl at the time and explained things, I might have split that marriage up years ago.' He winked at Pearl and she pulled her hand away, almost screaming with laughter. Cass remained straight-faced watching them. 'Listen to the music, Pearl!' In the background Carole King was singing 'You make me feel like a natural woman'. Charles grasped both Pearl's hands in his. 'That's what you do for me, Pearl. You make me feel like a natural woman.'

'Did you hear that, Cass?' said Pearl, her voice catching with emotion. 'That's the kind of lovely thing Gordon would never say.'

'Funny that!' said Cass. She didn't like Charles any more than she liked Charlene, but he was clearly working on Pearl. There was a definite frisson between them. Cass thought she'd muddy the waters. 'Are you married, Charles?'

He broke off from his cooing over Pearl. 'I was.'

Cass tried for a joke. 'Didn't she want to share her underwear?'

He looked her straight in the eye. 'She died.'

'Oh . . . I'm . . . I'm sorry.'

'I miss her,' he said, 'but it was years ago now.' Pearl nodded sympathetically and Charles turned to her. 'Me and Charlene just haven't found the right woman since.' There was a loud knocking on the plywood door and Pearl got up to answer it, patting his hand. Charles replaced his wig.

'Oh, Mum, I'm so sorry,' said Shirley flinging her arms around her mother as she opened the door. 'I feel so terrible, all this time I blamed you for leaving Dad and thought you were being selfish and he was so unhappy and all the time he was sleeping with that woman and you didn't even tell me and I'm just here to tell you that I will move in with you like you wanted me to and I won't be horrible to you any more and I'm going to be horrible to Dad because he's a bastard who let me be horrible to you and he deserves it and I just feel so horrible, I thought you'd ruined our family but the whole time it was him who was ruining it and I don't even know what my family is any more because everything I thought about it was a lie and I just think that I don't know what to think even though I've been thinking what to say for days.'

Pearl hugged her tightly. 'Oh, Shirley, what a silly state you're in.'

'I . . . you know I love you, Mum.'

'I love you too, Shirley, you silly chump.'

'I'm just so confused.'

'Of course you are,' said Pearl soothingly. 'But never mind that now.' She put her arm around her daughter and guided her into the flat. 'Dry your eyes and come and meet Uncle Charlie.'

Shirley followed her inside. 'Uncle Charlie? But didn't Uncle Charlie die when I was ten?'

Chapter 4

Family Outings

'Look at that, Florrie!' Andy held his baby high in the air, showing her the crowds at Brighton Pride. Thousands of people were pouring into Preston Park, meandering between rows of stalls and dance tents, lying together on picnic blankets, holding hands under rainbow flags and the strings of pink bunting that waved in the air. 'These are your people.'

Cass rolled her eyes. 'God, he's off again!' She was sitting at Andy's feet, trying to open a bottle of red wine with a penknife corkscrew.

'Oh, that's nice!' said Andy looking down at her. 'I'm trying to have a meaningful moment with my child here and all I get is heckled!'

'Meaningful moment, my arse!' Cass trapped the bottle between her feet and twisted the corkscrew. 'You just love the attention.'

He smiled. 'I know. If I'd realised a baby was such a man-magnet I'd have stolen one years ago.'

'You see,' said Cass, laughing. 'It's that kind of caring, socially responsible attitude that makes you such a perfect family man.' They had come by train to Brighton for their first holiday as a gay family. Gay Pride on Saturday, paddling, picnicking and partying for the rest of the week. Originally they were planning to rent a house together, but when Tony, Andy's partner, had decided to join them it seemed better for each couple to have their own space. So now Tony and Andy were staying in an expensive room at the Grand Hotel, while Cass, Anna and Florrie were camping in a shabby but colourful tent Cass had saved from her days at Greenham Common.

It was Anna's first time in a tent and she had spent most of the night awake with her face squashed against a nappy bag. After the shouting and partying on the campsite died down (about 3am) and she'd fed Florrie, she eventually got to sleep. She woke up again at five when the temperature dropped to near freezing. Fumbling among the bags wedged around her, she had found her clothes and emptied them in a heap over her sleeping bag. Then it started to get light. A baby-grow tied around her eyes helped a little, but at ten to seven, dreaming of being buried alive, and sweating under a pile of damp, creased clothing, she jolted herself awake. After that it was a slow crawl to consciousness. She was not in the best mood.

'Hey, Anna, aren't you glad we chose Andy as the father of our child?'

Anna was rummaging through the bags looking for sun-cream. 'What? Oh yes, perfect. Andy, do you think Florrie's too much in the sun up there? I think I might put some more cream on her.' She unzipped yet another bag and dragged out nappies, baby wipes and spare clothes in search of the Factor 35.

'Don't take Florrie off him now, Anna,' said Cass. 'He's showing her the wonders of Gay Pride.' She was pouring the wine into plastic beakers and held one out for Anna. 'Relax while you've got the chance. Florrie's having a great time up there, isn't she, Andy? She's finding out about her people.' Cass glanced up at the crowd and pointed to three bald men dressed in skin-tight black leather, being pulled along on a leash. 'Look, Florrie, here come some of your people now.'

Andy held Florrie to his chest. 'Those funny men are pretending to be doggies, darling. Take no notice of Mama Cass!'

But Cass was enjoying herself. 'And look, there's a hole in the back of their trousers so you can see their bottoms poking out. Just like doggies.'

Andy covered Florrie's eyes. 'Have they no shame! That whole SM look is *so* early '90s.'

'I've found it!' Anna held up the suncream. They both ignored her. Cass was laughing and looking toward the main stage. A cloud of pink chiffon was coming towards them through the crowd. 'Ah, ha. It's the best yet. Look, Florrie, Daddy's going to show you a ten-foot trannie.'

Andy balanced Florrie on his head and looked down at Cass. 'That's it. One more word from your *Little Book of Wisecracks* and I'm going home in a sulk.'

Above him Florrie was pointing and cooing at the transvestite stilt-walker making his way through the crowds in a giant pink ball-gown. His smiling, bearded face loomed over her and Florrie waved delighted arms.

'Hello, gorgeous,' he said. 'I'm Sister Bernadette, but you can call me Bernard.' He lifted her off Andy's head and held her in his arms. 'Would you like to come for a walk with me?' He gestured to Andy. 'Come on.'

Anna's mouth dropped open. For a moment they all just stared at the pink frill of Bernard's behind as he toppled towards the fairground with their baby. Then Andy jumped up and a second later Anna sprang after him, weaving her way through the jostling crowd. Cass stayed on the blanket, laughing at them both.

Within minutes Florrie was back. Anna was carrying her over one shoulder, looking noticeably shaken. 'Can you believe that? Him just going off with her like that?' Florrie howled and reached out for Bernard, who was still chatting with Andy.

Cass smiled. 'It was fine. Florrie liked him.'

'He was a complete stranger!' said Anna, sitting down on the blanket.

'He was part of the carnival. We were hardly going to lose him in the crowd, were we?'

Anna reached for the suncream. 'But he had Florrie at least ten feet off the ground. What if he'd tripped over?'

'Then she would have been squashed under fourteen stone of pink chiffon.'

'That's not funny, Cass.'

'Relax, Anna. It didn't happen. She's fine.'

Anna squeezed suncream onto Florrie's arms. 'You think I over-reacted, don't you?'

Cass rubbed Anna's back. 'A little.'

'So you think I'm over-protective?'

Cass kissed her. 'Only sometimes. You're tired, that's all.'

'And most people wouldn't flinch when their baby was taken off by a hairy fairy on pink stilts.'

Cass laughed. 'Just wait 'til she's a teenager.'

Andy appeared half and hour later with Tony at his side. 'Look who I found skulking round the dance tent? We send him off for a programme and he forgets all about us.'

Tony flashed a defiant smile. 'I got chatting to someone—'

'In the dance tent!' said Andy. 'I mean, isn't that the perfect place for a tête-à-tête, a veritable hub of the conversational arts.'

Tony lit a cigarette. 'So you think I forgot all about you?' He pulled a rolled-up programme from his back pocket and slapped it against Andy's thigh. 'As if I ever could! Now where shall we go?' He put his arm around Andy's shoulders and offered the programme to Anna. She stuffed it into the top of the padded nappy bag. 'Can we just go to the children's area? I'd really like a bit of quiet time to feed Florrie.'

Tony frowned. 'Quiet time? Anna, this is a festival, it's party time.'

Anna was gathering the piles of bags and trying to stuff

plastic toys into the tray under the pushchair. She scraped her hair with her fingers, tying it back with an elastic band. Her eyes looked puffy and grey. 'It may be party time for you, Tony, but unless I give Florrie a good feed right now my breasts are going to burst.'

Cass shrugged. 'Well, I guess bursting breasts clinch it, Tony. Unless of course your penis will pop if you don't get to the dance tent!' She picked up Florrie and strapped her into the buggy. 'Let's go check out the kids area.' Anna started to push the buggy away from the crowd and Cass picked up the rest of the bags. She gave the heaviest one to Andy who was bending beside the buggy still trying to hold Florrie's hand. He called back over his shoulder to Tony as they moved off. 'Come on, handsome, and bring the wine.' Tony watched them go. He grabbed the bottle, poured some wine into his mouth, then pushed his cigarette down its neck and dropped it back on the grass.

The children's area was small but well-meaning: a couple of plastic slides, half a dozen hula-hoops and a space to make flags.

'Isn't this sweet.' Andy grabbed a yellow hula-hoop. 'I was always fantastic at this when I was a kid. I had my first sexual experience with a hula-hoop.'

Cass took a pink one. 'Did you have to share that with us?'

'Don't worry, my mother cut it in half when I got sinful. Watch this!' He twirled around and the hoop dropped instantly to his feet.

Cass laughed. 'Oh yes, you and a hula-hoop. Sex on legs.' She had her hoop spinning around her waist, pierced belly button flashing on every twist.

Tony applauded as he came out of the crowd. 'Bravo, Cass, very good.' He stepped into the hula-hoop lying at Andy's feet and, holding him from behind, whispered into his ear. 'Let's try to keep it up together.' Andy smiled. 'Oh, if my mother could see me now!'

Cass left them to it and went to join Anna, who was sitting at a shady table, feeding Florrie and trying to make a tissue paper rainbow flag with her free hand. 'I thought Florrie might like it on her pushchair. What do you think?' She held it up for Cass to admire. Andy called over. 'Right, shall we move on then?'

'Already?' Anna shifted Florrie to the other breast. 'We've only been here five minutes.'

Tony shrugged. 'Anna, there are tents full of sweaty men here and you're keeping us in kindergarten.'

'What about the tents full of sweaty women?' said Cass, smiling at Anna. 'Maybe me and Anna could have a dance together while you two look after Florrie for a bit?'

Tony shook his head. 'We're not here to babysit.'

Anna could see Cass's hackles rise. She dropped her gaze back to the baby to avoid the row.

'No, Tony, you're not babysitters,' said Cass. 'Andy is Florrie's father.'

'And Anna is Florrie's mother.'

'I'm her mother too!'

Tony smiled. 'So with two mothers, why do you need us to look after the baby?'

'Stop arguing, you two!' Andy held out his arms. 'We're supposed to be celebrating here. Let's just stay together and go to the market. We'll buy some nice things for each other. Remember, the family that spends together . . .' Tony turned and left the play area.

'What?' said Cass, watching Tony go, and not in the mood for Andy's platitudes. 'Come on, Andy, the family that spends together does what?'

But Andy was distracted. He threw them an apologetic look and hurried after Tony who was striding into the crowd. Anna answered for him. 'The family that spends together, Cass, are friends together.'

'Fat chance,' said Cass.

Neither Cass nor Anna spoke as they picked up the bags,

the buggy and the baby and steered them slowly through the crowds of people sprawling on the grass. The market area was packed with traders selling clothes, jewellery, candles and herbal highs while people in sequins and feathers or T-shirts and jeans wandered around the stalls. Andy and Tony were standing ahead of them near a queue of women. Anna smiled at them as they approached, trying to break the atmosphere. 'Something looks interesting over there, shall we have a look?'

Tony smiled mockingly and gestured to the stall. 'That's Delia's Dildos. But we'll wait if you want to join the queue.'

'No thanks.' Anna blushed and steered the buggy round the other way but Cass was staring at Tony.

'I'll queue,' she said. 'I'd like a dildo.'

Anna thumped her as she passed. 'Leave it, Cass! Let's go.'

'Hey, Cass,' said Tony. 'Why be a dyke if all you want is a fake cock?'

'Hear, hear,' called a man in a turquoise body suit as he walked past. '*Pour quelle raison lesbiennes?* I've never seen the point of them.'

Cass shouted after him, enjoying the sport. 'That's because we're higher beings, beyond your limited understanding.'

'Yeah, right,' sneered Tony. 'Why don't you just admit you want a cock and go get the real thing?'

Anna was way ahead now and waiting for Cass to follow, but Cass could not let Tony have the last word. 'Because the real thing tends to have a boring bloke attached to the end of it. And believe me, Tony, no woman needs a man when she's got a full vegetable basket.'

'Stop!' said Andy, mocking squeamishness. 'Too much information.'

Cass took his arm. 'Well, you shouldn't start a conversation about dildos if you're scared of the hard truth.'

'Ha, ha. Remind me never to eat vegetables at your café again.'

Cass laughed and whispered in his ear. 'Just lay off the stuffed courgette.'

'Oh, please!' he recoiled. 'Do we have to know about your vegetable of choice?'

Anna wheeled the pushchair back. She'd been waiting by the T-shirts, avoiding the lewd banter. Florrie was crying. 'This is supposed to be a family day out, not porno *Ready, Steady, Cook*. Can we please just buy something nice!'

She turned the pushchair around and wheeled over to a stall selling flags. Cass jogged after her. 'Did you see that? I wiped the floor with him. I was laughing with Andy and Tony was well out of it.'

Anna rocked the pushchair, trying to settle the baby. She whispered back, 'It's not going to help, Cass. If you don't watch it, Tony could make trouble for us.'

'Just let him try,' said Cass.

'I'd say he's already trying. And you're right behind him, helping him do it.'

'I am not!' Cass looked behind them. Andy was clearly trying to persuade Tony to join them, but Tony was shaking his head. Andy found his wallet and took some money out.

'See that,' Cass nudged Anna. 'He's getting money out of Andy now. I can't believe Andy's having to buy him off. What kind of a relationship is that?'

But Andy didn't give the money to Tony. He ran up to them. 'Listen, girls, Tony's having a bit of a hard time. I think he feels a bit left out, poor love.' He was speaking so fast they had no chance to interrupt. 'So, I thought why don't we do the whole Pride thing as couples and start the family thing tomorrow. That seems fair to everyone.' He tucked the money in the pushchair, kissed Florrie's red angry face, and ran back to Tony, calling over his shoulder as he went. 'You buy that girl a present for me and we'll meet tomorrow at the hotel.'

Cass watched him go. 'I don't believe he's just run off like that.'

'Don't you?' Anna pulled Florrie out of the buggy and tried to quieten her. She was screaming.

'It's not fair. They get to party all day while we're left

holding the baby.' Cass took Florrie from Anna and held her over her shoulder, 'Not that I don't love her.' She smelt Florrie's nappy. 'But we do all the bloody work as it is. I thought they might at least give us a break.'

'You can still go partying,' said Anna.

'What? And leave you to cope on your own?'

'I'll be fine.' Anna put the bags in the empty buggy and began pushing it through the crowds. 'It's not me you should be worried about in this family, Cass. It's Andy.'

Chapter 5

Unwedded Bliss

'God, does that woman have a radar for scandal?' Cass was naked, hovering by the bedroom window, watching Doris Karloff skulking on the pavement below. Doris was standing guard outside her gate, arms crossed over her belted mustard coat, urine-yellow hair drooping over her shoulders. She was gazing fixedly at the student house.

'Probably,' muttered Anna from the bed. She rocked Florrie gently in her arms, watching her eyelids flutter into sleep.

'But how does she do it? How does she know that Johnnie's moving to Ruby's today?' Cass crouched on the edge of the futon where it butted against the window and pressed her face to the glass. 'I bet she sniffs out happiness. Smells it on people then sucks it out of them like a vampire.'

All the curtains were closed in Ruby's house. Cass turned back to the student house opposite. Johnnie would be moving all of twenty metres from his rented room to Ruby's house. 'Do you think it's going to be okay with Johnnie and Ruby?'

Anna placed Florrie gently on a heap of pillows beside the futon. 'Hope so,' she said. 'For Ruby's sake.'

'And what about us?'

'What about us?' Anna turned over and pulled the duvet around her.

Cass stared at her huddled shape. 'Are we okay?'

Anna groaned. 'We're fine.'

'But now you're working at the café we hardly even see each other.'

'We need the money.'

'I know that.'

'So let me sleep,' said Anna, pulling the duvet over her head.

Cass stared out at Doris patrolling the pavement. 'I feel like we spend our whole life either working or looking after Florrie. Anna, I feel middle-aged. Like suddenly I'm supposed to be grown-up and responsible.'

'You'll get used to it. I've always been grown up and responsible.'

'That's true.' Cass crawled back into bed, snuggling up to Anna's back. 'That's what I liked about you when we met.'

'Mmm . . .'

'You were irresistibly corruptible.' She began to stroke Anna's naked shoulder. 'I've always fancied sensible older women.'

Anna yawned. 'That's because your mother's such a mess.'

Cass leant forward, kissing Anna's shoulder and caressing her breasts lightly with her fingertips. 'True.'

'And if you're doing what I think you're doing,' said Anna, rolling over to face her, 'you can stop right there.'

'What?' Cass smiled, drawing her fingers across Anna's stomach and down to her thighs. 'I'm not doing anything.'

'I've had two hours' sleep, and I'm knackered.'

'Poor baby,' Cass leant up on her elbow, brushing her lips across Anna's nipple. 'It sounds like you need some looking after.' She let her mouth hover over Anna's, teasing her, blowing softly, not allowing their lips to touch. Anna murmured to be kissed, but Cass moved away. Reaching for the duvet, she pulled it over their heads as she pressed her body against Anna's, their breasts touching. In the warm darkness, she found Anna's mouth and parted her lips with her tongue. 'You just go to sleep,' she whispered. 'I'm taking care of you now.'

Across the road in the student house, Johnnie was coming out of the bathroom in combat trousers hanging low on the hip. He had a towel over his head and was squeezing water from his short dreadlocked hair. Shirley was waiting for him in the kitchen, standing beside a cardboard box on the kitchen table.

'I've packed this for you,' she said. 'It's all your kitchen stuff.' Johnnie dried his hands on the towel. Water was dripping onto his shoulders and he shook his head violently, spraying water around the kitchen. Shirley laughed, ducking behind the table.

'What kitchen stuff?'

'You know,' said Shirley, 'things you might need.'

'I didn't know I had kitchen stuff.' Johnnie peered into the box, and pulled out a jar of sea salt. 'You think I need salt?'

Shirley blushed. 'You might. And there's other things in there.' She reached in to show him, but he was already walking away.

'You keep it, Shirley. Anything in there you like, it's yours.' He didn't want to arrive at Ruby's with boxes of useless clutter. He wanted to travel light.

'But I packed it for you.'

'Thanks, Shirley, but Ruby's got it sorted.' He drifted into the hall where a small pile of his stuff (CD player, backpack, laptop) was stacked outside his door. Watching him saunter up the dark, narrow hall, his mind in a different place, Shirley realised that Johnnie had left her behind before he'd even moved out. He disappeared into his room and a shadow moved across the frosted glass in the front door. Shirley stayed at the kitchen table, wondering if she should unpack the box or just go back to bed.

The doorbell rang as Johnnie came back into the hall. He turned to answer it. 'You can have these CDs too, Shirley, I don't think Ruby's into jazz. Hey, Greg man.'

'Johnnie boy.'

They grasped each other briefly by the shoulders and Greg pulled the hem of his T-shirt out for Johnnie to read: "Dip me in honey and throw me to the lesbians." 'Anna and Cass got it for me from Brighton. What do you think?'

Johnnie raised his eyebrows. 'Dream on, man. Hey, do you want a couple of CDs?'

'Yeah,' Greg took them from Johnnie and looked at the titles. Shirley watched from the kitchen. 'Ta, mate. So you ready for the big move then?'

Johnnie hauled his backpack onto his bare shoulders. 'Sure am!'

'So when do you want to sort out the Harley?'

'Whenever.' Johnnie shrugged. The Harley was a scrapyard write-off that had spent most of the last year under blue tarpaulin in the front yard. 'It's not going anywhere, half the engine's still in my room.'

Greg sauntered down the hall and put his head around Johnnie's door. 'I've emptied the shed next door and everything. We can move it there now if you want.'

'No hurry.'

'Not for you maybe. I'm looking forward to this, mate. Getting a Harley's the best fun I've had all year.'

'You're a sad fucker, Greg.'

'Tell me about it.'

At that moment, Coriander, Greg's six-year-old daughter, jumped through the front door, ran down the hall and crashed into Shirley, who was eavesdropping in the kitchen.

'Cori! Where did you come from?'

'I was hiding outside. You didn't see me, did you?'

'I certainly didn't!' Shirley, embarrassed that Greg was more excited by the Harley than by her, was hiding her self-con-sciousness in exclamations. 'What a surprise!'

'Dad said you'd play with me while he gets Johnnie's bike.'
'Okay!'

Greg came up behind them and swung Cori into the air.
'Hi there, Shirley.' He held Cori above his head. 'I said you
could *ask* if she wasn't too busy.' He smiled down at Shirley
and her insides dribbled like chocolate in a hot car. 'It's no
problem,' she said. 'Honestly.'

Greg kissed Cori on the forehead and sat her down on the
chair next to Shirley. 'Cheers, Shirley.' He kissed her lightly
on the cheek. 'I'll take you for a ride when I get the bike going.
Show you that I'm still a young and sexy guy underneath.' He
laughed, mocking his fantasy self, and walked back down the
hall. Shirley watched his buttocks ripple as he followed Johnnie
onto the patch of gravel at the front of the house. She thought
about sitting on a throbbing motorbike behind that butt.

'What can we play?' Cori tugged at her sleeve. 'What can
we play?'

Shirley sighed, trying to hang on to her vision. 'Whatever.'

'What's this?'

'What?' Shirley focused on the face in front of her and saw
the box she'd packed for Johnnie still on the kitchen table.
'Would you like to help me unpack?'

Cori considered it. 'Is it a present?'

'Well, sort of. Johnnie left it behind.' She sat Cori on the
edge of the table so that she could search in the box. 'If you
find anything you like, you can have it.'

Cori brought out the tea towel Shirley had chosen specially
for Johnnie last Christmas. It had a portrait of Jimi Hendrix
on it. 'Would you like that, Cori?' The little girl nodded,
spreading the towel over the table to look at the picture.

The collection of objects in the box (a wok, tea towel,
calendar, mugs, various jars of spices and food) had no signifi-
cance for Johnnie. He could live with them well enough and
without them just as easily. Just as he could live without
Shirley. She pulled a mug out of the box and stared at it. It
was nothing special, green, gold and red stripes, a bit stained

inside, and she felt sorry for it. It was just like her, another household item that had made no lasting impression on him at all. She'd been nice to Johnnie and it had made no difference. She'd been nice to her family, and her mum had still left her dad, and her dad had still had an affair, and her Uncle Charlie had still come back from the dead wearing a dress. Perhaps that was what her life would be, people would come and go, and she would stand there being nice until she died.

'Can I have this too?' Coriander was struggling to pull the wok out of the box.

Shirley stared at her, slightly dazed. 'Um, yes.' She stood up to ease it out of the box. 'Are you sure you want it? What will you use it for?'

'I'm giving it to Dad to help him do cooking.'

Shirley smiled. 'That's a lovely idea, Cori, we'll give it to your dad as a present.'

Greg was nice. He was different from all the others. He was still living in his dead parents' house, with its ugly pink and grey stone-cladding on the front. Greg didn't leave things behind. Greg was like her, the type who got left. Cori's mother had left him when Cori was six weeks old. Cori had never even seen her. For five years Greg had waited for that woman to come back, Acorn, the self-proclaimed poet and eco-warrior. But now Shirley was there for him. They were taking it slow, but there was no doubt that she was the new woman in his life. He needed her. They both did, him and Cori. And she was going to be there for them. Always. She stared at the box on the table and thought about packing up her own stuff next month.

Then it struck her. Why was she even thinking about moving in with her mum? It was Greg who needed her. Pearl could take care of herself. Shirley sank back in her chair mulling it over. She was only moving to the café because she felt guilty. Because she wanted to be nice. But why should she? Being nice got you nowhere. Her mum wasn't nice. She'd lied about her dad, lied about Uncle Charles. What else was she lying about? No. Shirley didn't belong with her. She belonged next door. With Greg. She turned to Coriander who was arranging Johnnie's spice jars. 'Cori, does your dad ever talk about me?'

The little girl shrugged, uninterested. 'Sometimes.'

'Really?' said Shirley, more excited than she'd anticipated. 'What does he say?'

Cori lined up the spice jars in order of size, biggest to smallest, as if she hadn't heard. 'I mean, what I was thinking was, does your dad ever talk about your mum?'

Cori looked at her. 'My mum's a poet and she's going to be famous.'

'Oh, that's good!' Shirley had a nagging sense that she shouldn't ask Cori about her mother, but for once in her life she wasn't going to give up on what she wanted because it wasn't nice to ask. 'I suppose if your mum is famous she won't be able to live in your house with you and your dad.'

Cori shrugged and looked down at the table. She'd stopped playing with the jars.

'It's just that I've had a really great idea. I thought because I love you and I love your dad we could pretend that I'm your mummy.'

Cori frowned. 'But you're not my mummy.'

'No,' said Shirley, blushing. 'I know I'm not really your mum, I just thought we could pretend and it would be fun.' Cori looked thoughtful so Shirley pressed on. 'I could be the mummy, and your dad would be the daddy and you would be the little girl, and—' she took a breath, 'and I could live in your house with you and we'd be like a real family in the story books.'

Shirley was expecting Cori to throw her arms around her with joy, but she didn't. She put the wok on her head and sat perfectly still and quiet. 'Cori?' Shirley watched her anxiously. 'Cori? Have I upset you? I didn't mean to. It was just a silly idea.'

Coriander didn't move. Then she whispered from beneath the wok, 'Will you really be my mummy?'

Shirley bent forward to see into Cori's face. 'Would you like that?'

The wok nodded.

'Me too.' Shirley lifted her onto her lap. Coriander put both hands on top of the wok to hold it in place. 'I think if I lived with you and your dad we'd have loads of fun. We could play dolls, and make your daddy laugh and we'd all be really happy.' She gently lifted Cori's hands off the wok and took it off her head. 'What do you think?'

Cori nodded again. She still wasn't smiling.

'Well,' said Shirley, anxious and breezy, 'we'll just have to persuade your daddy to let me move in.'

Ruby stood at the edge of the window where she couldn't be seen and watched Johnnie as he and Greg pushed the bike out into the road. This is how she'd first seen Johnnie, almost a year ago, stripped to the waist, tinkering with that machine. She smiled thinking about it. She was on the phone to Anna watching some sad loser (she couldn't even remember his name) walking down the street and out of her life. And there was Johnnie, dark, young and beautiful, straddling that bike. She'd wanted him from that first moment. She'd fantasised about putting the phone down, going out into the street and daring to touch him. Watching him now, she had that same desire. But their relationship wasn't simply about pleasure any more. Johnnie wanted more from her than sex.

And here she was hiding behind the curtain in her own bedroom. She should be bouncing on the bed with joy, like any other forty-something woman with a young lover on his way. But she didn't feel like bouncing. She watched Greg laughing, sitting on the bike with his legs thrust in the air while Johnnie pushed him along the empty road. Doris was watching them too, arms folded, determined not to smile. God forbid that Ruby should end up like that. Doris was no advert for monogamy. Greg and Johnnie disappeared around the curve in the street. When they came back into the Close, Greg was pushing, Johnnie standing on the saddle, one hand on the handlebar, one leg in the air. He was looking up to her window, waving, showing off. She waved back, laughing and glanced at Doris. Did Boris once lark about to impress her?

Greg pushed the bike into the passage at the side of his house and they disappeared from view. But Ruby stayed at the curtain, gazing at the street. She knew she was making a mistake, that she was wrong to let Johnnie move in. Life was much safer if you knew where to draw the line. But Johnnie had refused to listen to her doubts. He wouldn't let her push him away. She might make the rules, shout the loudest, refuse him, abuse him, but somehow he managed to break her down and get what he wanted. With Johnnie she wasn't in charge. He said that they were two of a kind, that it didn't matter Ruby was a white woman almost twice his age. And he was right. But the closer he got, the more vulnerable she was becoming.

Johnnie knew things about her, things that she had told no one else. He knew more than the facts of her life – that her father had killed her mother twenty years before. He knew that she was a fraud, that her frivolity was an elaborate fake, and he wanted to reach beyond it. When her mother had been murdered, with soap opera irony, at the Christmas dinner table, Ruby had become someone else. She had not been a dramatic child, but as an adult her melodramatics had shielded her from the tragic farce of her past. Unlike the others, Johnnie was not deceived by sex or cynicism. He wanted to touch her where no one else ever had. And God knows there weren't many places left to try.

She examined her reflection in the mirror. Her face was saturated with the memory of her mother, forty-one when she died. She screwed up her features to make the lines appear, then painted over her mother's face with lipstick and kohl. For three years after witnessing her mother's death, life had been so painful that the sun on her face was like a slap. But she had learned. She had found a way not to care, to hide in hedonism, protect herself with burlesque. She went back to the window and waited for Johnnie until, at last, he walked across the road to her door. She went downstairs to let him in.

He stood on the doorstep with an old canvas rucksack slung over one shoulder and a streak of oil on his ribs.

'Hey, Ruby!' Greg called, kneeling on the pavement opposite. He was pulling snails off a blue tarpaulin and throwing them under the hedge. 'Aren't you going to carry him over the threshold? It is traditional on occasions like this, you know.'

Ruby laughed. 'Oh yes, and we're *so* traditional on this street. Isn't that right, Doris?' Doris, who was watching them from her gate sniffed and turned away. Ruby stepped back into the house and spoke softly to Johnnie. 'So, young man, you fancy coming over my threshold?'

'I'm just waiting for you to guide me in.'

She smiled, tracing her fingers over the straps across his shoulders. 'But you're much too big to squeeze into my narrow passage.'

He dropped the rucksack onto the patch of grass beside him, smiling at her smut, and not taking his eyes off her. They stood for a moment, neither of them moving.

'Once you move in, it will never be the same, you know that, don't you?'

He shrugged. 'For better or for worse.'

'What if it's worse?'

'It won't be.' Johnnie held her hands and stepped into the hall.

Chapter 6

Changing Rooms

Shirley rapped irritably on the painted glass of the café door. It was nine o'clock on a drizzly grey morning and The Cosmic wasn't due to open for another hour. For the third time, Shirley rung the bell labelled 'Pearl's Place' and waited for her mother's voice on the intercom. Pearl had told her to come over this morning to talk about decorating her room. And as Shirley still hadn't dared to ask Greg about moving in, even after her chat with Coriander, it looked like this was to be her new home. Shirley stepped on and off the doorstep, hair frizzing in the mist, finger pressed against the bell, hoping that two floors above her the noise was infuriating her mother, forcing her out of the flat and down the stairs to let her in.

She peered through a gap in the purple painted swirls. She could see Dee at the back of the café wiping tables. She knocked louder and called through the glass. 'Dee, it's me, Shirley. Can you let me in? Mum's expecting me.' Dee didn't even look up, and although Shirley suspected she was ignoring her, there was always the possibility that she hadn't heard. She looked for the letterbox. It was at the bottom of the door, four inches from the ground. Shirley bent over, trying not to drag her hair in the filthy puddles on the pavement, and opened it. 'Dee' she called, mouth against the draught-proof brushes, 'It's Shirley. Can you let me in please? Dee?' She paused, still bent double, to smile at a curious passerby.

Abruptly, the bolts were drawn back, and the door opened. Shirley looked up. Her mother was standing over her. 'Shirley, what are you doing down there?'

'I was trying to get Dee to let me in,' said Shirley, pushing past Pearl and into the café. She shook out her frog face umbrella and pulled wet strands of hair off her face.

Pearl closed the door. 'Well, she wasn't going to see you crawling in the dirt, was she? And anyway, you knew I was coming. You'd buzzed me.'

'That was ten minutes ago. You're supposed to tell people you're coming down. To let them know.'

'Honestly, Shirley, you're just like your father. He was always impatient. I was two seconds in the kitchen on my way down, telling Anna about your room. Oh wait 'til you see it. Wait 'til you see your room.'

Dee spoke up from the back of the café. 'Your mum's had decorators in.'

'Not decorators, Dee, designers.' Pearl buffed the edge of a table Dee had just wiped with the hem of her dressing gown. 'And you'll need a bit of polish if you're going to get a shine on these tables.'

Dee grunted and Pearl didn't pursue it. Instead, she led Shirley to the back of the café and up the stairs. 'You remember Sebastian, don't you, Shirley?'

'Who?'

'Sebastian. You met him that time with me last year. In Safeways.'

'Did I?' Shirley stared at the hard skin on her mother's heel as she climbed the stairs in her silver sandals.

'Yes, in the pet's aisle. That time Lucasta got an afghan.'

'Mum, I don't know who you're talking about.'

Pearl clicked her teeth. 'Sebastian. He's Lucasta's son. You must remember Lucasta from the Frinley Art Circle.' They'd reached the kitchen and Pearl led Shirley in. Anna was preparing salad. Buzz, wearing Pearl's flowery plastic apron over his new Tooting Hottentots T-shirt, was next to her at the sinks washing outsized saucepans. Pearl carried on talking without pause. 'That woman changed my life. Without her I wouldn't be standing here today.'

Buzz muttered to Anna. 'So now we know who to blame.'

Pearl beamed at them. 'Shirley's come to see her room, Anna. Isn't Sebastian just like his mother? So talented. I was telling Shirley. The ideas they have in that family. Same teeth, you know. My mother always said to me, she said, Pearl, you can always tell a lot about a person by looking at their teeth.'

Buzz clanked pan lids in the sink. 'That's horses.'

'You may scoff, Buzz, but if I'd listened to my mother I would never have married Gordon.'

'What's wrong with Dad's teeth?' asked Shirley.

Pearl pulled back her top lip and tapped her front teeth. 'False. They used to cross in the middle. Sign of a bad sort.'

'That's eyebrows,' said Buzz.

'Not where I come from. Now listen, Shirley, come on out of here. I've got a surprise for you! You won't believe it when you see your room. It's all designer. When I saw mine I practically had a seizure, but, you know, in a nice way.' She started up the stairs to the flat. 'You wouldn't believe what Sebastian's done for us. I said, Seb – he likes me to call him Seb – I said what you've done with that chicken wire and papier-mâché, it's like being on the television. Nobody would ever know that Roman pillar wasn't concrete.' She put her hand to her mouth. 'Oh, I'm giving it away.'

Shirley was appalled. 'I've got Roman pillars in my room?'

'No. Of course not. That's me. Wait 'til you see what he's done. I'll show you my room first.'

Shirley followed her mother into the flat. The front door opened into the lounge and kitchenette, and Pearl led her through it to the bedrooms on the other side. Pearl stopped outside her bedroom and opened the door with a flourish. Inside the room was painted a deep red and the window had been draped with red velvet curtains. On the far side of the room a row of old cinema seats had been fixed to the floor and black silhouettes of people's heads had been painted onto the wall behind them.

Pearl gestured towards them. 'That's my audience.'

The bed was on the other side of the room, surrounded by giant white pillars and raised from the ground. Two steps, also red velvet, led up to the mattress, which was framed by lavish drapes of white and red.

Shirley was speechless.

'It's ever so dramatic, isn't it, Shirley? It's just as I said to Charlene, I said, Lene, it's not that I'm not thrilled. I am. I'm thrilled. But as for sleep, I don't think I'll ever close my eyes in that room again. And Lene said, "Of course you can't sleep, you've never been to bed with an audience before." Oh, talk about laugh. Do you know what it is, Shirley?'

Shirley was still taking it in. She glanced at the small binoculars hanging from the headboard. 'A theatre?'

'It's a box at the opera. Seb said to me, he said, Pearl, I want to create your fantasy. I said, oh you cheeky thing, because we can have a joke like that. But he said, what's your *thing* in life, Pearl. And I said, Seb, I'd honestly have to say it was opera.'

'But you've never been to the opera.'

'It's a fantasy, Shirley. If I'd been, it wouldn't be a fantasy, would it?'

'But when Dad played Pavarotti you said it was a racket.'

'I told Seb that, I said, I don't like the singing or anything, it's the costumes I love, all the glamour.'

'And he didn't think it was odd that you've never been?'

'No, Shirley, you're missing the point. You see, Sebastian knew exactly what I meant. He said it's the *feel* of it I liked. And I said that's absolutely it. *It's the feel.* He knows me, you see. He just said, "Get me all the red velvet you can and leave the rest to me." '

Shirley was looking curiously at the drapes. 'Mum, aren't these–?'

'Yes, Shirley, they are. I took every curtain off those big windows in your father's house in Frinley.'

'I hope Dad didn't try and stop you.'

Pearl smiled. 'He was out at the time.'

'Serves him right.'

'And when we ran out of the velvet Seb dashed off to the market and like a flash came back with some Muslim—'

'It's muslin, Mum.'

'Anyway, I couldn't have thought of it without Charlene. She was with me all the way with this. And it's Charlene you've got to thank for your room, Shirley. I can't wait for you to see it.' Pearl led Shirley out of her room and closed the door slowly. 'Because Seb said, "You've got to think who Shirley is, what does Shirley love?" And Charlene says it straight away. Absolutely right.'

'He doesn't even know me,' said Shirley. 'I haven't seen him since I was ten.' She pushed her bedroom door, but Pearl had a grip on the handle and was keeping it shut.

'Listen, your Uncle Charlie loves you and he used to spoil you rotten when you were little.'

'Until Dad found out he wore dresses.'

'Yes, well, we needn't churn all that up now. The point is he hadn't forgotten your fantasy. Don't you remember how you always wanted a horse? Just you wait 'til you see it, Shirley. Go on, open the door.'

Pearl let go of the handle and Shirley twisted it with a heavy heart. The door clicked open and her mother pushed her in, switching on the bare light bulb hanging from the ceiling. 'Look, Shirley, it's a little stable.'

Shirley couldn't speak.

'Now Seb's only done the bed, so you can't get the whole of his vision from it, but look how clever he's been.'

In the middle of the floor a pair of second-hand bunk beds had been transformed using 4mm MDF. This had been staple-gunned around every side but one and curved over the top to give the impression of a roof. It had then been painted in metallic effect paint, and fake MDF wheels, with real tyres, had been attached to the bottom. Carefully painted on the back were a small number plate and a sign, SLOW FOR HORSES. Shirley's bed was a horsebox.

'Isn't he talented? You know, Shirley, I think Sebastian would go out with you if I asked him.'

'I don't want to go out with him. I don't want anything to do with him.' Shirley felt that Sebastian had personally insulted her by making her the most sexless bed imaginable. 'I've got a boyfriend.'

'Shirley, you've been out a couple of times with a married man from across the road. That's not what I'm talking about.'

'Greg's not married.'

'But Sebastian's so full of flair and imagination. He needs someone solid like you.'

'Thanks, yeah, I know that's how you think of me. Some-one's who's slow and looks like a horse.'

'Who said you look like a horse?'

'Greg doesn't think I look like a horse.'

'Nobody thinks you look like a horse.'

'He's asked me to move in with him.' Shirley said it without thinking, but she couldn't take it back now.

'Oh, I see where this is leading.'

'I love him.'

'Love? I've never heard such nonsense. He's twice your age.'

'He's not. He's twenty-eight.'

'And he's a father.'

'I love Cori too. We're going to be a family.'

'Oh, don't make me laugh, Shirley. He needs some help with the housework. You wait and see. It'll be babysitting for you.'

'That's not true. Greg loves me.'

'He's told you that, has he?'

'Yes!' Shirley lied.

'Shirley, you're fooling yourself. Listen, I don't want to fall out, but if you get involved with a married man, you are asking for trouble.'

'He's not married.'

'But there's still that child's mother. She's out there somewhere.'

'She left when Cori was a baby. She's never coming back.'

''Scuse me,' Buzz was standing at the bedroom door. 'You didn't hear me knocking. Someone to see you, Pearl.'

He stepped aside and Pearl and Shirley saw Gordon standing in the lounge, stiff as a soldier, one arm neatly behind his back. He was wearing a full evening suit and black bow tie.

Pearl walked straight over to him, hands on hips and roused for battle. 'If this is about those curtains, Gordon, I'm not in the mood—'

'It's not the curtains, Pearl.' He coughed and dropped to his knees. 'I'm here because I love you.' Shirley snorted, Pearl laughed, even Buzz rolled his good eye as he headed for the door. 'I want you back, Pearl,' said Gordon. He pulled his hand from behind his back and brandished a bouquet of red roses. Pearl and Shirley watched Buzz swerve to avoid the reams of florid ribbon, stumble against the leather sofa, lurch backwards in vegan disgust, and trample over the flowers in Gordon's hand.

Muttering about the exploitation of third-world flower workers, he walked out of the flat, leaving a trail of crushed petals in his wake. The Gates family all stared at the battered remains of Gordon's love offering scattered over the carpet. Pearl was the first to break the silence. 'And what about Spam Medley?'

'Pam Smedley,' corrected Shirley.

Pearl didn't take her eyes off Gordon. 'I know who I mean, Shirley.'

'It's over with Pam. It's you I want, Pearl.' Gordon had

never been a man to rush a decision, and he had thought about this one long and hard. Since discovering that Keith Smedley was about to die, he realised that despite Pam's perverse predilections, her charms were in no small part due to her being married. To someone else. It was Pearl he had shared his life with, Pearl he loved. 'I'll give up the life in Frinley, sell the business and move into this place with you.' Gordon had thought about this too. If he was to make a new life with Pearl, they had to be well away from Pam.

'You can't be serious, Gordon! You! Here! In the café!'

'I've never been more serious in my life. I've changed, Pearl. I've learned my lesson and I want to give us another go. If you can do it, I can.'

Pearl was silent, looking at him kneeling on her threadbare carpet surrounded by rose petals. She tapped her finger against her lip thoughtfully. 'Well, who'd have thought it!'

Shirley looked at her mother's face and was sickened to see a hint of triumph 'You're not going to take him back, are you? After everything he's done?'

'I'm thinking about it, Shirley.'

'What's there to think about? He's a bastard.' She stared hard at her dad. 'He lied to me for months.'

'I'm sorry, Shirley,' Gordon hung his head. 'I've been a very foolish man.'

Pearl watched him carefully. The way his grey hair curled up at the back of his neck. The way his suit fitted him perfectly across the back of the shoulders. 'I'm not saying he's not a bastard, Shirley. I'm just saying I'm thinking about it.'

Gordon knew he was winning. 'I could make you happy, Pearl.'

'Don't you think everyone deserves a second chance, Shirley? Even your father?'

'But you hated it in Frinley.'

'This isn't about Frinley, Shirley, it's about your father.'

'You said he was a boring git who made you miserable.'

'You're right, I did say that. But being alone at our age isn't much fun either, is it, Gordon?'

'I've missed you, Pearl.'

'Yes, well, on the odd occasion, I dare say I've missed you too.'

'We had our moments, didn't we, Pearl?'

Shirley looked from one to the other. 'I don't believe this! You think you can tell me how to live my life and look at you! You're as bad as each other! I hate you both! I'm going to live with Greg!'

She stormed out of the flat, pushing past the stumpy figure of her kneeling father and slamming the door behind her.

Pearl watched her go and sighed. 'You can get up off the floor now, Gordon. It's going to take more than crawling this time.'

Chapter 7

Goddess-Parents

Cass was leaning against the kitchen doorway, videoing a small crowd of friends and relatives gathered together in their garden. She pointed the lens at Anna, who was standing on the patio, trapped behind Cass's mother, and jiggling Florrie irritably on her hip. She didn't smile for the camera. Cass stopped recording, lowered the camcorder, and laughed at Anna's sulky face. 'Cheer up,' she said. 'We're doing the photos now.'

Anna had wanted to have a simple party to celebrate Florrie's half birthday: a couple of friends, the three parents and maybe, the grandparents. But Cass's mother, Sky, had managed to turn the whole thing into a New Age pantomime. It was also a month late, because Sky and husband Jeffrey were in Goa in August for a reunion of old travelling friends (Cass called them the SHITS – Sad Hippies in Their Sixties) so the party had to be in September.

Sky and Jeffrey had met in India in the early '70s when Sky was out there finding herself. After a night of pleasure with a Bombay rickshaw driver, she had found herself in Goa, pregnant with Cass, and with no idea who the father was or how to find him. She was on the lookout for a new man when she met Jeffrey, fifteen years her senior with a slight connection to Apple and an anecdote about George Harrison. He was just what she had in mind. They came back to England as the Bohemians of Buckinghamshire and spent most of Cass's childhood in a spiritual or chemical haze.

When Sky heard about the party, she had insisted on conducting a Wiccan ceremony for Florrie and her godparents, Ruby and Greg (now officially Goddess-parents). So Anna found herself herded into the garden among thirteen other people, forced to watch Sky squatting in a sari on the concrete. She was chanting over an arrangement of twigs, two candles, and a bowl of something grey and sticky that she'd set up on a tea towel right outside the backdoor. No one could get in or out of the house, and Sky had been there for close on twenty minutes. Anna could see her elderly parents smiling wanly from where they had wedged themselves behind the open kitchen window. Glynis and Ernie Jones had driven slowly all the way from North Wales to end up trapped against the trellis, a pair of wallflowers in their daughter's garden. Anna smiled at them, and her dad responded with a small wave. She could tell by her mother's pinched expression that she needed the toilet.

Behind Anna, Jeffrey had begun to erect his tripod ready for the photos. Anna could hear him muttering and struggling against the privet, but she resisted the polite urge to help. It wasn't that she disliked Jeffrey, with his long grey ponytail and embroidered Alice band, it was just that she was more concerned about her mother's view of his bendings and heavings. She stayed where she was, spreading her long linen skirt as wide as it would go, and smiling inanely. Jeffrey, at sixty-two, was only ten years younger than her parents, but whereas her mother and father were wearing matching slacks and a light cardigan, Jeffrey was wearing a suede waistcoat and baggy cheesecloth trousers with nothing underneath. He had abandoned underwear in 1967, so they all had a perfect view of his genitalia swinging back and forth like three mice on a trapeze.

Anna glanced at Tony standing motionless behind Jeffrey. He was glaring into nothing, ignoring Jeffrey's muttered apologies about the tripod. She looked at his face, at his mouth frozen in a half-sneer, and realised he was drunk. And taut with resentment. This was his one Saturday a month away from Luigi's restaurant, and it was clear that he didn't want to be spending it with them. Andy was standing next to him with his arm draped around his back, talking to Ruby and Johnnie. Tony turned to face her and she looked away.

'So, you young lovers,' Andy was saying. 'Do you like living in sin?'

Ruby blew smoke rings and passed her spliff to Johnnie. 'Of course. It's my natural habitat.'

Johnnie took a drag and put his arm around Ruby's neck, pulling her into his chest. 'This woman is the best sin that could have happened to me.'

Ruby laughed, her face pressed into Johnnie's jacket. 'Can you believe how corny this man is, Andy?' she said, struggling against Johnnie's hold. 'Give me a taste of that corn, baby!' She lifted her head and licked his face. He laughed, sinking onto the grass with Ruby on top of him, chewing his ear. Andy took the spliff out of Johnnie's outstretched hand and Tony stepped away as they rolled into his legs. 'Okay, children!' said Andy. 'We're supposed to be having a conversation about coupledom here, not demonstrating oral.'

Ruby sat up, smiling and smoothing her ruffled hair. 'If I was demonstrating oral, darling, I wouldn't have been giving head to his head.' She shuffled back to the garden wall and picked up her drink. 'And I'd have chosen a more promising audience than Glynis over there.' She raised her glass at Anna's mum who, upon hearing a whisper of her name, had inadvertently caught Ruby's gaze. 'But if we have to behave ourselves, let's have this grown-up conversation. You start.'

Andy stared down at her. 'I can't just perform to order.'

Ruby raised her eyebrows. 'Remind me to teach you sometime.'

'What? At the University of Vice?' He returned the spliff.

'No,' she said, passing it to Johnnie. 'I'm being totally sincere. I want to know about you and Tony. I hardly know a thing and I am going to be your Goddess-mother.'

'So what do you want to know, sweetie?'

'The highlights.'

'As in marriage, divorce, remarriage?'

'Sounds perfect!'

'Well, are you concentrating? Married four years ago, lots of sex and nights by the fire. Divorced two years ago, that's when Tony ran off to Italy and left me, lots of crying and Patsy Cline, you know the kind of thing. Remarried last year, that's when Tony realised he couldn't live without me and came crawling back.' He slid his hand into Tony's back pocket and Johnnie offered him the spliff. Tony took it, flattening the roach in his fingers.

'And that's when Andy told me he was having a baby with Anna. Wasn't that a surprise for me!'

'Of course!' Andy smiled. 'All us girls want babies. It's my ambition to be a housewife.'

Ruby laughed. 'You just want to be chained to the kitchen sink.'

'How did you guess?' Andy squatted down on the grass next to Johnnie.

'You forgot what came next,' said Tony, stroking Andy's hair. 'Happy ever after at the seaside.'

'The seaside?' asked Johnnie.

Tony blew smoke up to the sky. 'We're moving to Brighton.'

'But what about all this?' said Johnnie, gesturing to the people in the garden, to Anna and Florrie.

Tony shrugged and Andy interrupted. 'We have this fantasy of growing old together and ogling the bright young things on the beach.' He patted the ground next to him, but Tony didn't sit down. He was still looking around the garden.

'We're growing old together now,' he muttered. 'Look where we are.' He glared at Anna's elderly parents, Jeffrey adjusting his lens, Sky on the patio, Anna jiggling the baby. 'Straight grannies and gay breeders. The cutting edge of queer.'

'Just think,' said Andy, sharing his drink with Ruby, 'I'm thirty-seven now, by my fortieth birthday we'll have been together for seven years.' He gazed up at Tony. 'Hey, sweetie, you don't think we'll get the seven year itch when I'm forty, do you?'

Tony drew on the spliff. 'Only if you get fat.'

'I'm not getting fat!' Andy put his hand on his belly. 'Ruby, am I getting fat?'

'Don't make me the expert on fat and forty.'

'Of course you're not, darling,' he said, patting her arm. 'That was years ago.'

'Listen, fat-boy, I'll still be sexy at sixty. How about you?'

Andy shrugged. 'At sixty? Plain old seedy would do me. Or skinny. Maybe by sixty I'll finally make it to skinny. Do you think I should take up jogging?' He glanced around the garden. 'Greg, what do you think?'

Greg was sitting on the grass in front of them staring into space while Shirley and Coriander sat cross-legged next to him, playing a game.

'What?'

'Tony's worried about me being fat and forty.'

'I feel forty already.'

'Don't try to upstage me, Greg!' said Andy, crawling over to him. 'You're not even thirty yet, your ageing fears don't count.'

'Andy, I've been up half the night with Cori and I feel like an old man.'

'You know what you need, Greg, an au pair. Someone young and decorative around the house.'

'Yeah, thanks, mate, but I've got Shirley for that.' Shirley blushed, and concentrated on playing scissors, paper, rock with Cori.

'Yes, well, no offence to Shirley, but does she hoover up and look after the kids at the same time?'

'I could!' said Shirley, twisting around and wrapping Cori's rock fist with her paper palm. 'I could even move in.'

'There you are, Greg. You can stop moaning now and tell me if my belly looks flabby to you.' Andy lifted his shirt and pulled in his stomach. 'Do you think I should start early morning jogging?'

'Hey, kids,' Jeffrey said in a gentle, fraying voice behind them. 'Do we have a Goddess-Father here?' Greg raised his hand. 'Cool, and the Goddess-Mother?' Ruby stuck her hand in the air. 'Me, sir!'

Jeffrey nodded blearily. 'Hey right, yeah, sir, nice one!'

Ruby walked over and put her arm around him. 'Jeffrey – man – do you think you're up to focusing a camera?'

'Oh, yeah, yeah, no problem, you know, with the tripod. Okay then? Let's go for it.'

'Don't we need the baby?' asked Ruby.

'Yeah, Florence, right.'

Anna rolled her eyes at Ruby, and whispered as she handed Florrie over. 'Can you believe the state of him?'

Ruby smiled. 'I like him. I mean, wouldn't you anaesthetise yourself if you lived with Sky?'

Ruby and Greg took turns to hold Florence for the photo session, and then Andy and Anna joined them. Cass came later after Sky had finally allowed her to cross the sacred site on the doorstep. Shirley and Greg had a photo together, as did Ruby and Johnnie. Tony refused to join in the celebration of comfortable coupledom and slouched against the back wall, watching them. There were lots of family shots of Andy, Anna, and Cass with Florrie. Anna had a couple with her parents, a few more of just her and Cass, and then Jeffrey took several of Sky, alone and surrounded by different sets of adults and children. He was about to collapse the tripod when Shirley asked if he could take one of her with Greg and Cori. They all held hands, Cori in between Greg and Shirley with a big grin on her face.

When Jeffrey gave them the thumbs up, Shirley ruffled Cori's hair. 'I think that's going to be a lovely picture.'

Cori looked up at her. 'Can I keep it?'

'Oh yes. I'm sure Jeffrey will do one for you.'

'I want to take it to school.'

Greg interrupted. 'Okay, Cori,' he said, steering her away from Shirley. 'Why don't you go and tell Anna all about it?'

'You needn't have sent her off,' said Shirley, when he came back. 'I was happy chatting with her.'

He sat on the grass. 'I know that, Shirley, but I knew what was coming and I didn't want you feeling awkward.' Shirley squatted next to him, listening and uneasy. 'Cori's getting a hard time from some older girls at school. It's because she doesn't live with her mum. I just didn't want her involving you in it.'

'I don't mind.'

'I know you don't, but she's got it into her head that you're – well – I think with us being together and everything she's jumped to some wrong conclusions.'

'Oh.'

'It's a sort of a game for her, you know, choosing a new mum. That's why she wants the photo, to show them at school. But don't worry about it. It was only the other week that she started all this Happy Families stuff with you, and you know what kids are like, it'll pass in a week or two. I just don't want you to feel stressed by it.'

'Right.'

'And I didn't want you thinking that I'd said anything to her, you know, about you being her mum. Because I haven't. Honest.' He smiled, tracing a cross over his heart with his finger. 'I've told her you're at college, with your future ahead of you, and that we're just friends having fun. I've made it dead clear to her. She knows you're too young to take us on.

So don't worry.' He kissed her and sat back on the grass, absorbing the afternoon sun.

Shirley was thinking about Cori taking her photo to school and telling the bullies that she was her mum. She wanted to protect her, to make it come true, to live with Greg. Instead, she would be moving into the café, greeted by her mother's triumphant face as she crawled back, exposed, rejected, humiliated.

'Greg, you know what you were saying before about needing an au pair and how I said I'd really like to move in and help with Cori, well I meant it. And ages ago you said you could do with a lodger to help with bills, well I could do that—'

Greg opened his eyes. 'Shirley, are you asking me if you can move in?'

'I really need somewhere to live, Greg.'

Greg sat up. 'I thought you were sorted. Aren't you living with your mum at the café?'

'I was. But Dad's come back and he's got my room. They don't want me around.'

'Shit.'

'And I haven't got anywhere else to go. Mum just wants me out of the way, so she can get together with Dad.'

'And can't you stay where you are?'

'The new students are coming next week, and I've given my notice.'

'Andy will help you out. He is the agent.'

Shirley panicked. She started to cry. Greg put his arm around her. 'Listen, I'm not going to see you on the streets. You can move into our spare room. But we'd better tell Cori, so she doesn't get confused and think we're getting married.' He smiled, lifting Shirley's tear-stained, mascara-streaked face. 'Only joking.'

Anna touched him on the shoulder. 'Sorry to interrupt, Greg, but Sky wants to do the ceremony. Oh sorry. Are you okay, Shirley?'

Shirley nodded, wiping her face.

'It's just that we need Greg for a minute. I hope it's not going to be a terrible ordeal.'

Sky had arranged Ruby, Cass and Andy around the twigs, candles and bowl of paste.

'Oh, well done, darling,' said Sky in a low, melodic, ultra-sincere whisper that made Anna wince with irritation. 'Now we have our Goddess-Father and our birth mother. If you, Gregory darling, could stand next to the Goddess-Mother and hold hands, and Cassandra, you hold hands with the Goddess-Father, and Andrew, you are on the other side holding Ruby's hand. So do you see? We have an undulation of gender – from the male essence down to the female element and then back up again to the male principle. We are balancing the yin and the yang in little Florence's nature, harmonising the influences around her as a child.' She opened her arms and gestured to them all, with contrived humility.

'I myself will help Anna to perform her part in the ceremony as it's quite complex. I'm drawing on a number of influences from the movements of the planets above, to the energies in the soil below, and the different colours of our auras as we stand here together.' She smiled again, a sickly stretching of the lips.

'Anna, if you could first place Florence in the centre of our circle.' Anna looked at the collection of objects on the ground in front of her.

'Well, to be honest, Sky, I'm not really happy about Florrie sitting too near the candles. She's really at that stage of reaching out for things. I think it might be dangerous to leave her in the middle of all that.'

Sky shook her head. 'You must trust your daughter, Anna, as I have trusted mine to guide her own fate.' She looked over to Cass who, Anna knew full well, had a rather different perspective on that parenting technique. 'If Florence touches the candle, that itself will be a sign.'

'Yes,' said Anna, 'that's what I'm worried about, a sign of her getting burnt.'

Sky smiled with infinite patience. 'Anna, the flame is a sign of life, in all its varied power. You must think beyond the petty strictures of caution that you yourself have been taught by your parents, and that have left your own spirit so cramped. You must allow Florence to explore the wonders of life for herself. That is what my small ceremony—' Sky put her hand to her chest, '—my offering, is all about. Allowing Florence to embrace the world, and the world to embrace Florence.'

'I thought it was about asking Ruby and Greg to be God-Parents,' said Anna, exercising her cramped spirit.

'It is about Life within the Goddess. Now Anna,' Sky gestured to the space between the candles.

'Sky,' said Cass, 'if Anna feels better holding Florrie I think we should go with that.'

'I see.' Sky was clearly irritated and trying not to show it. 'Well, I'm sure the Goddess will still smile upon us. Anna, could you manage a few words in praise of the Goddess, asking her to bless your child?'

'What?' Anna was thrown. 'You want me to just make something up?'

'No, darling, I want you to speak from the heart.'

Anna could feel the bemused presence of her parents behind her. She had wanted to show them her happy, ordinary family life, and thanks to Sky they would be going back to Wales with the impression that not only was she queer, she was also part of a New Age cult. Jeffrey was bobbing about encouragingly behind Sky. Ruby, Cass and Andy were barely suppressing their laughter. Only Greg was taking any of it seriously. He looked at Anna sympathetically. She spoke to him. 'Please, um, Goddess, can you help Florrie to live a happy, fulfilled life.'

Sky was clearly disappointed. 'Well, perhaps the others could add something more thoughtful later. If anyone writes or knows poetry, please bring that to the gathering. Anna, you must daub the potion onto the family's open palms as they add their blessings. If everyone can hold their hands palm upwards, that's it, towards the sky, darlings.' Sky held out her palms. 'Me first, then Anna.'

Anna transferred Florrie to her hip and picked up the bowl of grey paste. She tried to stop Florrie getting her hands in it, but Florrie thought it was food and started crying when it was pulled away from her. Sky had to speak over her howls and sobs.

'Great Mother, who feeds us from the blood and belly of the Earth, waters us from the milky breasts of the sky, and soothes us with the soft pillows of . . .' This was drowned out by Florrie's screams as Andy lifted her away from Anna and the paste. 'Give this child fecundity of flesh and soulfulness of spirit.'

Anna dabbed the potion onto Sky's hands. It had the texture, and something of the smell, of mashed pilchard. 'Help these adults surrounding the child to be like the great trunks that surround the sapling.' Sky brought her palms together in a silent clap.

Anna scooped some more potion onto her fingers and smeared it over Greg's open palms. He smiled, watching her. 'I just want to say that I'm honoured to be part of this family, and I'll always be there for you. For all of you,' he added, nodding to the others in the circle.

'Said like a true trunk,' said Ruby holding her hands out for the paste, 'and that goes for me too.'

'Well,' said Andy, still holding Florrie and refusing to be pasted. 'I'm going to impress you all with culture. My wish is that my daughter will really live, and live in ways that we can't imagine. For as the great Oscar said: "To live is the rarest thing in the world. Most people exist, that is all." '

'Hypocrite!' Tony was sitting against the wall at the end of the garden. 'Standing there like the proud father.' He stood up, slipping to the left and crushing a glass under his boot. 'I'm through with this.'

'Tony!' said Andy, giving Florrie to Anna. 'That's enough!'

'Yeah, off you go, Tony,' yelled Cass. 'Just piss off and leave us all alone.'

'I'll go when I'm ready,' he said, staring at her. Behind Cass, Anna was ushering their parents and some of the others into the house. 'Hey, Anna,' Tony shouted, as she disappeared into the house, 'I don't think your pretended family is working, do you?'

'It works fine,' said Cass, 'without you. You'll never be part of it.'

Johnnie and Andy had hold of Tony's arms and were half-helping him, half-hauling him up the garden. 'You think I want to be a boring breeder like you?' Tony said as he came towards her. 'Your family's nothing special, Cass. It's ordinary. Do you hear me? You bitches aren't radical, you're sad.'

Cass stepped out of his way as they reached the back door. 'Get out, Tony! You're pissed.'

'I'm going,' he said, shaking Johnnie off and holding the doorframe. 'And by the way, we're moving to Brighton.' He looked into Cass's face. 'Oh dear, hasn't Andy told you? Not as important as you think, are you?'

'Andy! What's he talking about?'

'Sweetie, listen, it's not like that. But we need to talk, I'll come back later.'

Tony winked at her as Andy pulled him into the kitchen. 'Looks like I win.'

Chapter 8

Ladies Night

'I'm going to make an announcement in the café tonight, Gordon, so make sure you're on your best behaviour.' Pearl was standing in the bathroom doorway, watching Gordon admire his reflection in her full-length mirror. Turning to the side, he tucked the white T-shirt into his jeans and flexed his biceps. Pearl tutted at his vanity and went off to collapse the ironing board. He called after her. 'I'm always on my best behaviour.'

'You know what I mean, Gordon. I'm talking about Buzz.'

He grunted. In the mirror, a trim, silver-haired Marlon Brando sneered back. 'Old Buzzard brain?' he said, smiling at himself. 'The man's a weirdo.' He swaggered over to the kitchenette. 'And that eye of his, bobbing about like an olive in a martini. How anyone can eat looking at that, I'll never know.'

'I hope you haven't said that to him,' said Pearl, passing him a mug of tea across the breakfast bar.

He sat straddling one of the high stools. 'Of course I haven't, Pearl, what do you take me for?'

'Because you don't want to infuriate him.' She put a plate of toasted sandwiches between them and sat down. 'Not if you want to move in properly.' He winked at her and she held up a warning finger. 'Three weeks, Gordon, that's what we said. Three weeks starting yesterday. A trial. And you'll be spending them in the stable room.'

He nodded. 'Taking it slow, Pearl, I understand.' A minute later, he reached over the last slice of toast and took Pearl's hand. 'Just being with you, Pearl, being here, it makes me feel twenty years younger. I've got new clothes, a new look. You've shown me the way, Pearl, you really have.'

'Have I, Gordon?'

'Oh yes! And as for you!' He walked round to her side of the breakfast bar, still holding her hand. 'I haven't seen you look this sexy in years.' Pearl glanced down at the low-cut purple swirl dress she'd got from the market. It was too young for her. She'd only bought it because the colours matched the café. 'They'd throw you off the streets if you wore that in Frinley.'

'Really, Gordy?'

'Oh yes.'

Pearl laughed as he led her out of the flat. At the door, Gordon kissed her gently on the cheek. 'I'm proud of you, Pearl.'

'You sweet talker!' She slapped him on the chest, but they still held hands all the way down the stairs.

When they opened the door at the back of the café, Buzz was making tea for a solitary customer, a middle-aged woman in a yellow woollen hat and torn brown overcoat. Gordon glanced down at the small piles of copper coins she'd stacked on the table and the plastic bags at her feet as he strolled past. 'Hello there, um, Buzz,' he said as they reached the counter. Buzz ignored him, not looking up from the tray he was arranging. Pearl noticed that he'd put two flapjacks under a napkin. Gordon leant on the counter. 'Hey,' he laughed, 'I

don't think we'll be seeing much profit from that table tonight.'
Buzz stared at him, fixing him with one eye as the seconds
ticked past. Gordon shifted uncomfortably, gesturing helplessly
at Pearl when Buzz finally looked away and picked up the tray.
Pearl rolled her eyes and marched past him to the back of the
counter. 'Buzz, where's Cass? I've got something to tell you
all.'

'She's there,' said Buzz, pointing to the window on his way
to table five. Cass struggled through the front door carrying a
chalked-up blackboard.

'Pearl, did you put this out?' she asked.

'I did,' said Pearl. 'I'm advertising tonight's theme. Monday
night is Ladies Night. We agreed that.'

'Pearl, we agreed you could resurrect Women Only Nights.'

'I know. But Women Only sounds so ugly, don't you think
so, Gordon?'

'Absolutely,' said Gordon, straightening up.

Cass barely glanced at him. 'Pearl, if you put a sign out the
front saying "Ladies In Here Tonight" the only customers
you'll get are perverts.'

'Oh!' She looked at Gordon. 'I didn't think of that.'

'Obviously,' said Cass, reaching for a cloth.

'Well anyway. It's a very exciting night for me. My first
theme evening, and I have an announcement.'

The door pushed open and Dee walked in. 'What you all
standing here for?'

'Pearl has an announcement,' said Cass rubbing the
blackboard.

'Make it quick, Pearl. I'm upstairs tonight.'

'Well,' said Pearl, looking around for Buzz to come back to
the counter. 'Jasbinder and Anna should be here really. But I
can always talk to them later.' She coughed. 'I wanted to let
you all know that Gordon and I are having a trial upstairs.'

Dee sat down. 'What trial? Jury trial, horse trial?'

'Marriage trial, Dee,' said Pearl, taking Gordon's hand. 'And
I'd like to put Gordon forward as a volunteer for the café.'

Silence. Buzz stared at Cass, one eye on her, the other swooping excitedly from floor to ceiling. 'No fucking way!'

'Now, Buzz,' said Pearl, ' I knew you wouldn't like the idea, but Gordon is a good worker and he won't interfere, will you, Gordon?'

'No. Absolutely not. Just do as I'm told.'

'Toilets need cleaning,' said Dee.

'Ha, ha!' said Gordon, on his best behaviour. 'Very funny.'

'Who's fucking joking?' said Buzz.

'Ah, I see,' said Gordon. 'Well, I think that's more of a job for Pearl, don't you? I don't have much experience with toilets.'

'Too busy shitting on the workers,' said Buzz, jaw twitching. 'Sexist bourgeois git.' He slammed his apron on the counter and walked out into the street. Dee stamped off to the kitchen. Cass picked up Buzz's apron and put it on. 'It's not going to happen, Pearl.'

'Surely, Cass, you'll give Gordon a trial.'

'No.'

'He's not asking for money.'

'I know that, Pearl, but he's blatantly racist, sexist, capitalist and homophobic.'

'I don't think that's exactly fair,' muttered Gordon.

'Sorry, Gordon,' said Cass. 'You're not our kind of guy.'

'But that's prejudice,' said Gordon, outraged.

'Yeah, crap, isn't it?' said Cass. She picked up the blackboard and wrote 'Women Only Night' in bold yellow letters.

Pearl propped the blackboard up against the front of the café, smarting from the collective's response to Gordon, and galled by the crudeness of the newly chalked sign. She marched back into the café. 'The state of that sign, I'll be surprised if we get a single person through that door tonight, male nor female.'

'We don't want men,' said Cass, rearranging the counter display, 'that's the point.'

'But you've still got to draw people in, Cass. Not frighten them off with militant feminism.'

'Pearl,' said Cass, not bothering to look up. 'We've been through this before. If you want to redo the sign, then redo the sign. But women only means women only. Not ladies, not men and not women wannabes, okay?'

'And what's that supposed to mean?' said Pearl, grabbing the chalk.

'You know who I'm talking about, Pearl, and I'm just letting you know, if he comes tonight, he'll have to go upstairs. I won't let him stay in the café.'

'Who's she talking about, Pearl?' asked Gordon.

Pearl's stomach lurched, and not for ideological reasons. Among the invitations she'd sent out to local women's groups and self-help meetings, Pearl had posted a couple of her own. One to Lucasta in Frinley and one to Charlene. She looked at the clock. Six-thirty. If Charlene decided to come, she had less than one minute to get Gordon upstairs before his brother turned up in a dress. 'I think you should go back upstairs now, Gordon. You don't want to be down here with all the lesbians.'

'Good point,' said Gordon, heading immediately for the back door. 'Not that I'm prejudiced,' he added, turning around and looking pointedly at Cass.

'Course you're not,' said Pearl, pushing him on through the café. 'I know that.'

They had reached the back door when the first customers arrived. A group of women, friends of Cass's from the tattoo parlour across the road, crowded around the counter. Behind them, in a new wig, green lace blouse and matching skirt, was Charlene. 'Pearl? I made it, lovey, I'm here for Ladies Night.'

Gordon wasn't quite through the door. He looked back. 'What the—?' He gripped the doorframe. 'Charles? What the bloody hell . . .?'

The women at the counter went quiet. Both men were shouting the same question.

'What the fuck's he doing here?'

As soon as he stepped foot into the flat, Gordon confronted Pearl. 'Why the hell didn't you tell me Charles would be here?'

Pearl followed him in, breathless from the furious gallop up the stairs. 'I forgot, Gordon. I sent Charlene a little note when I did the invitations.'

'It was sort of a surprise,' said Charlene. She was standing beyond the open door, not coming into the flat.

'Too bloody right it was,' said Gordon, stamping furiously across the lounge, glaring at his brother. 'And what the hell do you look like?'

'I was here for Ladies Night,' said Charlene, holding herself with touching dignity.

'For God's sake,' muttered Gordon. He grabbed a bottle of whiskey and poured himself a drink.

'I think we'd all like one of those, Gordon,' said Pearl, pointing at the bottle.

Charlene stepped further back along the landing. 'Pearl, I wouldn't have come if I'd known Gordon was here.'

Gordon grunted.

'I'm sorry, Lene,' said Pearl, following her out onto the landing. 'It's all happened so quickly.'

Charlene nodded. 'So it seems.'

'Gordon and I are trying to make another go of things.' She pulled the door behind her. 'He's staying a while.'

'But I thought it was over,' Charlene whispered. 'You said you didn't want him back.'

'I know, but Gordon's not so bad really. And I promise we'll stay friends, Lene.'

Charlene smiled. 'We won't, Pearl, not now.'

'Don't say that, Lene.'

'How can we? You've seen what he's like with me. It's best if we just say goodbye now. You've made your choice, Pearl.'

Pearl held her arm. 'Listen, Lene, you just stay right where you are. Gordon isn't telling me who I can be friends with.' She kicked open the door behind her. 'If I get back with Gordon, he's got to accept you for who you are.' She winked.

'What?' Gordon spluttered from inside. 'Accept him? I'll never accept him!'

'Her, Gordon', said Pearl, going back into the flat. 'Charlene's a her.'

'For God's sake, Pearl, it's a man. He's got a dick under that dress.' Gordon slammed his glass onto the breakfast bar. 'Do you want me to show you?' He charged towards the door, but Pearl grabbed his T-shirt with her nails. 'There's no need for that, Gordon. Charlene is leaving.'

'I think there's every need!' He pulled away from her, tearing the back of his new white T-shirt. Pearl rushed to the door and blocked his way to Charlene. 'No, Gordon!' He pressed his weight against the doorframe, but didn't knock her out of the way. 'I know you don't like it, Gordon, but Charlene is my friend. Don't ruin things between us now, just when we're getting our marriage back together.'

Gordon held his ground, scowling at his brother, standing there at the top of the stairs in frills.

'Please, Gordon, I don't want you two fighting. Now go back inside. Let's try to sort this out.'

'How can you be friends with that?' he said, pointing to Charlene.

'Very easily, now please let's sit down.' Gordon refused to move, and for a moment they all stood there, staring at each other. Then Gordon released his grip on the doorframe and Pearl led him back to the flat. 'My brother the freak,' he muttered as he slumped on the sofa.

Charlene moved back to the door. 'I realise this must be a little strange for you, Gordon,' she said, 'after all these years.'

'A little strange? More like a bloody nightmare.' Pearl poured him another drink and sat next to him, waving to Charlene, gesturing for her to come inside.

She hovered at the edge of the room. 'Pearl invited me to the café a while ago. We got on straight away didn't we, Pearl?'

'From that first day.'

Gordon was staring at Charlene. 'And what are you then, some kind of poof?'

'Oh no, Gordon,' Charlene looked him straight in the eye. 'Both Charles and Charlene prefer women friends.'

'I can have dinner with Charles and go shopping with Charlene,' said Pearl, smiling.

'I see,' said Gordon. 'So not satisfied with being a pervert, you're also making a play for my wife.'

'Oh, for goodness sake, Gordon,' said Pearl, 'now you're being ridiculous.'

Charlene said nothing.

'Right,' Pearl stood up. 'I think we should sort this once and for all. Lene, I think we need Charles in here. You'll find Gordon's things in the stable room. Change into something of his.'

'I'm not having him in—'

'Be quiet, Gordon. Do you want Charles out of that dress or not?'

Gordon watched his brother mince out of the room in high heels. He slumped further into the sofa. 'For God's sake, Pearl. How can you be friends with that thing?'

'Because *she* is fun.'

'But *he* is my brother.'

'I know that, Gordon.'

'This is too much for me, Pearl,' said Gordon, draining his drink. 'I can go so far and no further. Buzzard Brain, Deadpan Dee. I did my best. But Charles is beyond my limit.'

Pearl sat on his lap and stroked his hair. 'Perhaps if you just talk to him?'

'What about? Make-up?'

'I know it's hard for you, Gordy, but Charles is your brother. Remember when you were boys? You always told me you adored him.'

Gordon shrugged.

'He's still the same person underneath.'

'Underneath what? Frilly knickers?'

Charles came out of the bedroom, wearing Gordon's flannel trousers and a dark blue blazer. He was taller than his brother, but narrower across the chest. He made Gordon's conventional wardrobe look clownish. Pearl had to suppress a giggle.

Charles didn't sit down. He stood behind the armchair and stared at Pearl sitting on Gordon's lap. She slid off and sat next to Gordon on the sofa.

'I'm prepared to make the effort here, Gordon, because you and Pearl are the only family I've got.'

'Really? I thought you had a twin sister?'

'Gordon,' Pearl said. 'this is a chance for you and Charles to talk, not bicker.'

'Charlene is part of who I am, Gordon. She's always been there, even when we were boys.'

'So you did *this* when we were boys?' Gordon waved his hand in the air to indicate a vague sense of femininity. 'Did you dress up?'

'Yes, but I also looked after you, Gordon. For years I let you follow me around—'

'Doing your dirty work.'

'You were my little brother. We were children.'

'I bet you two got up to some pranks, didn't you, when your dad was out?' Pearl said, helpfully. Gordon stared at his feet. For a while no one said a word. Pearl put her arm around Gordon, giving him a squeeze. Charles coughed. 'Do you remember that time I made us chips and set fire to the kitchen curtains?'

Gordon spoke to the floor. 'That battle-axe next door dragged them down and threw them out the window. You got the strap for that.'

'You see, that's something, Gordon,' said Pearl. 'You need to cling on to these memories.'

'Here's one then,' said Gordon, still not looking up. 'Do you remember calling me a pansy at school?' Charles stopped smiling. 'Do you remember that? All the other kids joined in. I was always Pansy Gates after that.' Gordon was looking directly at his brother now, and Charles was shifting uncomfortably.

'And do you remember why?'

Charles nodded. 'Because you wore Mum's scarf.'

'After she died, Charles. I was six.'

'We had tough times, Gordon, but I wasn't a bad brother. I saved you from some scrapes. I was handy with my fists.'

'And isn't that the biggest joke? My skinny brother, the hardest man in Mansfield, wanted to be a girl.' Gordon snorted at the irony and sat back on the sofa. Pearl stroked his arm, watching memory colour his face. Suddenly he hauled himself to his feet. 'You wore her clothes.'

'What?' Charles backed away from the chair.

'You dressed up in our dead mother's clothes. Didn't you?'

Charles raised his hands. 'You don't understand, Gordon.'

'You filthy bastard.'

'I missed her too, Gordon. She would have understood me.'

'She would have hated you.'

'No, Gordon, you hate me. You hate me because I embarrass you.'

Gordon walked slowly around the chair towards him. 'You don't embarrass me, Charles, you appal me.' He raised his fists and smashed into Charles's shoulder. Pearl screamed for him to stop, but Charles hit back, catching Gordon on the cheek, knocking him over the back of the armchair. 'You know what, Gordon,' he said, standing over him, breathing hard and wiping the blood from his nose. 'You appal me too. You cheat on your wife, betray your family, and have the nerve to judge me.' Walking away as calmly as he could, Charles left them in the flat and headed down the stairs to Women Only Night in his brother's ill-fitting clothes.

Gordon watched him go. 'That's the end of it, Pearl.'

'Gordon—'

'No, Pearl. This is where I stop. I will not have him in our lives. Either you get rid of Charles or our marriage is over. It's him or me.'

Chapter 9

Moving On

'God I forgot what a dump this house was!' Lou pushed open the front door and stepped onto the worn brown carpet of her new home. 'We could have got a mansion for this price at home.'

'It's London, Lou,' said Will, following her inside. 'I don't care if we're living in a toilet. We've fucking escaped, darling.'

She smiled at him. She had dyed red hair and thick black kohl around her eyes that spiralled out to her temples. 'I didn't think we ever would.'

He grinned. 'Me neither.'

'And here we are!' She stuck her arse towards him. 'Rural England, kiss my pretty white ass!'

'Pleasure!' He bent forward, lips pursed. 'Life starts here, sis!'

Upstairs, Shirley was packing her clothes into a black bin liner when she heard voices. She opened her bedroom door. A blond man in a beaded blue skirt was prancing about in the hall while a thin woman leant against the wall, laughing at him. He pulled her towards him and they jumped around in circles, holding hands, singing, 'We escaped, we escaped.' Shirley watched them for a moment from the top of the stairs before stepping quietly down.

'Hi!' she said when she reached the bottom. They didn't hear her, so she slammed the front door to get their attention.

The woman looked up first. 'God, who the hell are you?'

'Shirley,' said Shirley, holding out her hand.

'Will,' said the man. He waved at her breathlessly from the end of the hall, and Shirley noticed the green varnish on his short nails. The woman grabbed Shirley's hand and shook it once, hard, like she was trying to ease a cramp. 'Lou! Where did you come from?'

'I live here,' said Shirley.

'What?' Lou glared at Shirley and then opened the front door. 'Mike,' she yelled. A man's head appeared from the back of an old blue van parked outside. 'Mike, stop unloading. There's a problem.'

'There's not,' said Shirley from the hall. 'I'm moving out today.'

'When?' Lou turned on her from the doorway. She was taller than Shirley and her red hair was cut with geometric precision into two half moons over her eyebrows. She stared down at Shirley through the curls of kohl around her eyes. 'We were told the house would be empty by twelve today.'

Shirley looked at her watch. It was 12:10. 'I'll be gone soon. I'm only going next door,' she glanced at Will. 'I'm moving in with my boyfriend.' He smiled but Lou leant back through the door. 'Mike, ring the agent. Tell him there's a problem.'

'I've just told you there's not,' said Shirley, gesturing to Will. 'Doesn't she believe me or something?'

'Lou, darling,' he said, moving forward and taking her by the elbow. 'Shirley will be gone in an hour. We don't need to bother our lovely agent.'

'I told you,' said Shirley, 'when Greg, that's my boyfriend, gets home from football, I'll just go. Everywhere is empty except my room.'

Lou studied her for a while then headed for the stairs. 'Will, I'm going to check the rooms upstairs. I think the back one had the best light for a studio.'

'That's my room,' said Shirley.

Lou hung over the banister near the top of the stairs and looked down at her. '*Was* your room, Shirley. We're paying for it now.' It was the first time Shirley had seen her smile.

Will laughed at Shirley's stunned expression. 'Oh God, don't worry about Lou. She just doesn't realise how scary she is. Oldest twin, you know, squashed me in the womb and all that. Anyway, meet our friend from home, Mike. He really isn't scary, are you, Mike?'

'What?' Mike hovered in the doorframe. He was overweight and the only one not wearing a skirt.

'You're not scary,' said Will.

'Not me,' said Mike. 'But there's a real creepy woman across the road just staring at me.'

'That'll be Doris,' said Shirley, 'Doris Karloff.'

'Oh,' said Mike. He stood there, waiting to be told what to do.

'Let's have a drink to celebrate our new life. You too, Shirley. Mike, where's the champagne Mummy gave us? Not that we should drink a drop when you think what it's done to her.'

Shirley didn't care about Mummy and her champagne. She wanted to make sure Lou wasn't rifling through her stuff. She turned to go up the stairs. Will stopped her, grabbing her arm. 'Hey, Shirley, is that the agent outside?'

She glimpsed Andy through the open door. 'Yeah.'

'He's dead sexy, isn't he? Best get rid of him though, before Lou throws a tantrum.' He picked up the hem of his skirt and ran into the street. 'Andy! Hi.'

Shirley hovered with Mike, both of them stuck for something to say. Shirley glanced at him, backed up against the wall, avoiding her eye, and realised how far she had come. It wasn't her standing on the edges of life, waiting for something exciting to dribble in her direction. She wasn't sleeping in a horsebox. She made things happen. She was moving in with the man of her dreams. After thirty seconds of thickening silence, Shirley gave up on politeness and left Mike chewing his lip in the hall.

Andy had been hoping to avoid the new students. He'd told the office he was checking on the house, but really he'd come to see Anna and Cass. And he didn't have much time. He hadn't seen them or Florrie since the party and there were things he needed to say. He stopped and faced the blond boy crossing the road. 'Is everything okay with the house, um—?'

'Will, and yeah, it's cool. There's no need for you to come inside.'

'That's good.'

'I just wanted to ask you something.'

'Uh huh,' Andy couldn't help looking at his watch.

'It's just, I was wondering if you knew of any good pubs, you know, where I could meet new friends, I mean . . . men friends.'

Andy felt the vulnerability of this beautiful boy in a skirt, but he didn't have time for him now. 'Sorry, Will, I can't help you. I'm here to see my daughter and I'm in a bit of a rush.' It sounded like a brush off, but Andy couldn't help that. He had other things on his mind.

'Oh,' Will blushed, and hung his head. He fiddled with the beads hanging from his waist. 'I thought you were : . . that you'd know . . . I'm sorry.'

Andy glanced up the street to where Tony was waiting for him. They were going to have lunch together after his visit to the girls. 'Talk to my friend there. He knows all the places to go.'

He left Will standing on the curb and walked up the path to number 96. Cass answered the door. 'Hi, sweetie,' said Andy brightly.

'Oh, it's you. I thought you'd gone to Brighton.'

'Okay, I deserved that. I should have come round sooner. I did phone.'

Anna called from inside. 'Cass, stop arguing and let Andy in.'

Andy followed Cass up the hall, past the framed photos of his daughter and into the sitting room. She spoke without looking back. 'So! Are you really moving?'

He stood in his best suit, in the doorway, feeling on trial. 'We found a flat yesterday.'

'You didn't waste any time.' Cass sat next to Anna on the futon sofa, both of them staring at him. Judge and jury.

'I'm an estate agent, remember.'

'When will you go?' asked Cass.

'Christmastime.'

Cass shrugged and looked away. Anna stared at him in silence. Eventually she spoke. 'What about Florrie?'

'She'll be fine . . . she'll have great holidays.' He walked across the floorboards and lifted Florrie from her rainbow play mat.

Anna watched him. 'She doesn't need holidays, Andy. She needs a father. She needs you.'

'She's got me. It's an hour away on the train, let's not forget that, girls.'

'So we pack the pushchair in the guard's van and send her off,' said Cass.

'Obviously not,' said Andy, holding the baby.

'What then?' Cass asked. 'We bring her to you? And when do we do that? We're working every shift we can at the café. I'm supposed to be there now.'

'I'll visit you here.'

'How often?' Cass demanded.

'Look, I think we're getting ahead of ourselves, girls. Can I just sit down?' Andy took a pile of toys off the armchair and sat with Florrie on his knee. 'We're not getting divorced or anything.'

'Aren't we?' said Anna. 'That's what it feels like.'

'That's because we're so ordinary,' said Cass. 'Not queer enough.'

'Shut up, Cass,' snapped Anna. 'That won't help.' She dragged her fingers through her hair. 'I thought we were making a family, Andy. I thought we were in this together. A lifetime commitment, isn't that what we said?'

'I'm still committed.'

'From fifty miles away. That's not what we planned and you know it.'

Andy shrugged. 'Things change, Anna. You can't plan against the future.'

'She's seven months old, for God's sake. How did things change so quickly?'

'No need to answer that,' muttered Cass.

'That's how!' said Andy pointing at Cass. 'You've had a problem with Tony from the moment he came back.'

'Yeah, because he was determined to wreck our family. You heard what he said: "I win".'

'He was drunk,' shouted Andy. 'He didn't mean those things.'

'Of course he did,' yelled Cass. 'We should never have asked you to be the father.'

'Well, thanks a fucking lot!' Andy put Florrie on her mat and walked out of the room.

'Stop!' Anna jumped up from the sofa and went after him. 'Andy, come back. Cass didn't mean that.' She held his arm and shouted to Cass from the hall. 'Go and make us coffee, Cass. I want to talk to Andy.'

Cass appeared at the sitting room door. 'I'm not the one breaking up this family.'

'Shut up, Cass, and make the coffee. You've said enough already.'

Cass stormed into the kitchen, and Anna led Andy back into the sitting room. She shut the door behind them.

'So you're really going?' She stood by the door, arms crossed. Florrie was sitting happily on her mat.

Andy nodded. 'Anna, sweetie, try to see it from my position. I love Tony, I don't want to lose him, and I don't want to lose you three either. But you know what Cass is like.'

'Don't blame Cass for this, Andy.'

'I'm not, but it's never going to work if we're all in London.'

'What with it being such a small town?'

Andy sat on the armchair. 'You know what I mean, Anna. I've hardly slept this week. I don't want to leave my gorgeous flat, but what can I do? This seems the only way to keep this family together.'

'By pulling it apart.'

'By giving us some distance.'

'And Tony fancies Brighton.'

Andy nodded, staring at the floor.

'Well, we'll just have to make the best of it, won't we?'

'It's not as bad as you think, sweetie. I'll be commuting for the first six months until I get transferred at work. I can see Florrie every day.'

'I want Florrie to have a father, Andy.'

'She will.'

'I mean a relationship.' She sat on the sofa and held out her hand. He took it in his. 'I want her to know you, Andy. I don't want you to be just some man she can get money off when she's older.'

'Is that what Cass wants?'

'Cass thinks Florrie will do fine with two mums.'

'She'll do brilliant.' He squeezed her hand.

'I want her to have a dad too.'

'So do I, Anna. I'm not abandoning her. Brighton is only an hour away.'

'I want you to see her, Andy. A lot.'

'I will. Every month.'

Anna stared at him, dropping his hand. 'Twelve times a year.'

'Anna, don't hate me for trying to save my relationship.'

She looked into his face. 'I don't hate you, Andy.'

'She does.' He glanced at the closed door.

'She's upset.'

'I do love Florrie, Anna, but I have to change the balance in my life.'

'And that's what you've done.' Anna looked at Florrie, sitting in front of them on the floor, banging a green plastic cup. They sat in silence for a while, watching the child they'd made.

'I have to go,' said Andy. 'Tony's waiting for me outside.'

'Right.' Anna stood up and opened the door for him. 'Cass, Andy's leaving. Say goodbye.'

Cass stood in the kitchen with a tray of cups in her hands. 'What about the coffee?'

'I'm sorry,' said Andy, letting himself out, 'I have to go.'

When Andy got out onto the street Tony and Will were still talking together, laughing at the end of the street. Andy ran over to them, barely acknowledging Greg, who was walking home, sweaty and dirty, from football practice with the Balham Bhajis.

Tony held his arm out to Andy as he came up to them. 'They give you a hard time?'

He grabbed at Tony's sleeve. 'What do you think?' He pulled him along the street. 'Come on. Let's get out of here. I need a drink.'

Tony turned back to smile at Will. 'See you around.'

Chapter 10

Breakfast News

'Morning, darling.' Gordon tapped lightly on Pearl's bedroom door. He had already made his bed in the horsebox, showered and changed into clean, silk pyjamas. Now, for the second Saturday in a row, he was hovering, cologned and hopeful, with toast and tea on a tray. Saturday mornings had always been a good time in their married life and Gordon knew it was only a matter of time before he could leave the horses behind and start spending his nights at the opera.

'What?' Pearl's voice sounded groggy behind the closed door. 'Gordon, is that you?'

He opened the door a crack and peered in. The audience watched him silently from the far wall as he stepped across the room to the crimson drapes around the bed.

'Morning, darling. I've made you breakfast in bed.' Gordon slid the tray through a gap in their old lounge curtains. 'Hope you like it.' Pearl looked at him. The morning's letters were wrapped in an elastic band on one side of the tray; the *Daily Express* was neatly folded by the teapot, and two cups snuggled against the plates of toast.

'I see you've brought yourself a cup, Gordon. Were you thinking of stopping?'

'Only if you don't mind sharing.'

Pearl stared at him for a moment and then sat up against the pillow, smoothing her nighty and pulling the lacy straps back over her shoulders. With the tray balanced on her lap, she poured two cups of tea and handed one to Gordon, smiling, 'And where were you thinking of drinking it, Gordy?'

The only chairs in the room were in the fold-down theatre row so Gordon took his cup and walked to the other side of the room. He lowered a seat, the hinge groaning, and perched on the edge. Pearl looked at him and laughed. 'Are you just going to sit in the audience and watch me?'

He stood up awkwardly. 'I'll get a chair.'

Pearl smiled at his shy formality. 'Don't be soft, Gordy.' She pulled back the blankets. 'There's room in here for two.'

Gordon coughed. 'Well, if you're sure.'

'I think you deserve breakfast in bed after what you said last night.'

'Really?' he smiled. 'What was that?'

'About Charles.'

'Oh,' Gordon climbed the two steps. 'I just said I'd write to him, Pearl, not that I've changed my mind.'

'I know that, Gordon, but putting your feelings in a letter might help. It's a start.'

Gordon snuggled in. He didn't want to talk about Charles. The rumpled sheets and the smell of Pearl's warm perfumed body made him feel boyishly excited. 'I've missed you, Pearl.'

'I know you have, Gordon. I've missed you too. It's been nice you being here.'

'I've missed our Saturday mornings, when Shirley was at her riding lessons.'

Pearl smiled coyly. 'I don't think it's right for us to be talking about such things when you're here next to me in bed, do you?'

'I think it's exactly the right time,' said Gordon, moving the tray to the foot of the bed. 'After all, I'm still a rather distinguished gentleman, and you're still a rather buxom wench.'

'Opera singer,' Pearl corrected.

'Exactly, a rather naughty opera singer who hasn't been practising her scales.'

Pearl giggled.

'And now you're going to be taught a lesson.'

'Are you going to teach me?'

'Oh yes.' Gordon ripped open his pyjama jacket, revealing a triangle of grey hairs on his chest. 'For I am the arrogant Lord Gates and you have run away from my advances once too often.' He pulled down the straps on her gown. 'I'm going to spank your bare behind, you little hussy. And then—' he let Pearl sink under the covers, '—and then I'm going to kiss it all better.'

On the tray, waiting for the moment when they would resurface, pink and breathless, smiling and sweaty, for a sip of cold tea, was the bundle of letters. In amongst the postcards from Lucasta and the newsletters from Pearl's food clubs was a plain white envelope, postmarked Frinley-on-Sea. The card inside, tastefully printed in gold over a gloss black background, announced the sad departure of Keith Smedley (much-missed husband and father) and invited the Gates family to pay their respects at his cremation the following Friday. There was no personal message from the widow.

Shirley could hear Greg ambling down the stairs as she poured the milk over three bowls of Coco Pops. He strolled into the kitchen in his boxer shorts, draped his arms over her shoulders and kissed her, resting his head on hers. Shirley wriggled in his arms. 'Careful, silly, I'm making us all some breakfast.' She put the biggest bowl in his hands. 'That's for you, Daddy Bear, and this little one's for Cori, she's in the lounge watching TV.'

Coriander didn't move when her dad gave her the bowl and plonked himself next to her on the sagging brown sofa. She was staring at the telly, cuddling Mr H, the teddy Shirley had given her the day she'd moved in. When Shirley came in Greg heaved himself along the sofa, throwing tattered cushions onto the floor, Cori pushing him along so that Shirley could sit between them. The three of them watched cartoons, Greg and Cori drinking chocolate milk out of the bowl, Shirley sucking hers off the spoon. Greg teased her with his foot, tickling her leg, and wrapping his bony toes around her fleshy ankle. Shirley giggled and slapped him. 'Stop it!'

'What? I'm not doing anything.'

'Yes you are, isn't he, Cori?'

Cori threw herself across them, spilling the dregs of Shirley's cereal over Greg's boxers. He leapt up, brown milk dripping from his legs, while Shirley and Cori laughed.

'Quiet!' Greg yelled at them. He was pointing at the television. Shirley turned to look. A woman was sitting cross-legged on the studio floor telling the presenter about a new after-school programme. 'It's called "Eco-Pops" and it's going to be fantastic. We've got eco-friendly competitions, wildlife advice, green projects that everyone up and down the country can join in with; phenomenal things to make out of recycling – art, robots, even houses, and we'll be meeting some of the great people who make them.'

Shirley was watching Greg's face. He looked like he had seen a ghost.

'And of course we've got poetry, we'll be reading your poems about the environment, and a few of mine, and the best of yours we're going to make into songs with the top stars in the business. So if you care about the planet and you want to write a song for your favourite pop star, this is the show for you.'

'Hey,' said the presenter, twinkling at the wrong camera. 'Doesn't that sound great? Will you treat us to a poem now, Acorn?'

'Acorn?' Shirley looked again at the woman on the television. She wasn't beautiful. She had a big mouth and lots of teeth. Her hair was long and plaited into tight braids that kept falling over her eyes. She flicked the hair off her face. 'Let's see if I can make one up for you. Just to show you all how easy it is. I know, a limerick. They're always fun.

> *'There was a young planet in space*
> *That had a most beautiful face*
> *But we spoiled her air*
> *And we didn't care*
> *So now that's the end of our race.'*

The camera returned to the smiling presenter. 'It's pretty serious, guys. Thanks, Acorn. She's amazing, everyone, she just makes that stuff up in her head. And we'll certainly be watching "Eco–Pops" every day this week at four o'clock.'

Greg had lifted Cori into the air. 'You see that lady, Cori, that famous lady on the TV, that's your mum, Cori. She's made it, she's really bloody made it. I knew she would. What do you think of that, Cori? I told you your mum was going to be famous.'

Cori was squealing, over-excited by her dad dancing her around the room, covered in chocolate milk. It was a while before Greg remembered about Shirley. She had got an old tea towel from the kitchen and was mopping the sofa.

'Come on, Shirley,' he said, holding his arm out to her. 'Join the dancing. Me and Cori are celebrating.'

Ruby yawned, tousling her hair, which sleep had styled into a lopsided quiff. The smell of food had dragged her out of bed and into the kitchen. 'So what are you cooking for me?'

Johnnie smiled at her from the hob. 'Sausage.'

'Are you tempting me to be crude?' she said, strolling over to him and leaning into his naked back.

'Always.'

'So I have found Mr Right.' She kissed his neck and looked over his shoulder at the sausages, bacon and mushrooms in the frying pan. 'What have I done to deserve this?'

'Nothing.' He held her hands to his mouth, kissing her palms. 'It's eat now, pay later.'

'I see.' She leant over him for a while, watching him flip the bacon with a wooden spoon, then wandered over to the kettle to pour herself a lukewarm coffee. 'And is there going to be extra interest added to my late payment?'

'Oh yes!' He grinned, pointing the wooden spoon at her. 'Lashings!'

'No way!' She backed off, laughing. 'No way are you whipping my ass with that thing.'

'You wait, girl.' He threw it back in the pan and turned down the heat. 'I've got plans for you today.'

'So can I sit down?' asked Ruby, grabbing her coffee, and moving to a chair. 'Or do you want me naked on the table garnished with two fried eggs and a rasher of bacon?'

He smiled at her. 'I'm using a plate. But you eat how you want.'

Ruby sat down and reached for her cigarettes.

'Post's on the table,' said Johnnie, not turning around. 'It's all for you.'

Ruby pushed the letters aside. 'I'll open them later, there's nothing import . . .' She trailed off. Among the credit card offers and charity appeals one letter stood out. It was an ordinary envelope, manila with a typical address label, but the red frank mark jolted her. She put down the cigarettes. Johnnie was looking at her.

'You all right, babe?'

She nodded and he turned back to the pan, cracking eggs that hissed and spat in the fat. Ruby picked up the letter and opened the flap. Inside was a printed solicitor's letter and a smaller blue envelope that slid out onto the table. Her name was handwritten across the front. She stared at it, at the rough black letters on cheap blue paper. She hadn't seen that writing for more than twenty years. The solicitor's letter was still in her hand. She tore it to shreds and jerked the blue envelope away from her. It fell silently off the table and onto the floor.

'The usual crap?' asked Johnnie, not turning away from the pan.

Ruby lit a cigarette, fingers shaking. 'Yeah. All bollocks.'

'Shove it in the bin then and I'll bring the plates over.'

Ruby cleared the table, gathering the shreds of papers and throwing them all into the black plastic sack under the sink.

'Right, woman, you are in for a feast,' said Johnnie, putting the plates on the table. Ruby didn't answer. She was leaning over the sink, staring into the black bag. 'Ruby, are you okay?'

'Course, why shouldn't I be?'

'Come on then,' Johnnie forked egg and mushroom into his mouth. 'Get it while it's hot.'

'Just give me a minute.' Ruby walked back to the table and stubbed her cigarette in the ashtray. She watched him eating as she lit another. 'I'm not hungry, Johnnie, you have mine.'

'What? No way! I made it for you.' He pulled out a chair for her and noticed the envelope on the floor underneath. 'Here's a letter for you.'

Ruby moved away. 'Bin it. It's crap.'

'But it's handwritten.' He picked it up. 'Aren't you going to read it?'

'No.'

'Who's it from?' He turned it over in his hands.

She kept her back to him, leaning against the sink. 'My father.'

'What!' Johnnie stared at the envelope in his hands.

'His solicitor sent it. It means he's dead.'

'Fuck!' Johnnie slid back his chair and went over to her, but she brushed him off, refusing to turn around.

'It's all right, Johnnie, I don't need sympathy. I'm fine.'

He stared at the curve of her back as she swayed against the sink. 'So did they send you a letter?'

'I tore it up.'

'I'm really sorry, babe.' He put his hands on her shoulders. 'What did the solicitor say?'

'How the fuck do I know? I told you, I tore up the letter.'

'Didn't you read it?'

'Apparently not.' She dragged on her cigarette.

'Ruby, you've got to read it!'

'Why?'

'To see if he's dead or not.'

'I'm not interested.'

'Well, I am.' Johnnie tried to turn her to face him, but she stiffened at his touch. So he bent down next to her and pulled out the black sack from under the sink. It rubbed against Ruby's legs, but she ignored it, so he emptied the paper out and gathered the torn shreds of the solicitor's letter. He took them to the table to piece the letter together, and read it silently when he was done. Ruby turned around to watch him.

Dear Ms Gold,

It is with deepest regret that I must inform you that Jack Gold, of no fixed abode, passed away earlier this year in January 2001. In accordance with his wishes we are forwarding the enclosed document, which he bestowed to our care on 15 December 1996 following his release from HMP Brixton. Mr Gold left a small estate that he bequeathed to you as the sole beneficiary. Please contact this office at your earliest convenience to arrange the reading of Mr Gold's final will and testament. Yours in deepest sympathy,

pp. Mr Stokes
Stokes, Coffin and Hand

Johnnie sat back looking at Ruby. 'He is dead. He died last winter.'

She dropped her cigarette into the sink. 'Well, at last some good news.'

'He wrote you that letter when he got out of prison. That was five years ago, Ruby.'

Ruby was silent.

'And he left a will.'

She clapped her hands. 'Oh goodie, I'm an heiress! Throw it away, Johnnie, I don't want to know.'

Johnnie picked up the blue envelope 'But, don't you—'

'I said throw it away!' She snatched the letter out of his hands as he came towards her. 'He's dead now. That's the end of it. It's over.' She struck her lighter and held the envelope over the flame. The edges caught, but Johnnie grabbed the burning letter and doused it in the sink.

'If you do that you'll never know what he wrote.'

'So?'

'So you'll always wonder.' Johnnie went back to the table, the damp, singed letter in his hands. 'It will haunt you.'

'No, it won't,' said Ruby, walking towards him. 'You don't get it, Johnnie. I don't care what it says.'

'That's not true.'

'You calling me a liar?' She leant over him, hands gripping the edge of the table.

'I'm saying I know you better than that. I think you need to read it.'

'Well, you're wrong.'

'Okay,' Johnnie pushed the letter across the table towards her. 'Burn it.' He leant back in his chair with his arms crossed behind his head. Ruby looked at the letter lying between them.

'You burn it,' she said. Johnnie didn't move. 'I don't want to read it. Why should I read his shit?' Johnnie shrugged. Ruby bit the side of her finger. 'It's not going to help, Johnnie.'

'What will?'

'I don't know. Nothing. Not this.'

'But this is here. You either read this letter, or you burn it, or you put it away somewhere like a time bomb.'

Ruby sat at the table and reached for the cigarettes. Johnnie grabbed her hand. 'I'll help you, Ruby. It'll be okay.'

She lit two cigarettes and gave one to Johnnie.

'Do you want me to read it for you?' he asked.

'No.' She shook her head, reaching for the envelope, her hand trembling. 'Look what he does to me, after all these years. It's a piece of paper from a dead old man and I'm a wreck.'

Johnnie moved behind her and massaged her shoulders. 'You have to deal with it, Ruby, and move on. This is your past.' He leant forward to kiss her cheek. 'And I'm your future.' She smiled and held his hand as she smoked her cigarette to the stub. She pressed it into the ashtray. 'Okay. Let's read it. You read it.'

Johnnie sat next to her, tore open the sodden envelope and carefully unfolded a single sheet of thin blue paper.

My Dearest Ruby

I won't ask you to forgive me because I don't deserve it. I will never forgive myself. I loved your mother and I love you. Always. I get released tomorrow but I won't try to find you. I know you don't want to see me. If you did you would have visited me sometimes during these long years. You've probably got a husband and children of your own now, I bet. I'm only writing this letter, Ruby, because before I die I want the chance to tell you that I love you and that I'm so sorry for what I did. I feel like I'm talking to you now, Ruby, like I did when you were a little girl. Do you remember those years? I think about them every day. It's the memory of you that's kept me going in here. We were happy in those days. You loved me then. Perhaps when I'm gone you'll be able to remember those times again.

God bless my daughter,

From your loving father,

Jack Gold

P.S. I have some things of yours. Mr Stokes will make sure you get them when I'm gone.

'That's it.' Johnnie folded the letter and put it back in the envelope. Ruby was shaking. He touched her arm. 'You all right, babe?'

'The man is trying to fuck with my head from beyond the grave.'

'Yeah. I suppose at least he was sorry.'

'Sorry! He was a nasty psychotic bastard who battered my mother to death at the Christmas dinner table. I should think he was fucking sorry.'

'You know what I mean.'

'He wanted me to feel sorry for *him*, Johnnie. To regret never going to see him. Well, tough shit, Dad!' She snatched the letter from the table and waved it in the air. 'All this does is make me bloody glad I stayed away.' She screwed up the letter in her fist and jammed it into the ashtray. 'Time to burn it.'

'Are you sure you want to?'

'Too fucking right.' She pressed her lighter against the letter, rotating the ashtray until several red holes were eating into the blue paper. A green yellow flame began to crawl around one side. Within seconds the letter crumpled into a heap of white ash and the last floating grey flakes were curling up to the ceiling light. Ruby lit another cigarette, took one deep drag and crushed it in the ashtray, mixing shreds of tobacco with the letter's remains. She brushed her hands together.

'All gone.'

'You sure you're okay, Ruby?'

'You were right, Johnnie. Now I know when my father left prison he was the same bastard as when he went in.'

'The past is behind you, Ruby.'

'And my future begins now. I want a fantastic breakfast and a damned good fucking, please.'

Chapter 11

The Wake

Pearl stared out of the car window at the Smedleys' bungalow. It hadn't changed. Pale yellow bricks, plastic window boxes, white plastic front door (ajar today, inviting the mourners in for tea and sandwiches). The garden had the same manicured lawn hemmed in by the same relentless ranks of petunias. Pearl had always hated those gaudy plants. Over the years she'd come to see them, with their timid leaves and trumpeting flowers, as being like the Smedleys' marriage: Keith wilting in the shadows; Pam pink and brutal on top.

Gordon yanked the handbrake and turned off the ignition. He hadn't wanted to come, but now he was sleeping in the opera box, Pearl had ways of persuading him. She put her hand on his knee. Shirley was sulking too, sitting behind them in the back seat. Pearl had insisted that attending this funeral was to be a show of Gates' family unity (Shirley's rent cheque was depending upon it) and she was not having the grieving widow, that vamp in velour, thinking the Gates were too scared to show their faces at Keith's wake. Pearl Gates could take on Spam Medley any day. Even the day she was burying her husband.

'Right then, we'd better go in.'

'Do we have to, Pearl? We made an appearance at the ceremony. Everyone's seen us.'

'So the worst is over, Gordon. We'll just go in, give our commiserations, and then it's straight back to Balham.'

The front door was propped open with a golfing trophy, the Frinley and District Cup. Gordon recognised it even before he read the inscription and ushered Pearl through the door. She glanced down as she stepped over the threshold. 'Is that one of Keith's?' she asked 'Fancy it being a doorstop at his own funeral.'

Gordon coughed, making way for Shirley. 'That's typical of *her*!' said Shirley to her mother.

'No respect!' added Pearl.

Gordon hesitated on the concrete steps outside. The cup wasn't Keith's. It was his. And Pam's. Tournament winners in the Millennium Couples Cup. Keith's frozen shoulder had kept him out of the competition so Gordon had stepped in to partner Pam. Not for the first time. The doorstop was there for Gordon.

It had been several months since he had last seen Pam and his previous visit, before either of them knew about Keith's illness, had involved a roll of cling film and a bottle of massage oil. He stepped inside. Pam's collection of antique sugar tongs was hanging from the picture rail in the hall. Gordon tried not to think about the unsavoury games they'd played with them over the years.

'I never did like the way she lined these walls with knick-knacks.' Pearl was ahead of him, leading Shirley through the glass doors, and into the dignified hum of post–crematorium chitchat.

There were about twenty people in the lounge, standing on the parquet floor or sitting around the smoked-glass dining table. Most of them were from the golf club. A few smiled when Gordon came into the room. Pam was nowhere to be seen. Pearl and Shirley found the nibbles and started chatting to the women hovering around the table. Gordon nodded to Barbara Barlow, who was waving at him from the low-slung sofa, and patting the cushion next to her. He noted with relief that Barry wasn't with her, but made no effort to go over. Barbara stopped gesturing and struggled up, nose first. She had the pinched, reddened look of a woman who had gone through life with nostrils two sizes too small. 'Gordon!' She kissed him on the cheek. He smiled, inwardly recoiling as she brushed his cheek with her exposed nasal passage. 'Pam will be so pleased you've come. She was talking about you earlier. We were all so shocked.' Barbara's voice was in itself alarming, a grinding monotone peppered with erratic shrieks. Gordon felt a twinge of panic. Surely this woman didn't know about his affair.

'Shocked?'

'Keith. Fifty-eight. It could have been you, Gordon,' opening shriek sinking into monotone.

'Thankfully, it wasn't.'

'I don't suppose Keith was thankful.'

'No, I don't suppose he was.'

They stood awkwardly for a moment until Barbara broke the silence. 'We're all so pleased about you and Pearl getting back together.'

'Thank you, Barbara.'

'What was that freak place she went to? The Cosmic Centre?'

'Cosmic Café.'

'Oh. She's got out now, has she?'

'It's a restaurant, Barbara, not an asylum.'

'But she did go a bit . . . you know, didn't she? Change of life and everything.'

'Pearl just needed a change of scene.'

'I see. So when are you both coming back to Frinley?'

'We're not sure.'

'Oh? Why's that?'

Gordon shifted from foot to foot. 'Pearl needs to make financial arrangements. You know how tricky these things can be.'

'Especially with those types. If it was me, Barry would get the police in.'

'And who could blame him,' Gordon muttered, turning away to look for Pearl. 'Well, I'd better mingle.' He could see Shirley sitting by herself at the table. Barbara was still talking.

'It's the children I feel sorry for.'

'Pardon?'

'Young Nick and Jack, teenagers without a dad.'

Nick Faldo Smedley and Jack Nicklaus Smedley. Gordon remembered sitting in the clubhouse with Keith when the news came through from Pam at the hospital. Twin boys. Was that really more than thirteen years ago?

'Well,' said Gordon, edging away, 'at least you're here for them.'

'That's the thing about Frinley,' said Barbara, taking hold of his arm. 'We all stick together. Barry's with the boys now, cheering them along.'

'Shouldn't they be left to themselves today? I remember when my own mother died—'

Barbara interrupted. 'No, no, Gordon. You have to keep children occupied at a funeral. Pull their leg a bit, have a joke. Stops them thinking. They'll only get sullen if you don't, and you know how churlish Pam's boys are.'

'Well, I'm sure Barry's tomfoolery is just the ticket.'

'Oh, yes. Barry's been practising his magic show from the moment we heard Keith had died.'

Pearl was in the kitchen with Lucasta, teacher and guru of Frinley's Art Circle. She was examining Pam's new country kitchen. It was the top end of the Kitchen Thinks range on Frinley High Street, several notches up from last year's new units in Pearl's marital home. Pearl cast an envious eye over the breakfast island, the hanging pan rack, the mahogany work surface and butler sink. She whispered to Lucasta, who was supervising vol-au-vents.

'I see Pam managed to get her kitchen done before Keith died.'

'Ha!' Lucasta scoffed as she open the fan oven. 'Apparently, Pearl, it was Keith's last wish to see the kitchen refurbished.'

'That's handy.' Pearl raised an eyebrow as she passed Lucasta a tray of frozen pastry.

'And look what the ghastly woman's done.' Lucasta switched the trays and shut the oven door, sweeping the dangling ends of her Bloomsbury bandana away from the cooked pastry. 'Disaster. I offered to help. I said to Pam, Sebastian will help you conceptualise.'

'He's so talented.'

Lucasta held her free hand to her forehead. 'She threw the offer in my face.'

'She didn't.'

'Oh yes.'

'The cheek.'

'I told her. I said, Pam, I have a vision. Think Kandinsky, I said, think Duchamp.' Pearl didn't catch the name in the breathy excesses of Lucasta's accent. 'Bless you,' she said.

'You're with me, aren't you, Pearl? I knew you'd understand.' Lucasta pointed to the backdoor. 'Willow screening, granite, a bicycle wheel.' Pearl nodded vigorously at every suggestion. 'I mean,' said Lucasta, rattling her beads, 'what is a modern day kitchen if not a Duchamp Ready Made?'

Pearl had a flash of uncertainty. She rubbed her head against her shoulder in a gesture poised between a nod and a shrug.

'And what, pray, does Pam Smedley then do?' Lucasta stared hard at Pearl, who continued with the enigmatic head rolling. 'She copies a picture from *Homes and Gardens*, takes it straight to the Kitchen Thinks and Bob's your Uncle.'

'No flair,' said Pearl, relieved to be on surer ground.

'Exactly, Pearl, that's what Sebastian said. "Ma," he said "where's the flair there?"'

Pearl hoped Lucasta hadn't seen her admiring the pan rack. 'Nowhere,' she said. 'Not a sniff.'

'Her own fault.' Lucasta draped her hand on Pearl's arm as she took the hot tray through to the lounge. 'Sebastian thought you were wonderful, by the way.'

Pearl smiled and helped herself to a hot vol-au-vent.

In the lounge, Gordon was still trapped with Barbara. She had lowered her voice to such an extent that she was barely audible. 'She's outside,' she whispered, glancing over her shoulder.

'Who?' said Gordon, turning around. Barbara clutched his shoulder. 'Don't look,' she hissed, 'it's Pam.' Gesturing for him to move closer, she began to communicate through mime. Gordon watched as she cupped her hand and tilted it towards her face, her mouth silently shaping the words. 'Three sheets to the wind.' Pam was drunk. Gordon's horror of Barbara was overwhelmed by his dread of Pam. It was time to leave. His fragile reunion with Pearl was too precious to risk. He looked around for his wife and realised that Pam was staring at him through the French windows, looking resplendent in a puce twin-set with black accessories: hat, bag, shoes, and golf club. She was practising her swing on the lawn. She curled her index finger. Gordon was summoned.

His hopes that decorum would restrain Pam and prevent her from making a scene were lost in the bunker. He decided to grab Pearl and make a run for the door. He dashed into the kitchen and found her looking in the fridge.

'Pearl, we'd better go. Pam's drunk.'

Pearl brought out a plate of salmon and put it on the draining board. 'I'm not running away from Pam, Gordon. Let her do her worst.'

'But Pearl, this is Keith's funeral.' Gordon wanted to beg. 'It's not the occasion for a confrontation.'

'Leaving so soon, Gordon?' He turned around. Pam was silhouetted against the back-door frame, golf club in hand.

'Yes. Pearl and I simply came to pay our respects.'

'Well, here I am, the grieving widow. Why don't you pay your respects to me?'

Pearl spoke first. 'Pam, I know we've had a bit of a falling out, and we're not friends, but I hope you know how sorry I was to hear about Keith.'

'I'm sure you were.'

'He was a good man,' continued Pearl.

'Unlike Gordon.' Pam leant on her club.

'Now, that's not called for, Pam,' said Pearl. 'Gordon may have strayed from the path in recent months—'

'Recent months?' Pam laughed. 'Is that what he told you?'

Gordon grabbed Pearl's hand. 'We're leaving.'

But Pearl stopped by the breakfast island. 'I'll have you know, Pam Smedley, that Gordon and I are back together and our marriage is stronger than ever.'

'Well, that wouldn't be hard, Pearl Gates. Your marriage has been a sham for years.'

'That's enough, Pam,' Gordon hissed. 'Pearl and I have a future together.'

'And what about my future?' Pam stumbled forward to the breakfast island, letting the golf club clatter to the floor. 'What about my boys' future?'

Pearl softened. 'I feel sorry for you, Pam, but your family's future is not Gordon's responsibility.'

Pam raised her voice. 'Gordon, I will not allow you to walk away from me. Not now. Not after all these years.'

'What does she mean "after all these years"?' said Pearl, turning to Gordon.

Gordon ignored her. 'I've made my decision, Pam. I want to be with Pearl.'

'Who says you have a choice? There are things even you don't know, Gordon.'

Pearl was getting nervous. 'Gordon, what's she talking about?'

'I don't know, Pearl, but I've heard enough. Let's go.'

Pam reached up and grabbed the pan rack. Saucepans and various implements hanging on butchers' hooks dangled from suspended wooden rails. She swung them fiercely, one hand on the wood, the other gripping a potato masher. A storm of utensils clattered over their heads.

Shirley raced in from the lounge. 'What's happening? Is anyone hurt?'

'It's all right, Shirley,' said Gordon. 'Pam's just rattling her sabre.'

'We can hear everything in the lounge, you know,' Shirley said. 'They're all listening to you fighting.'

'Well, let's make this interesting for them.' Pam looked Gordon in the eye. 'The twins are yours, Gordon.'

There was a collective gasp from the lounge.

Pearl looked from Gordon to Pam. 'You're lying!'

'Tell her, Gordon.'

'Tell me what?'

'Tell her how long we've been together.'

'Gordon?' Pearl asked nervously.

'It's over, Pam,' said Gordon.

'How long, Gordon?' Pearl insisted.

Gordon hung his head, a beaten man. 'Fifteen years. I'm so sorry, Pearl.'

Pearl slumped onto a barstool. 'Fifteen years? Shirley was just a child.'

At the mention of her name, Shirley was roused to speak. 'I don't believe this. Everything about my life's a lie. My whole family's a lie. I'm not even a fucking only child.' She stamped through the lounge, hitting out at Barbara Barlow when she attempted a consoling hug.

Pearl stood up. 'I have to go. Shirley's upset. She needs me.'

'Pearl, let me come with you, please.'

Pearl shook her head.

'Let me explain.'

'There's nothing to say, Gordon. Your life is here now.'

'No, Pearl. I love you.'

'Too late.' She kissed him on the cheek with a dignity sustained by shock. 'Goodbye, Gordon.' She turned away from the glint of triumph in Pam's eyes and walked through the familiar faces gawping in the lounge.

Chapter 12

Heaven Sent

'We're taking you out.'

'Sorry?' said Anna, holding the front door open. Ruby and Greg were squeezed together on the doorstep, sheltering from the rain slanting across the roofs opposite. It was a dreary evening in October, windy and cold.

'Get your glad rags on,' said Ruby. 'You and Cass are going out.' She hurried down the path and back to her house across the street.

'What?' Anna called after her. 'Now?'

'I'm coming for you at ten,' Ruby shouted, without looking back.

'We can't just go out,' said Anna to Greg, watching an empty crisp packet swirl up the path and land in a damp cluster of leaves. 'It's bloody miserable out there. And what about Florrie?'

'It's okay, Anna, I'm babysitting. It's all arranged.'

'That's really kind of you, Greg, but to be honest, I'm not really in the mood. I'm kind of knackered, you know how it is.'

'Yeah.' Greg smiled sympathetically. 'But you're going anyway.'

At 10:25 Anna was sitting in a seat on the tube. The train jerked and rattled along the track and Anna held her arms tightly across her chest, stiff with the effort of not brushing against the people next to her. On one side a grey-skinned woman, her nose peppered with blackheads, sat with a large wire cage perched on her lap. It was stuffed with shredded newspaper, which twitched and rustled when the train stopped at Clapham South. On the other side, an old man was coughing into a handkerchief. Anna wanted to go home. Cass was standing further down the carriage, laughing with Ruby. They were swaying against the rails, crushed among the standing bodies heading for a Saturday night out. At Clapham Common, Ruby pushed through to the open door, leant out and whistled loudly.

'Is this us?' asked Anna, getting up from her seat. It was seized instantly by a small woman in a pink jumpsuit.

'No,' said Ruby, squeezing back into the carriage. 'We're just picking up.' As she spoke, Andy jumped through the doors behind her, breathless from running down the platform at Ruby's signal.

'Surprise!' said Ruby.

'Ruby!' Cass shouted over the crowds of people filling the train. 'What's going on?'

'You've been set up,' yelled Ruby, cheerfully. 'Can't talk now!' The doors had shut and the train was lurching into action. 'Bollock me later!'

Anna grabbed hold of the rail as the train moved off. She was facing Andy, who mouthed 'I didn't know!' over the heads between them. She nodded and looked away, smiling at him only once when they were jolted into eye contact. Cass was behind her, hanging onto a strap she could barely reach, anchoring herself by holding Anna's coat. As the train juddered down the Northern Line, Cass stared at her green DMs. She didn't speak until her boots had stepped off the train and onto the platform at Charing Cross.

'Well,' said Ruby, as she saw them get off the train. 'So far so good.'

'What!' said Cass. She spoke into the rush of air as the train plunged into the tunnel. 'What the hell are you playing at, Ruby?'

'I'm giving you a Saturday night out. My treat.'

'I mean inviting him without telling us.'

'I thought it would be fun.'

'Well, you were wrong,' said Cass, walking away from them and towards the opposite platform.

'Thanks for that, Cass,' said Andy. 'I've been set up too, you know. I thought I was meeting Ruby and Greg, not you.'

'Perhaps we'd better go home,' said Anna, glancing at Cass. The other passengers had drained away and their raised voices were echoing along the empty platform. 'I don't think any of us are up to this.'

'Of course you are,' said Ruby. 'You three lovely people need to kiss and make up. Greg thought you should talk so we fixed you up with a counsellor for the evening.'

'I don't think talking will help,' said Andy. He was sitting behind them on a bench set into the curved wall of the platform.

'What's there to say?' shouted Cass. 'Andy's bored with parenting and he's running off to the seaside.'

'Is that really what you think?' he demanded.

'No, Andy, that's how hurt she is,' said Ruby. 'Okay, darlings, these are the options. Number one: be proud, go home, don't speak, watch your family fall apart. Number two: indulge Ruby, whinge and moan, be friends again, happy ever after.'

'I don't think it's as simple as that, Ruby,' said Anna. She was leaning against the tiled wall, looking pale in the cold, underground light.

'Of course it is! Now, there's a little place near here that's perfect for family therapy. Are you coming?'

'No,' said Cass.

'I really don't think—' said Anna.

Ruby interrupted. 'Then the Goddess-Parents will have to launch Plan B.'

'What's that?' Andy asked.

'You'll find out if you go home. Oh, the fun we'll have if we get to Plan D.'

'I get it,' said Cass, moving closer as the platform started to fill with people waiting for the next train. 'You're threatening us. If we don't come now, you'll be on our backs, hassling us and setting us up all the bloody time.'

'Like you wouldn't believe, sweetheart,' Ruby winked.

'This is out of order, Ruby. You've got no right—'

Ruby raised her arms in supplication. 'I serve the will of the Goddess, Cass.' The ground rumbled. 'Hear her anger!'

'It's a train, Ruby!' said Cass.

'It's a sign,' said Ruby. 'She says get thy arses moved now or a plague of tripping tweenies will come out of that tunnel and fall upon your heads.'

Ruby led the way out of the station and into the streets and alleys of Charing Cross. It was still raining and the orange lights reflected the city in the wet pavements. She stopped to light a cigarette and Anna sheltered her with her umbrella. 'You told me counselling was prostitution for liberals.'

'It is.' She flicked a dead match across the pavement. 'Forty quid to moan and groan with a stranger without any of the "was it good for you" malarkey.'

'So what kind of family therapy are we getting, Ruby?'

Ruby smiled, walking ahead. 'The unorthodox method.'

'I feared as much.'

Andy and Cass shuffled behind, not speaking to each other. 'How much further?' Andy asked.

Ruby stopped. 'We're here.'

'But this is . . . I thought you said we were going to talk.'

'Nah! Greg thinks you should talk, but that's all bollocks.'

Ruby was fumbling for her purse. 'What you three need is a dance and a laugh. Come on, I'm paying.'

They stepped under the railway arches into the flame-red décor of Heaven. Ruby had taken them clubbing.

'This is the deal,' she told them as she took her coat off, revealing an eye-wateringly tight red basque. 'Make friends before my tits pop out of this thing and you win the car.' Shouting over the noise, she led them to the main dance floor. Anna took Cass's hand and kept her close as they weaved across the floor to a space in the crowd. Cass was still sulking, so Anna held her by the shoulders, and rolled her hips against her. 'Come on, Cass,' she yelled. 'When's the last time we got to do this?' The music was throbbing through the floor. Cass smiled, pressing herself against Anna's pelvis so that their bodies were rotating in rhythm. When the next track faded in, she was already waving her arms and jumping to the rhythm, her piercings sparkling in the half-light. She hugged Anna and shouted in her ear, 'Good old fucking Ruby.'

Anna circled around, looking at the people dancing near her. A skinny boy in a crop top and hipster flares, a few white T-shirts and jeans pounding to the rhythm, a red-faced woman in full leather. She revolved back to face Cass, who was wiping sweat from her forehead, and they danced together until Anna glimpsed the red of Ruby's basque bouncing towards them through the crowd. She blew the damp hair away from her face as Ruby and Andy reached them. 'Told you,' yelled Ruby. 'It's therapy.' Anna smiled. Andy was hovering behind Ruby, eyeing up the crop top. He leant forward. 'I'm glad I came, Anna.'

'Me too,' she said.

The rhythm slowed, and for an uncomfortable few seconds they all swayed awkwardly to a single drum beat. Andy shimmied across to Cass, waiting for the beat to surge. When it did he danced like a maniac in front of her. She didn't smile, but she didn't move away either.

Three hours later, Cass and Andy were still on the dance

floor, camping up a barely recognisable version of the tango. Ruby had saturated them both with alcohol and they had decided, while strutting their stuff, that Brighton was practically on the doorstep, that Florrie loved the seaside, and that they were going to be a fantastic family no matter who or what life threw at them. Anna was dancing with Ruby, watching her wobbling out the of top of her corset, and flirting outrageously with the muscle-bound bull-dyke dancing beside them.

'Ruby, that woman's going to come over in a minute.'

'What woman? Oh her. Do you think I've pulled?'

'I think you're pissed,' shouted Anna. 'Come on, let's go for a coffee.'

She half-dragged Ruby off the dance floor, holding her up as they pushed through the bodies and stumbled to the coffee bar.

'Sit down, I'll get us something sobering.'

Anna came back ten minutes later with two coffees, one of them black and strong. She gave it to Ruby. 'Here! This will make you feel better.'

Ruby nodded blearily and took the coffee.

'I know you're so pissed you won't remember a word, but thank you, Ruby.'

Ruby sipped the coffee. 'What for?'

'For this! For making us come here tonight. If it wasn't for you, I think Cass and Andy would have ended up hating each other, and now look at them. I know I'm pissed and sentimental and everything, but you're a fantastic woman, Ruby. You've saved our family.' Anna leaned over and wrapped her arms around Ruby, kissing her on the head. 'Florrie has the best Goddess-Mother ever. I fucking love you, Ruby.'

She slid back onto the seat next to her. Tears were rolling in mascara streaks down Ruby's face. Anna smiled, sipping at her coffee. 'Look at the state of us, hey, what a pair of old lushes.' But Ruby carried on crying, silent tears turning into heaving sobs. Anna stopped smiling. 'Ruby! What is it? What's the matter?' Ruby mumbled something, keeping her head down so that her face was hidden by her hair, and Anna fumbled in her bag for tissues. She pressed one into Ruby's hand. 'Tell me what's wrong.'

Ruby wiped her face and reached for her cigarettes. 'I don't know why I'm in such a fucking state,' she said. 'I haven't seen him for twenty years.'

'Who?' Anna asked. 'You . . . you're not talking about your dad, are you?'

Ruby nodded. 'He's dead.'

'Well, for God's sake.' Anna put her arm on Ruby's shoulder. 'Of course you're going to be upset.'

'I don't give a fuck about him.' She moved Anna's arm away. 'I hate him. It's just . . . I don't know why it's got to me so much . . . but he died sleeping rough. Hypothermia.'

'Oh.'

'He'd been on the streets for four years, ever since he got out of prison.'

'I see.'

'Why should that bother me? I mean, why should I give a fuck about that? There are good people out there, young people in doorways. I walk past them every bloody day and what do I do for them? Fuck all. And then there's him, that bastard. And, you won't believe this,' she dragged hard on her cigarette, 'but I feel guilty about it.'

'That's natural, Ruby. He was your dad.'

'He was a bastard.'

'Yeah, an evil bastard who was also your dad. It's not easy to get your head round. No wonder you're upset.'

'But it's not getting any better, Anna.' They sat quietly while Ruby smoked her cigarette. Anna finished her coffee, watching her. 'I went to the solicitors yesterday,' said Ruby. She was tracing patterns on the table with her finger. 'For the will. I got everything. And do you know what that was? What they found on his body?' She looked up at Anna. 'A photo of me and my mum, and a necklace I used to wear when I was a kid, little yellow beads on elastic. I didn't even know he had it.'

'He loved you.'

'Yeah, and that's the thing, isn't it? I loved him. Do you know that? I loved him when I was a kid. Even though he hit my mum. I see that necklace and I remember how I felt and I feel sick, Anna. I'm so angry.' She dropped her head in her hands. 'I'm talking bollocks.'

'No you're not, Ruby.'

'And you know the worse thing.' She didn't look up. 'That bastard left me a letter and Johnnie read it, and . . . oh, it doesn't matter.'

'Ruby, have you thought about getting counselling?' Anna asked, taking her hands.

Ruby smiled. 'What? You mean like going to Streatham for a £40 head job?'

'No, seriously, I think you should go and see someone. Get some help.'

Ruby moved her hands. 'I've done all that. It makes no difference. It's still all in your head, waiting for you. It's not more talking I need, Anna, it's liposuction.' She smiled. 'If they could slice open my head and get the Hoover in there, suck all the shit out, I'd do that. I wouldn't even ask for anaesthetic if they'd do that.'

'You could have a lobotomy.'

'I've tried. Bloody GP got sniffy and wouldn't do it. Uptight cow.' Ruby laughed. 'Anyway, don't look so bloody worried, Anna. The bastard's dead and buried. He can't hurt me now.'

'That's right, Ruby, it's all in the past.'

'Over and bloody done with.' Ruby brushed her hands together.

'And you're moving on. You're a new woman.'

'Right on, sister!' They gave each other a clenched fist salute and Ruby lit another cigarette. She took a drag. 'You see, when two good women get together, not even a psychotic murdering piss-artist father can keep 'em down.'

Chapter 13

Show and Tell

'Okay, comrades,' said Buzz, 'tonight's the night. The parasite press are in the café, the Hottentots are a happening sound. Ours is a radical future.'

Buzz, after a modicum of success selling the Tooting Hottentots' home-produced CD over the café counter, had promoted himself from friend of the band to manager. And he'd decided it was time to launch them onto the Indie music scene. He rang the music papers and all the local rags and told them that the Hottentots were the twenty-first-century Clash. The response was unexpectedly lukewarm. He was hoping for *NME*, *Mojo*, *Kerrang!*. He got Martin from the *Tooting Free Advertiser*, Christine from *Balham Library News*, and two student papers from Greenwich and Southside New Universities. Martin, Christine and one of the students were sitting at a side table that Buzz had reserved for the Press.

Cass walked up to the stage. 'I see all the hacks are here, Buzz,' she said, smiling.

'Good turn out.'

'It's local roots, Cass, that's how it all starts. From the people.'

Gizmo, the Hottentots singer, nodded confidently, shaking his blond dreadlocks. The waist-length dreads were part of the band's image. Mutley, Gizmo's brother, had red ones, Kevin's were purple and Skank's were the original black.

'It's a cool school, sister,' said Mutley.

'What?'

'Life,' said Buzz.

' "Cool School". New song, you know,' said Mutley. 'People in the world, like, learning, about each other, the planet, it's a cool school.'

'I'm groovin' with you,' said Cass, giving him the thumbs up.

'Yeah, like, the band, you know.'

'I do,' said Cass.

'Yeah, like, Kev, you know, he's, like, Jewish, and Skank, he's, like, Jamaican and me and Gizmo, we're, like, Anglo, so it's, like, a cool school, you know, for the music.'

'Mutley,' said Cass. 'The Hottentots make a big noise.'

'Hey, sister,' said Skank. 'It's a serious sound.'

'It's a global groove, Cass,' said Buzz, bouncing with enthusiasm. 'Our music's like a new globalism, crushing corporate imperialism. Jew and Gentile, Black and White, Third, Second and First World. It's the sound of the planet, Cass.'

'They're all from Tooting, Buzz.'

'Tooting's a happening place.'

'This amp's fucked,' said Kev and Buzz jumped onto the stage.

Cass looked back to the other end of the café. People were still queuing to get past Dee on the door and there was no one behind the counter. Pearl should have been serving, but she was sitting on a stool, talking to Shirley, and taking no notice of the Hottentot groupies swarming around her. Cass pushed through the crowded tables, and squeezed past Pearl's stool at the side of the counter. Pearl sucked her breath in to let Cass through without pausing from the verbal post-mortem on her marriage, which had now entered its third day.

'I still don't believe it, Shirley. All those years and he was having it away with Pam Smedley.'

'Pig!' said Shirley.

'On the golf course!'

'Sleaze-bag!'

'Those boys are your brothers!'

'Bastard!'

They sat in silence, Pearl swigging from the bottle in her hand. 'Cass, when you've got a minute, another two of those Spanish lagers.' She turned back to Shirley without waiting for Cass's frantic reply. 'At least Keith didn't live to see the day!'

'If he hadn't died when he did, you would have taken Dad back.'

'Thank you for that reminder, Shirley.'

'I did tell you, Mum.'

'I know you did.'

'But you wouldn't listen.'

'Shirley, you're beginning to get on my pigging wick.'

Cass passed the bottles over and Pearl drank most of hers in five long gulps. She belched loudly when she put the bottle down on the glass-topped counter.

'Mum!' said Shirley, wafting her hand against the whiff of lager.

'It's no good, Shirley. I'm past caring what people think of me. I'm already a laughing stock in Frinley.'

Shirley had no words of comfort.

'I know that lot of old,' said Pearl. 'I bet their tongues are flapping like fish in a bucket.'

'At least Spam-face will get the worst of it,' said Shirley.

'She doesn't care! She'll milk it for all it's worth.'

'Cow!'

'That woman's got no shame, Shirley.'

'Slut-bag!'

'And all the time she was my best friend!'

'Bitch!'

'And you know what will happen now, don't you, Shirley?'

'You told me all day yesterday.'

'That's right. Your father will move in with Pam and bring up those two boys.'

'But you don't know that for sure, do you, Mum?'

'I do.'

'He hasn't told you.'

'Told me? Course he hasn't told me, Shirley. He hasn't dared show his face.'

'So he might—'

'Might nothing!' interrupted Pearl. 'Not when Pam's got him on the hook. Your father's not going anywhere now.'

'So you won't take him back again?'

'Shirley, what kind of fool do you take me for?'

'Just checking.'

'Well don't.' As Pearl was speaking, Shirley was barged from behind and thrown forwards. She swore loudly and turned on the youth behind her. His face was plump, pink, and pock-marked, and Shirley recognised him instantly, right down to his Ozzy Osbourne T-shirt. Ugly Iain from college. Shirley had successfully avoided him since the house party a year ago when she woke up to find him next to her in bed. 'Hello, Iain.'

'Shirley! I didn't know you were into the Tots.'

'The what?'

'The band, the Hottentots.'

'Oh, them. I'm not. My mum's got a flat above the café.'

'For real? Wicked! Your mum must be cosmic.' He snorted at his joke.

Shirley didn't laugh. 'Not really.'

'I heard that, Shirley,' said Pearl, belching.

'I'm the Press,' said Iain, showing her Buzz's hand-drawn Press Pass. '*Southside Student*. Do you read it?'

Shirley nodded, affecting boredom. 'Sometimes.'

'Well, you know Cheap Gigs McGuire. That's me, Iain McGuire. I get to see free gigs all the time.'

'Is that why you're never in lectures?'

He gave her his card, pointing to the word 'journalist' in the bottom corner. 'That's my education, Shirley. I'll tell you about it sometime. We could meet up for a drink.'

'No thanks, I've got a boyfriend.'

'So?' said Iain.

'So I don't want to go for a drink.'

'Please yourself!' He shrugged. 'If I don't see you around, you can read about me when I'm famous.' It was his favourite line, well worn and wearing thin.

'Pillock,' said Shirley, turning back to her mum.

'He seemed quite nice to me, Shirley. And he liked you.'

'God, don't make me puke, Mum. He's a worm. Everyone at college knows he'd sell his granny.'

'Nothing wrong with trying to get on in life, Shirley,' said Pearl, watching Iain sit down at the Press table. 'You could do with some of his oomph.'

The sound of microphone feedback rang through the café. Buzz turned down the amp and tried again. 'Brothers and Sisters, Comrades. Tonight we present the Hottentots in their home venue, The Cosmic, for the first night of the international *Shit Happens* album tour. So let's give the Tots a real South London welcome.'

The fans clapped and whistled, the guitar vibrated through the tables and Gizmo began mumbling the lyrics of 'Cool School'.

On the door, Dee was taking a £5 note from Charles. 'Hello, Dee.' He shouted over the noise of the band. 'I don't suppose you recognise me without a frock on.'

She looked up at the straight-looking, middle-aged man in front of her. 'Not Charlene?'

'Charles, my dear. This is my day wear.'

She stamped his hand with an impression of Lenin's head. 'Stick to the dresses, girl.'

Charles saw Pearl at the counter with Shirley and pushed his way towards them. 'Pearl, Shirley, I'm so sorry.' He stood above them with his arms around their shoulders. Shirley was rigid with embarrassment.

Pearl nuzzled his suit. 'You were right about Gordon, Charles.' She yelled over Gizmo's groanings. 'He betrayed me, he betrayed us all.'

'You mustn't blame yourself, Pearl.'

'I bloody don't! He was a rat. I married a rat!'

'A bastard,' shouted Shirley.

'But fifteen years . . .' Charles sighed.

'Don't!' said Pearl, sitting up. 'Honestly, I couldn't squeeze out another tear if Shirley's life depended on it. I'm past caring, Charles, I really am.'

Shirley dodged away from Charles's embrace and he put both hands on Pearl's shoulders. 'You're a very brave woman, Pearl,' he said, enunciating each word over the music. 'And you've got friends and family around you now.'

The Hottentots finished their first track.

'I don't know what I would have done without Shirley,' said Pearl during the applause. 'She's been marvellous.'

'Thanks, Mum,' said Shirley, smiling.

'I mean, we've talked for three days solid, haven't we, Shirley? And she's been right here with me. In the café.'

On stage, Gizmo yelled a quotation from the *Communist Manifesto* and the conversation was lost. Pearl got up and went behind the counter to get Charles a glass of wine and a flapjack. Charles turned to Shirley, putting his arm around her again. 'And how are you coping, young lady?' he shouted.

Shirley shrugged and shouted back, 'Don't know really.'

'Must be difficult for you.'

Shirley wanted to wriggle out of his grasp. 'Suppose so.'

'Talked to anyone?' He leaned forward, shouting into her face. 'Friends? Boyfriend?'

'Just Mum really.' She had told Greg, on the phone, and he had been kind to her. But for the last week he and Cori had watched nothing but videoed repeats of 'Eco-Pops'. She could hear Acorn's voice in the background when she phoned. It was a relief to stay the weekend with her mum. At least she didn't have to look cheerful. She could moan all she liked.

'And how are you getting on, living with your boyfriend?'

'Great!' Shirley glanced at Pearl with Cass behind the counter.

'Pearl tells me he's got a daughter?'

Shirley nodded.

'Nice?' He shouted.

'Great.'

They gave up trying to make conversation over the noise and listened to the Tots. Gizmo had his back to the café and was shouting expletives into the mike; Mutley was thrashing his drum-kit at the back, and the electric violin and guitar were competing for the best feedback. Charles didn't move his arm off Shirley's shoulders.

After three tracks and a chat with the manager, Iain felt he had enough to write up for *The Southside Student*. He said goodbye to his fellow journos. No one answered. Martin and Toby, the other student, were rocking to 'Roll on Revolution' and Christine still hadn't come back from the toilets. Iain pushed through the tables towards the door. Shirley was at the counter. A man old enough to be her father had his arm around her, and she wasn't enjoying it. Iain felt a stirring of interest. He studied Shirley's face. She looked uncomfortable, embarrassed, smiling only when the old man looked at her. His journalistic instincts told him that here was a story. Prostitution perhaps? He could see the beginning of an in-depth feature. Was Shirley paying her way through college by selling her services to older men? Was she using her mum's flat? Was it a mother and daughter enterprise? After all, what kind of parent would live above The Cosmic? He scribbled the outline on his pad, and moved into the queue for drinks. He stood with his back to Shirley, listening.

Shirley was thinking about 'Eco-Pops'. She drummed her fingers against the counter, trying to pick out a rhythm in the Hottentots' music. Greg didn't love Acorn. He was only thinking about Cori when he taped her programmes and bought all those TV guides. And even if he did love her, it didn't matter, because Acorn was long gone and Shirley was there to stay. She was the woman in Greg's life now. Greg was just confused by seeing Acorn appear on the TV. She leant forward to Charles.

'Do you watch children's TV?'

He shook his head.

'You know my boyfriend's got a child, Coriander.'

'Unusual name.'

'Yeah,' Shirley smiled. 'Coriander Smith, silly isn't it? Well, her mother's on TV.'

Charles nodded, impressed.

'And she's never even set eyes on her own child.'

He mimed shock. Behind Shirley, Iain had crossed out 'Prostitution' and was scribbling excitedly.

Shirley leaned forward again. 'She left when Cori was a baby and she's never been back.'

Iain was willing Charles to ask the question that he couldn't: who was it, who?

'Why?' shouted Charles.

'She's trying to save the planet.'

Charles looked dumbfounded. Who? Who? pleaded Iain silently.

'How?'

'Don't ask me,' answered Shirley. 'But now she's on the telly, Greg thinks she's great.'

'And what do you think?'

'She's a cow,' said Shirley with authority.

'Sounds it,' said Charles. 'What's her name?'

Iain's pencil twitched in his fingers.

'You won't have heard of her,' said Shirley and sat back on

her stool. They sat in silence until Pearl joined them with Charles's drink.

'Do you want the flapjack? Because I'll eat it if you don't.'

'You have it,' said Charles, sipping the wine. 'Shirley was telling me about the woman on TV.'

'What woman on TV?'

'The one who left her baby,' he said.

'I didn't know about that. Was that in my *Chat*, Shirley?'

'No, no,' said Charles. 'This is her boyfriend's child.'

Pearl rounded on Shirley. 'You didn't tell me that child's mother was famous.'

'She's not famous.'

'What does she do then?'

'Only a bloody children's programme.'

'I told you it was trouble, Shirley.'

'How can it be trouble? She's not been back for six years.'

'And what does Greg think about it?'

Shirley shrugged.

'He's got feelings for her, hasn't he? That's why you've been here with me.'

'That's a lie. I was being nice to you after everything with Dad.'

'And what if she comes back?'

'For God's sake, Mum!' Shirley shot up from her stool. The music had stopped, but Shirley kept going. 'Acorn abandoned Coriander when she was six weeks old. She's not coming back now.'

She pushed her way through the crowd and out of the door. Iain watched her go. He kissed his notebook and put it in his pocket. He'd just got his ticket to the tabloids.

Chapter 14

The Dawn Chorus

Never before had Andy jogged down Cavendish Road with such speed. But then, never before had he had such gossip. Under his arm he had an assortment of doughnuts (chocolate, raspberry, apple) and tabloid papers. If he was quick he just had time to get to Anna and Cass's for a spot of early morning hilarity before work. And he had a corker for them. He hugged the papers against his chest. He didn't normally go in for girly-gossips at 6:30 in the morning, but he had to tell someone what he'd heard in the newsagents. And Tony wouldn't be home for hours. He had worked late again at Luigi's, and stayed over in the flat above the restaurant.

He stopped on the corner of Madrigal Road where the street veered to the left and the last five houses clustered together in the Close. Dropping the newspapers and the bag of dough-nuts on the pavement, he leant over, gasping for breath until the gripping pain in his throat began to subside. He didn't want Anna to think he was having a heart attack when she opened the door. Bent double, he became unbearably conscious of the sweat collecting around his groin in the lycra all-in-one.

Before he presented himself at the door, he was going to need a discreet scratch and a jiggle. He looked down at his suit, trying to work out the best way in. Up the leg or down the chest? He glanced around to make sure he wasn't about to traumatise a papergirl, and shoved his hand down the front. Then, across the road, someone opened the front door of no. 97, the student house. The blond boy, Will, came out wearing an orange silk dressing gown and snogging a man in a black leather jacket. Andy crouched down next to a row of green bins. It wouldn't go down too well at the office if a tenant reported him skulking around their house, fumbling with himself. The lover drew back and Andy saw the side of his face, tanned, high cheekbone, dark eyebrow. It was Tony.

Andy's first thought was not betrayal, but panic. He mustn't be seen. He scrambled into the narrow space behind the dust-bins next to him, his heart thumping. Looking through the gap between the bins he saw Tony walk past, three feet away, in jeans and the new Versace boots he'd bought him the month before. Andy was dazed. He slumped down, squatting in the rancid remains of a Chinese takeaway. How could Tony betray him? The past months ran through Andy's mind. Tony wasn't happy, Anna and Cass had made him feel like shit, but they'd dealt with that. They were moving to Brighton, away from the girls. They were starting again. It couldn't have been Tony. They'd found a fantastic Georgian conversion on the seafront . . . And anyway Tony was in Croydon, sleeping above the restaurant in Luigi's spare room. He had jumped to all the wrong conclusions because of a pair of boots. He had only glimpsed him after all and how many men in London had dark hair, or a tan, or high cheekbones? How many gay men wore Versace? He was getting upset over nothing. It wasn't Tony.

He pushed the bin away and stood up. The back of his legs felt clammy and cold. He wiped at them with his fingers. Orange gunk. He had congealed sweet and sour seeping through his lycra. He plucked at his suit to pull it away from his legs and hobbled to Anna and Cass's front door. It was a while before Cass answered the bell, wearing men's stripy pyjamas, her hair sticking up like a pink fuzzball.

'Andy?'

'I've had an accident.'

'Oh, my God! Are you hurt?' She opened the door. 'Come in. You look terrible.'

'Not that kind of accident.' He turned around and pointed at his bum. '*That* kind of accident. Sweet and sour sauce.'

She peered at it. 'Yuk!'

'More than yuk, sweetie. It's gone everywhere. The hairs around my arse feel like raffia matting.'

'So how did you manage to sit in that?'

'Don't ask! Just me being a dizzy queen and getting myself in a stupid tiz. Can I use your bathroom?

'Sure. Have a shower! We're bound to have something that'll fit you upstairs.'

Andy gave her the papers and doughnuts. 'And, I've got the most fabulous gossip for you, but you must promise you won't read these until I come back down.'

'Promise.' Cass dumped the doughnuts in the kitchen, made coffee, and went upstairs to tell Anna they had a visitor. She was sitting in the rocking chair in Florrie's room, staring through the gap in the closed curtains.

'Andy's here,' said Cass.

'Quick, Cass. The Karloffs are in the garden.'

'He's in the shower.'

'I think they're doing one of their rituals.' Anna moved the chair away from the window and gestured for Cass to peep through the gap.

'Oh God, not this again,' said Cass, wandering over. 'Did you hear what I said about Andy?' She looked out the window. Doris and Boris were squatting naked on their lawn. 'We can't just watch them, Anna.'

'Yes, we can. I missed it last year. I want to see what happens. Move over.'

'You know what happens,' said Cass. 'I told you.'

'I know.' Anna put her eye to the curtains. 'But I can't help myself. I know I shouldn't look, but I can't believe they really do it. It's just bizarre.'

Cass moved away. 'I've seen enough.'

'I think Sidney's having problems with his balance,' said Anna, excitedly. 'He must be getting a bit old for all this crouching. Yep, there he goes. Rolled over.'

Cass picked Florrie out of her cot. 'Has he rolled in anything nasty?'

'Not sure. Doris is helping him up. No, he missed their little offerings. Now what are they doing?'

Andy came into the bedroom wrapped in a towel. 'Have you girls got anything I could put on while my clothes dry?'

'Sorry, Andy, I'll get something now,' said Cass, carrying Florrie out of the room. 'Doris and Boris are doing their stuff out there.'

Anna waved Andy to the window. 'You remember we told you about the sacred barbeque and Doris and Boris burning rubbish, and shitting on the lawn. Well, it looks like this is the bit we missed last year. The end of the ceremony.'

Anna stepped back and pointed Andy to the gap in the curtain. He put his eye to the crack. 'Are those little holes what I think they are?'

'Yeah, they've done that bit. What are they doing now?'

'Boris has gone in the shed. Wait.' He fought Anna back. 'He's got a rabbit. Are you allowed to hold them by the ears?'

'What's he doing with it?'

'Hold on. Doris is moving one of those gnome things. Hey, there's a big hole under it.'

Anna ducked underneath him and poked her head through the curtain. 'Let's see. Oh no, are they forcing that poor rabbit down it?' She turned her head away from the window. 'I didn't want to see that.'

'They've put the gnome back on top,' said Andy, the curtains around his shoulders.

'The rabbit will die,' said Anna.

'It won't if there's air,' said Cass from behind them. 'Rabbits are burrowers, remember.' She threw an old pair of sweatpants and a jumper at the back of Andy's head.

'Unless . . .' said Andy, turning around and picking them up. 'Unless something down there eats it. Some creature from the depths. An alien being that lives on rabbit blood.'

'That's what they want to happen,' said Anna, gripping his arms. 'The Karloffs think there are aliens underground. They sang about it last year. You don't think it's true, do you?'

Cass laughed, 'Anna, you're freaking yourself out.'

'We live next to mad people,' said Anna. 'What's freakier than that?'

'Living above aliens?' said Andy, putting the pants on under his towel. Anna had a last look out of the window. The garden was empty.

'Come on,' said Cass. 'You two need some coffee.'

Andy sat at their kitchen table with the papers stacked in front of him while Cass poured coffee and unwrapped the doughnuts. 'Jesus, Andy. Are you sure you've got enough here?'

'We'll need them. Wait 'til you see what I've got for you. I couldn't believe it when I realised who they were talking about in the newsagents. Okay, I've found it. Look at this!'

TV's Acorn Abandoned Baby

Acorn, of 'Eco-Pops' fame, abandoned her six-week-old baby and has never been back to see the child. Is this feminism gone mad? We're all familiar with career women and super-mums, but what kind of woman gets a career 'saving the planet' by dumping her child like so much toxic waste? Aren't we saving the planet *for* our children? Poets are supposed to be the legislators of the world, Acorn is one of the world's let-downs.

'Oh, my God!' said Anna, bouncing Florrie on her knee. 'How did they find out?'

'Wait! It gets worse.' He picked up another paper and shuffled through to page seven. There was a picture of Acorn in the bottom corner, a publicity shot pre-'Eco-Pops' when her hair was still a ball of frizz with a bow on top. 'Look at this little gem.'

TV Mum's Shame

Call this woman an Earth Mother? Earth Monster more like! 'Eco-Pops' Acorn dumped her baby and ran off. She wanted to SAVE THE PLANET with poetry. What a joke! Acorn, this is for you – Shut up and go home!

'Does Greg know?' said Anna, snatching the paper from him.

Andy shook his head. 'Not unless he's read the papers this morning.'

'Then we're going to have to tell him.'

'You're joking,' said Cass, picking up the other paper and looking through it.

'But he's bound to find out, Cass.'

'He might not,' said Andy. 'It might blow over in a day or two.'

'I feel really sorry for him,' said Anna reading the story again. 'He's so proud of Acorn's success. He thinks he's helped her to be a poet by bringing up Cori.'

'I can't believe they're still writing this stuff,' said Cass, hitting the paper in her hand. 'All this about Acorn is just sexist bollocks! They're trying to force women out of work and back to their babies.'

Anna shrugged and drank her coffee.

'What's that meant to mean?' said Cass, mimicking her gesture.

'Nothing.'

'So you agree with *The Daily Hate* now?'

'No,' said Anna. 'But you know how hard it's been for Cori without a mum. Acorn should have told them where she was.'

'And what about the men who leave their kids?'

Anna kicked Cass under the table and nodded her head anxiously towards Andy. He was stuffing the last of his doughnut into his mouth. Cass gestured helplessly. 'All I'm saying is that men run out of their children's lives all the time and they don't get in the papers.'

'Maybe they don't claim to be saving the world, sweetie,' said Andy, reaching for another chocolate doughnut. 'I agree with Anna. Acorn deserves all she gets.'

'I didn't say that, Andy.'

'These papers don't give a toss about Acorn, anyway,' said Cass. 'They're just having a pop at feminism. Again.'

Anna sipped her coffee. 'You've got to feel a bit sorry for her, though.'

'Why?' demanded Andy.

'Because of all this.'

'Then she shouldn't have betrayed Greg.'

'Well, she didn't exactly betray him, Andy,' said Anna, reaching for an apple doughnut to share with Florrie.

'So why did she leave? I'll tell you. Because there was another man.'

'I don't think so,' said Anna.

Andy laughed dismissively. 'You're telling me there wasn't another man behind his back? Maybe more than one?'

'Why does it always have to be about a man?' asked Cass.

Andy slammed his coffee onto the table. 'Because it is! That bitch was just thinking about herself. She didn't care who she hurt by sleeping around. People like her are all the same.'

Anna and Cass exchanged glances. 'She wanted to be a poet,' said Anna. 'They made an agreement when she was pregnant. Greg knew she was going to leave. He didn't want her to go, but she didn't deceive him. I thought you knew that, Andy.'

'She abandoned her child!'

'She must have thought a clean break was best,' said Cass.

'She just didn't want a baby spoiling her fun.'

Anna shrugged uncomfortably, 'Well, I suppose that's not the worst thing in the world.'

'How can you say that about a child? How can walking out of her life be good for Florrie?'

'Cori,' said Anna.

'What?'

'You said Florrie.'

'Did I?'

'Yes.'

'I meant Cori.'

'We know,' said Cass.

'Anyway,' said Andy, looking at his watch, 'I'd better go. Keep the papers. I've seen enough sleaze for one morning.'

Chapter 15

Common Ground

Anna wheeled Florrie's pushchair into the street and towards the common, the papers from Andy stashed in a bag with juice, bananas and nappies. 'Right, my little darling,' she said, leaning over the buggy, 'how would you like to go on the swings?' Florrie smiled and gurgled, kicking her legs. She was wearing an orange flowery coat and bright red wellies. Anna smiled at her, almost tempted to go and get the camera. She looked back to the house and caught a glimpse of Ruby staring through her window at the end of the Close. Anna checked her watch. Eleven o'clock. Turning around, she steered Florrie over the road to Ruby's front door. 'Let's invite Ruby, shall we? We haven't seen her all week.'

It took a while for Ruby to answer the bell. 'Hi,' said Anna, as the door finally opened. 'I didn't know you were off work today. Are you okay?'

Ruby let go of the front door and went back to the kitchen at the back of the house. She was wearing a red towelling dressing gown and her dark hair was scraped back in a novelty hair band.

'I rang in sick.'

'What's wrong?' said Anna, following her inside. She wheeled the pushchair into the hall and unstrapped Florrie. 'Have you got a bug or something? You don't look well.'

'I'm fine,' said Ruby. 'I'm taking a sicky.'

Anna carried Florrie into the kitchen. There was a vodka bottle, half empty on the draining board, and a full glass on the table. She sat down with Florrie on her lap and Ruby lit a cigarette. Anna watched the smoke drift towards them. 'What about coming to the park with us? We're going to the swings. It'll be fun.'

Ruby smiled at Florrie. 'And how is my little swinger?' She held her small hand, stroking the chubby fingers.

'Oh, she's fine. But we've had a right morning. Andy was round at six with doughnuts and Doris and Boris were doing their ritual shitting in the garden. So, you know, just an ordinary day.'

'Sounds like my idea of fun.'

'And there's something else, it's about Greg. Andy showed us something and now I don't know what to do for the best. I was hoping to talk to you.'

'All right, Anna?' said Johnnie. She swivelled around and he walked into the kitchen in his underwear.

'Oh, hi, Johnnie. I didn't know you were here as well. I thought you were at Uni today.'

He shrugged and took one of Ruby's cigarettes from the packet on the table. 'Didn't feel like it.'

'Oh well, if you two had planned a day together, me and Florrie will leave you lovebirds to it.'

Neither Johnnie nor Ruby spoke. Johnnie filled the kettle from the tap, Ruby stared at the table. Anna stood up. 'Okay, we'll be off then.'

'Stay for a coffee,' said Ruby. 'Johnnie'll make it.'

Anna glanced between her and Johnnie. 'I should be getting to the park.'

'Sit down.' Ruby pulled on Florrie's welly. 'It's nice to see you.'

Anna watched Ruby take Florrie's boots off and stand them gently on the table. She smiled and sat down. 'Okay, I'll have a quick cup of tea.'

Johnnie opened the stainless steel tin next to the kettle. 'There's no bags.'

'Well, look in the cupboard,' said Ruby without turning around.

He opened the white cupboard above his head. 'There's none in here either.'

'And what, that's my fault, is it?'

'I'm not saying it's anyone's fault, Ruby, I'm saying there's no teabags.'

'Coffee's fine,' said Anna. 'I don't know why I said tea.'

'You said tea because you wanted tea,' said Ruby, scraping her chair across the floor as she stood up. 'And as Johnnie can't seem to manage that, I'll make it for you myself.'

'Fine,' said Johnnie, throwing a teaspoon across the kitchen and into the sink. 'You make the sodding tea.'

'Just watch me.' Ruby yanked open the cupboard in front of Johnnie, banging the door into his legs. He was pouring boiling water into his cup and jumped back, splashing hot coffee over the counter. 'You wanted tea, Anna?' She produced a dusty jar of instant tea from the back of the spice rack. 'You've got tea.'

Johnnie stared at her coldly. 'So that's another fucking point to you, Ruby.' He stormed out of the kitchen and Ruby slammed the jar onto the work surface. Anna concentrated on Florrie. When she looked up Ruby was leaning over the kettle.

'Are you okay, Ruby?'

Ruby turned around, pulling the loose strands of hair away from her face. 'I'm fine, darling.' She smiled. 'And don't look so worried. I don't expect you to drink this muck.' She threw the jar of tea into the dustbin. 'How about we just go to the park?'

On the common, Ruby took the pushchair and raced past the row of expensive garden gates, all covered in graffiti and razor wire, towards the park. Anna walked slowly behind, watching her whizzing Florrie around, making faces and singing to her as she weaved around the path, avoiding the couples in business suits. Anna stopped to give some change to a teenager lying on a bench in a sleeping bag, a rucksack under his head, a dog at his feet.

When she reached the park, Ruby had lifted Florrie into a swing and was pushing her gently to and fro. Anna closed the metal gate and wandered over to them.

'You can leave her there, Ruby. She loves it. She goes all dreamy.' Ruby stepped back, lighting a cigarette, and followed Anna to the painted wooden roundabout. They sat together watching Florrie happily dangling her legs in the swing. 'What's going on, Ruby?'

'What do you mean?'

'All that business with the tea. Are you and Johnnie going through a hard time?'

'Anna, darling, please don't start worrying about me. I couldn't bear it.'

'But I am worried about you, Ruby. I've been worried since Saturday, when you told me about your dad.'

'Only since then?'

'Ruby!'

'It's fine, Anna.' She dragged on the cigarette. 'I got a little drunk and emotional. That's all.'

'And you feel better now?'

'Completely.'

'It's just that . . . don't get cross with me for asking, Ruby, but were you drinking this morning?'

'The tea. I confess, I had the last teabag.'

'I'm not talking about tea, Ruby. I saw the glass on the table.'

'What glass?'

'The one with the vodka in it.'

'Not vodka, Anna, water.'

'Ruby, you hate water.'

'But it's so good for the skin,' said Ruby, getting up and moving away from Anna towards the swings. 'Didn't you know? Models drink at least fifty gallons a day.'

Anna followed her. 'Don't run away from me.'

'Who's running?' said Ruby, pushing Florrie.

'You just seem—'

'A mess?'

'That's not what I was going to say.'

'Of course you weren't, Anna. You're far too nice to hurt my feelings.'

'I was going to say you don't seem happy,' said Anna, perching on the empty swing beside Florrie.

'And are you happy, Anna?'

'We're not talking about me.'

'We are now. So answer the question. Are you and your lovely family happy?'

'Yes. Thanks to you. But I still think—'

'I know you do, darling, but please don't be boring. Tell me about this new scandal.'

Anna paused. 'I know what you're up to, so don't think I don't.'

Ruby shrugged. 'I'm an open book.'

'But I've got to show you the papers.' She jumped off the swing and rifled in the basket under the pushchair. 'It's terrible, Ruby.'

'What is?' said Ruby, walking over.

'I just feel so sorry for Greg.'

'Tell me, woman. The suspense is dreadful.' Ruby sat on the roundabout, kicking it around with her feet.

'This!' Anna pulled out the papers and gave them to Ruby as she circled around. 'Look what they've said. "TV Mum's Shame, Acorn Abandons Baby." ' Ruby studied the papers as the roundabout slowed to a halt.

'They all know about her leaving Cori,' said Anna, sitting

next to her. 'What shall we do? Do you think I should tell Greg?'

Ruby kicked against the ground until they began to move again. 'No.'

'So you think it will blow over?'

'I doubt it.' Ruby was reading the *Sun*.

'Ruby, I need some advice here. Greg still loves Acorn. He'd do anything for her.'

Ruby put the papers down. 'Would he give up his daughter?'

'What?'

'Would he let Acorn take Cori?'

Anna stared at her. 'No, of course he wouldn't. But Acorn doesn't want Cori, Ruby.'

'Doesn't she?' Ruby stood up and went back to the swings.

'No way, she's never even come back to visit.'

Ruby shrugged. 'She will.'

Anna gathered up the papers. 'You think she'll come back?'

'The woman needs to save her career, Anna. Her daughter's right there where she left her. What do you think she'll do?'

'But, she couldn't, I mean . . . we have to warn Greg.'

'It won't do any good, Anna, not if he still loves her. Greg has to deal with the past in his own way, just like the rest of us.' Ruby heaved Florrie out of the swing. 'And no one ever said it was easy.'

Chapter 16

As Seen on TV

Shirley yawned and snuggled up to Greg, reaching over his chest to switch off the alarm. 'Come on, lazy. It's half-seven.' Greg moaned and rolled away. 'It's your turn to make the coffee,' she said, sliding her hand across the sheet and tickling his back.

'Leave me alone, Shirley.'

Shirley giggled, tickling him again, pushing him across the bed until he tumbled onto the floor. Without speaking, he dragged himself up, grabbed a pair of boxer shorts and slouched out of the room. Shirley curled up on the bed with the duvet up to her chin watching him, and listening as he plodded down the stairs, scratching and farting. 'I heard that, smelly!' she said, swinging out of bed and bounding down the stairs after him. 'I know, let's have breakfast and stories in bed,' she called to Greg as he disappeared, grunting, into the kitchen. 'I'll get Cori's *Barbie* comic.' She darted into the front room and opened the curtains to look for it. There were men outside with cameras, clicking, flashing. Their voices pounded through the glass.

'Tell us about Acorn, Greg!'

'Is little Coriander there?'

'What do you think about your mum being on TV, love?'

Shirley yanked the curtains shut.

Greg, still half asleep, was making two instant coffees when Shirley ran into the kitchen. 'Greg! Something's going on outside. There's all these men asking about Acorn.'

'What?' Greg scratched his chest, yawning.

'Acorn.' Shirley yelled. 'Come on Greg, wake up.'

'Acorn?'

'They've got cameras and everything. I think they must be from the newspapers.'

'She's not here.'

'I know that, stupid. They're asking for Cori.'

'What! Why?'

'I don't know!' she said, pulling his arm. 'Just come and look!'

'I'd better tell them Acorn doesn't live here.'

'No, don't go out there! They're taking photos of everything.'

Greg trekked upstairs. 'Don't worry, I'll get some trousers on.' He came down in jeans, pulling a jumper over his head. His hair was ruffled and he hadn't shaved. Even to Shirley's eyes he looked rough.

He opened the front door to a barrage of shouting and flashing. 'Greg, where's your daughter?'

'Have you got any words for Acorn?'

Shirley was hiding in the front room, listening as Greg tried to speak over the confusion. She peeped through a crack in the curtains at the side of the bay window. There were at least fifteen people there with cameras and recorders, several of them women.

'Guys! She doesn't live here. You've got the wrong house.'

'And what do think you about that, Greg?'

'Are you angry?'

'Do you hate her for walking out?'

'What? No! What's going on?'

'Come on, Greg,' shouted a reporter from the back of the group. He had thin greasy hair and a taunting mouth. ' "Celebrity Mum Abandons baby". Did you think we wouldn't find out?'

Greg stared at them for a moment, then turned around and slammed the door. He was shaking. 'What the fuck's going on?'

Shirley rushed into the hall and put her arms around him. 'I don't know.'

'I've got to wake Cori.' He glanced over the top of her head and up the stairs.

'Yes, and I'll make her breakfast.' Shirley could feel her excitement rising. Just her and Greg, trapped in the house, besieged by the media. Her face was glowing. It was her chance to be indispensable.

'Yeah,' said Greg. 'Then I'm going to find Acorn. Warn her.'

'What!' Shirley drew back.

'They're out to get her, Shirley. I've got to warn her.'

'No you haven't!' The phone started ringing on the table next to her. 'Don't answer it!' she said.

But Greg's hand was already on the receiver. 'It might be her,' he said, picking it up. *'What's your daughter think about her mum, Greg?'* asked a male voice. He held the phone out to Shirley. 'Listen to them, Shirley. They're pigs. Acorn needs me!'

He jogged up the stairs, leaving Shirley with the receiver in her hand. *'Hello?'* said the voice. *'I just want to help you put your side of the story. It's only fair.'*

'Piss off,' she shouted, and slammed it down. It began ringing immediately. She picked it up. 'I told you to leave us alone!'

'It's Acorn. Don't hang up.' The voice was breathless. Shirley hung up.

'Take it off the hook, Shirley,' said Greg as he came down

the stairs with Cori in his arms. 'They're not going to leave us alone.' It rang again as he was talking and Shirley grabbed it. Greg took it out of her hand. 'I'll deal with this,' he said, gesturing for her to take Cori into the kitchen. 'You girls get some breakfast.' He waited for the kitchen door to close behind them before shouting into the receiver. 'We've told you to leave us alone, all right? We've got nothing to fucking say.' Shirley dumped Cori at the kitchen table with the Coco Pops in front of her and raced back to the closed door. She listened at the crack. It was Acorn, she could tell by the dazzle of Greg's silence.

'I need milk.' Cori looked up at her. 'And a bowl. And a spoon.'

'All right.' Shirley snatched a bowl off the draining board and plonked the milk on the table. 'Now you can pour it yourself.' She went back to the door. Greg's voice was trembling. 'Wow, it's really you.' She could hear him shuffling on the mat. 'Same as ever, you know me, nothing changes . . . I've seen it, yeah. You look great . . . We watch it together, you know, me and Cori . . . She's fantastic . . . What? . . . Really? You mean it? . . . Yeah, she'd love that. She talks about you all the time . . . Today? You can't, Acorn, there's photographers here, you know, reporters . . . Course I do, you know I do.'

'Where's my spoon?' Cori was sitting on the table, her bowl full to the brim with milk and cereal. 'You didn't give me a spoon.'

Shirley glanced around. 'In a minute.'

'But how can I eat it?'

'Just go and get one.'

'I can't reach. They're all in the sink.'

Shirley gritted her teeth. 'All right!' She dipped her hand into yesterday's washing-up water, pulled out a spoon and dried it on a tea towel. 'Now just eat.'

When she went back to the door there was no sound in the hall. She pushed it ajar. Greg was standing, smiling, still holding the receiver in his hands. She went over to him. 'Is everything all right, Greg?'

'Huh?' He looked down at her. 'What? Oh yeah. Acorn's coming . . . to see Cori. Shirley, you get her dressed. I've got to have a shave. Look at the fucking state of me.' He threw himself up the stairs so fast his feet barely touched the treads.

At nine o'clock Shirley was sitting by herself on the sofa in the front room, chin in her hands, elbows on her knees. The curtains were closed behind her, but she could still hear the reporters outside chatting to each other, occasionally calling out questions or banging on the door. Greg was pacing the hall in his sexiest shirt, smoking a joint to calm his nerves. Shirley could smell his aftershave, the one she had bought him, as he walked up and down.

'Look at me, Shirley!' Cori pranced into the room, wearing her favourite dress, a sequined sack Ruby had bought her. She began singing the 'Eco-Pops' theme tune, and dancing around the coffee table.

'You look lovely,' said Shirley, managing a smile.

Outside there was a sudden commotion. Cameras whirred into action, and reporters could be heard running away from the house. Shirley looked out from the curtain. Across the road Acorn was getting out of a car, carrying a simple wicker basket. She smiled at photographers, shaking her hair-beads for the cameras.

'She's here,' said Shirley. Her voice sounded dull, but Greg didn't seem to notice. He charged into the room, leaping onto the sofa and dropping his spliff on Shirley in his eagerness to look out the window. Shirley fumbled for the roach in the cushions next to her and threw it in the ashtray.

'Is this shirt okay, Shirley? Do I look all right?'

She nodded, reaching up to kiss him. 'You look fantastic.'

'And you've been great, Shirley.' He hugged her, looking out of the window over her head. 'Okay, Cori?' He turned back into the room. Coriander was bouncing up and down on the rug. She ran into his arms and he picked her up, carrying her towards the hall.

'Greg,' said Shirley as they reached the door. 'Just remember that I love you, Greg.'

He glanced towards the front door, impatient to answer it. Acorn was knocking. 'Thanks, Shirley,' he said, not catching her eye.

Shirley opened the curtains. Outside the cameras were in spasm and Acorn was standing on the step, smiling at the reporters. Her teeth looked even bigger in real life and the beaded plaits in her brown hair made her head rattle. 'Oh, Greg,' she said, turning to him as he opened the door behind her. 'Where is my darling?' Cori appeared from behind Greg's legs in the doorway and Acorn knelt down. 'Coriander?'

Cori nodded.

'I'm your mummy, Coriander. Acorn. Can I hug you?'

With Greg's big hands on her shoulders, Cori edged towards her prodigal mother. The cameras snapped and clicked as Acorn held out her hands and touched Coriander's cheek. 'Look at you, you're beautiful.'

Cori smiled, staring at Acorn's shoes.

'Do you like pop music, Coriander? Would you like to meet your favourite pop star and be on television with me? I'll do all that for you. Just give me a hug.'

Cori stepped forward and Acorn grasped her, spinning her around in the cramped front garden, over the heads of the kneeling photographers. What a happy family scene, thought Shirley, as the journalists laughed at the giggling mother and daughter.

'How does it feel to be with your daughter, Acorn?'

'Have you missed her?'

'Have you come back for her?'

'How will this affect your career?'

Acorn refused to answer any of their questions. She was overcome with emotion. Holding Cori's hand, she smiled at the reporters, biting her knuckle to hold back the sobs. Then she led her daughter into the house. Greg beamed at her as he moved out of the doorway and shut the door behind them.

'I am terrible person, Greg,' she said as soon as they were inside. 'I've failed as a woman. I've failed you. I've failed my child.'

Shirley stood in the front room watching them through the gap in the door. Acorn was sitting on the bottom stair with Cori on her lap, while Greg stood against the wall, Acorn's basket at his feet.

'You haven't failed, Acorn. Look at you, look at everything you're doing on TV.'

'Greg!' She put her hand to her breast. 'I've realised that without you and Coriander, I'm like a shell.' Behind the door, Shirley rolled her eyes. 'Everything is nothing, because I'm empty, empty inside. My life is meaningless. And what's happened in the papers has opened my eyes to my emotional and spiritual starvation. Greg, I've been pretending to be happy and really—' she pressed her fist to her forehead, lip wobbling, '—I was lying. Lying to myself. Leaving you two was the worst mistake I ever made.'

'I . . . I don't know what to say,' stumbled Greg, moving towards her.

'Greg, baby, don't say anything.' She held out her hand and Greg knelt forward to hold it. She pulled him nearer. 'Give me another chance, Greg. Take me back. Let me be a mother to my child.'

'I—'

'Greg, honey,' Acorn pressed her finger to his lips. 'I've written a poem for you. You know I can only express my spiritual side in my art. It's the story of my journey as a woman and poet. I'd like to read it for you.'

Greg knelt on the floor, gazing at Acorn as she passed Cori to him and stood up. She gestured for him to move back with the basket and stepped onto the bottom stair. Shirley slunk back into the front room.

'Hey, do you remember how I always performed my poetry on the stairs, Greg?'

Shirley couldn't see Greg's reaction, but she wanted to vomit. She watched Acorn test the banister and clear her throat before curling into a ball on the bottom step. She spoke into her knees.

> 'I am the Acorn!
> A seed in Nature's world –
> A mere girl
> A leaf to be unfurled.'

She raised one arm towards the ceiling and waved it from side to side.

> 'I am the sapling!
> Bending in the breeze –
> Fighting for the planet
> That man's brought to its knees.'

She clung to the banister with both hands, arms outstretched, head bent back. Cori clapped wildly.

> 'I am the tree!
> Clinging to the Earth –
> Changing children's lives
> With the power of my verse.'

She climbed two steps up the stairs and curved over the banister, pulling her stomach under her ribs.

> 'I am the great oak!
> Hollowed from within –
> A shell of a woman
> Parted from my kin.'

Finally, she laid out her full length on the stair, speaking into the worn patch of carpet, all fluff and string, on the edge of the top step.

'Will I be the fungied stump?
Lost in the forest's gloom?
Never to see the blossoming
Of the Acorn from my womb?'

She sat up and Cori ran up the stairs into her arms. They sat together on the top step, looking down at Greg.

'That's how I feel, Greg,' said Acorn, wiping tears and carpet fuzz from her cheeks. 'It's up to you now. I'm the hollow oak with her little acorn at her side.' She stroked Cori's head. 'If you want to cut me down, the axe is in your hands.'

Greg stepped forward and glanced at Shirley watching them from the front room. Acorn followed his gaze. 'Who's she?'

'Um, that's Shirley. She's got the spare room upstairs.'

'I see, a lodger. You wouldn't mind moving out, would you, honey, so Cori's mother can come home?'

'Actually I'm Greg's girlfriend,' said Shirley.

'Girlfriend?'

'Shirley moved in a few weeks ago,' said Greg.

'But we've been seeing each other for nearly a year,' said Shirley, glaring at Greg.

'So, it's not too serious then,' said Acorn, sitting with Cori on her lap. 'You understand, honey, Greg and I have a spiritual bond, like with nature, through our child.'

Shirley looked at Greg, but he was avoiding her gaze, staring at the floor.

Acorn smiled. 'Can I speak to you woman-to-woman? Can I do that, Shirley?'

'No,' said Shirley.

'It's important for all of us to understand,' said Acorn. 'To really understand what the mother–daughter bond means.'

'It didn't bother you until last week,' said Shirley.

Acorn appealed to Greg. 'I've tried, honey. But where I am emotionally right now, I can't deal with someone who won't acknowledge the bond here.'

Greg guided Shirley into the front room. 'Shirley, we need

to talk.' He closed the door and sat next to her on the edge of the sofa. 'I don't really understand what's happening out there, Shirley. Acorn says she wants to come back and she wants to be with me and Cori.'

'You're not going to take her back, are you?'

'I don't know. I don't know what to think. Acorn's Cori's mum.'

'But she abandoned her.'

'And now she's back.'

'So tell her to get lost again.'

'I can't do that, Shirley.'

'Why not?'

'Because Cori misses her. You know how much Cori wants a mum.'

'I can be Cori's mum.'

'Oh, Shirley, that's sweet and everything, but Acorn is Cori's mother, and she's sitting outside with her now, asking to come back.'

'Yeah, she just walks in after six years and expects everything to fall into her lap. Expects you to just jump up and . . . and . . . kiss her arse.'

'Shirley, it's not like that. Be honest. Have you ever seen Cori so happy?'

'Yes,' said Shirley. 'She was just as pleased when I moved in.'

Greg sighed. 'I don't want to hurt you, Shirley, but we both know that's not true. Cori loves you, but Acorn is her real mother. She needs her. I think that for Cori's sake I have to make a go of it with Acorn.'

'No,' said Shirley. 'I love you.'

'I'm sorry, Shirley, you're a sweet girl and we've had a great time, but I've got no choice. You must be able to see that.'

Shirley started to cry, pulling away when Greg put his arm around her.

'There's no nice way to say this, Shirley, so I'm just going to have to spit it out, but if Acorn comes back . . . well, I think you should move out.'

'No, Greg.'

'We can't all live together, Shirley, it wouldn't be fair on anyone. I'll help you find another room.' He stood up. 'Maybe now your dad's moved out, you can go back to the café with your mum?'

'No!' she cried, but Greg was already standing by the door. Shirley was facing heartbreak in the horsebox.

Chapter 17

Street Fighter

'Andy!' said Cass, standing at the front door in her pyjamas. 'What the hell are you doing here?'

'I've come to see you,' he said, stepping inside.

Cass closed the door. 'But it's gone twelve o'clock. Florrie's been asleep for hours.'

'I know, sweetie, I'm the midnight booze fairy, here to keep you company through the cold lonely hours.' He held up two bottles of wine.

'I was in bed,' she said, but Andy had already disappeared into the sitting room. When Cass joined him with two glasses and a corkscrew, he was sitting on the sofa in the dark with the curtains open behind him.

'Why are we in the dark?'

'Atmosphere,' he said. 'You can light a candle if you want, though.'

'Andy, is something going on?'

'No.'

'So you're only visiting out of hours now? Either the crack of dawn or the middle of the night?'

'It's the perfect time for a midnight feast, sweetie.' He emptied his pockets, producing a dozen packets of chocolate and sweets. 'We can be like two schoolgirls in the dorm. No snogging though, I've heard the stories!'

'God, look at this stuff,' said Cass. 'I thought you were trying to keep in shape. Jogging and everything.'

'I've given that up. I'm back on the binge-vomit regime. It's part of my celebrity lifestyle.' He opened the wine and Cass lit candles. Andy's face looked drawn in the flickering light.

'You sure you're okay, Andy?'

'Of course, darling. Why do you ask?'

'Well, it's Saturday night and you're here stuffing your face. I just thought it might—'

'Sweetie,' he interrupted, 'can't we share a midnight feast without you thinking I'm having a nervous breakdown?'

'Sure,' Cass shrugged and opened a chocolate bar, dipping it into her red wine. Andy swivelled to look out of the window behind him.

'If you're looking for Anna, she won't be back from the café until gone one.'

'I'm not looking for anyone, darling, just admiring the stars.'

Cass ate her chocolate, sitting cross-legged in the armchair. 'Tony working?' She tried not to sound too interested.

'He's had to stay late at the restaurant.' Andy turned to face her. 'That's what it's like in the catering trade, isn't it? You go in for the lunchtime shift and don't get home until four in the morning?'

'Not at The Cosmic.'

'You know what I mean, Cass, in normal restaurants.'

'It depends. If you're some poor sod with no work permit then it's exploitation city. But Tony knows what's what. He should tell them to go fuck themselves.'

'Oh, I'm sure he does, sweetie,' said Andy, turning back to the window. 'I'm sure he does.' The street was quiet with no lights shining from the houses. A cat sat licking itself on the wall outside. Cass grabbed a packet of M+Ms and snuggled into the chair.

When Anna got back at 1:30 Andy met her at the door with his finger to his lips.

'They're both asleep.'

'Hi,' she whispered, 'I didn't know you were coming round tonight.'

'Spur of the moment thing.'

She followed him into the sitting room. Cass was sprawled in the chair in her pyjamas, chocolate melted down the front. Anna smiled. 'Wild night I see. I'll take her to bed.'

'I'll pour you a glass of wine.'

'Um, okay, but I'm pretty shagged, Andy. The café was packed tonight. Cass, wake up, I'm taking you up to bed.'

When Anna came down the stairs the hall was dark. Andy was crouching behind the front door, looking through the letterbox.

'Andy, what's—'

'Shush!' He waved her over.

She crouched next to him, whispering. 'What's going on? Is it the Karloffs?'

He shook his head. 'Look through here,' he said, holding open the letterbox.

Anna pressed her face to the door and peered through the gap. She could see one of the new tenants across the road kissing a man on his doorstep. She turned back to Andy. 'What are we looking at? Gay men?'

'Look again, Anna, see who it is!'

She turned back to the letterbox. The two men were going into the house, still kissing, fumbling for the light switch. The bulb brightened just before they pushed the door closed. She snapped the letterbox shut.

'Did you see them?' Andy asked.

'I'm not sure.'

'Yes you are,' he said. 'It was Tony, wasn't it?' He walked back into the sitting room and Anna followed.

'But how could it be him? I thought you were—'

'So did I.' Andy was sitting on the sofa with his head in his hands. 'I've seen them before.'

'When?'

'A couple of times, the other morning when I was here.'

'What? Why didn't you say?'

'Would you expect me to? After the last few weeks?'

Anna shook her head. She sat in the armchair opposite Andy, facing the window.

'I came back, the next night. Tony said he was staying at the restaurant, so I waited for them. I hid behind some bins until four in the morning.'

'Oh Andy!'

He started to cry.

'Have you said anything to him?'

'I didn't want to believe it.'

'Maybe you're wrong. Maybe it's just someone who looks like Tony.' She gave him a crumpled tissue from her pocket.

He took it, squeezing her hand. 'You're so sweet for trying, Anna.' He wiped his eyes. 'Guess where I had my dinner tonight?'

Anna shook her head. 'Don't know.'

'Luigi's! The fabulous Luigi's of Croydon.'

'Oh.'

'Remember that place?'

Anna nodded.

'Last time I went I was pretending to be straight, this time I was pretending to be happy.'

'Tony wasn't there?'

Andy shook his head. 'He lied to me, Anna. Lovely little Stefano, my waiter, told me Antonio doesn't work Saturday nights. So I dutifully ate my *tortellini ai funghi* and then I came here, to watch my lover with another man. How sad is that?'

'It's one up from the dustbins.'

Andy smiled. 'So kind of you to say so.'

'What are you going to do?'

'What can I do?'

'Challenge him.'

'I can't do that, sweetie, he might leave me.'

'But you can't carry on like this.'

'I won't risk losing him for a little affair that will fizzle out next week.'

'And what if he does it again, with someone else?'

'Who says he will?'

'He's done it before.'

'Thank you. Thank you for rubbing it in.'

'Andy, I'm not, I'm—'

'I know, I'm just . . . If only I could be different, you know, have an open relationship? Every other fucking gay man does it. Why do I have to be so pathologically monogamous?'

A light from the bedroom opposite shone out into the street. The curtains were open. Anna tried not to look up. 'Maybe you should become a lesbian?'

'Funny, that's what Tony says.'

Anna glanced behind him across the street. Tony was at the window. Andy saw her eyes move and swivelled around.

'Bastard!'

Anna stood up. 'We shouldn't be watching this, Andy. I'm going to close the curtains.'

'No!' Andy grabbed her hand. 'I want to see.'

'Why? It won't do any good. If you're not going leave him, Andy, then you have to ignore it, not torture yourself with voyeurism.' She pulled the curtains and moved back to the armchair, taking her wine with her. Andy didn't move.

'What happens when you move to Brighton?'

'What do mean?'

'I mean what happens if Tony has an affair and you're in a new town, without your friends?'

'I learn how to cope, I'll be mature.' He was still kneeling on the sofa, facing the closed curtains.

'I see.'

'Anyway, I'm trying not to think about it. This might be a last fling, you know, before we get married.'

'I didn't know you were getting married.'

He turned around. 'It's going to be on the beach at sunrise, just us and a few friends . . . I didn't think you'd—'

'It's all right, Andy, I understand.'

They sat in silence. Andy poured himself more wine.

'You know what I don't understand, Andy. Tony was never going to keep this affair secret, was he? Think about it. It was only a matter of time before Cass or me saw him and then what would we have done? If we'd told you, after everything that's happened, we might have fallen out for good.'

'What are you saying, Anna? That this is all about you?'

'No, of course I'm not saying that. I don't know what I'm saying. It just seems kind of dangerous for Tony to have an affair with someone who lives opposite us and is one of your tenants. It's like inviting us to find out.'

Andy shrugged.

'I mean, did he just meet him in a club and not know where he lived?'

'Anna, how the fuck do I know how he met him?'

'So you think it's a coincidence.'

'I really don't want to think about it, if that's okay with you.'

'Can I tell you what I think?'

'If you must.'

'I think Tony's punishing you.'

'Anna—'

'He's punishing you for making up with me and Cass, for us being a family again. I bet this affair started after that night at Heaven.'

'Okay, Anna, you're not helping. I'd like to stop talking now.'

Anna sipped her wine slowly. 'Do you want some music on or something?'

'No, I just want to sit here.'

Andy opened the second bottle of wine and held it out to her. 'More?'

She shook her head. 'Not for me.' She rubbed her eyes. They were stinging with tiredness.

'Please yourself. Go to bed if you want.'

'That's okay, I'll sit here with you.'

'There's no need.'

'I know, I want to.'

He shrugged and poured himself more wine. They drank in silence.

When Anna opened her eyes, the room felt cold. A draught was blowing in from the hall. Both wine bottles were lying empty on the coffee table, surrounded by sweet wrappers, and the curtains were open. She stood up. She could hear shouting in the street. 'Andy!' She rushed to the door. Andy was in the middle of the road.

'Come on out then, you bastard!' he yelled, staring up at the window opposite. Anna ran out after him. The night was cold and her breath made ghostly clouds in the stillness of the streets.

'Andy, come on,' she said, reaching out to him. 'This isn't going to do any good.'

He shrugged her off. 'You wanted me to challenge him.'

'Not like this! Come on. Come inside!'

'No!' he shouted, moving away from her. 'Stay out of it, Anna.' He walked over to the student house and hammered on the door with his fist. 'Come on then, Tony. You knew I'd find out! Why are you hiding now?'

One by one, the lights clicked on in the bedroom windows around the street. Anna saw Ruby's face appear at her curtains and waved her over.

'Come on, Tony! You bastard!' screamed Andy. He ran back into the street and looked up to the window. The light was on. 'I know you're up there! I saw you fucking with him, like I was meant to.'

The front door opened. Tony was standing there, bare-chested in jeans and a leather jacket. 'Shut up, Andy!'

Andy stared at him. 'Shut up? You go fucking behind my back and I have to shut up?'

'You're drunk!' Tony's voice was angry. He stepped out onto the path. He had no shoes on, but didn't seem to notice the cold gravel. Anna moved back to the safety of her front gate, noticing that Cass had turned their bedroom light on. Andy backed away from Tony, towards Ruby's house.

'Of course I'm fucking drunk, you're pulling my fucking life apart.'

A voice behind Anna made her jump. 'This is disgusting!' Doris was stamping her feet on her doorstep. 'I'm ringing up the police.'

'No, please don't do that, Doris, Ida, I mean, Mrs Prestwick.'

She was fully dressed in thick tan tights, lace-up shoes, the mustard coat and a turquoise headscarf. Anna wondered if she slept like that.

'Don't come near me!' yelled Andy in the street. 'Don't you fucking come near me!'

'Is he the father?' said Doris, pointing at Andy, who was clinging onto the lamppost at the end of the street.

'Listen, Ida, he's just a bit tipsy,' said Anna, watching Ruby walk over to him. 'But we're getting him inside now. There's no need for the police to be involved.'

Tony was walking slowly up the street towards Andy. 'It's over,' he said. 'It's been over for weeks.'

'Liar!' spat Andy.

Doris narrowed her eyes. 'You shouldn't have a baby in that house, I told you.'

'Yes, I know you did, Ida,' said Anna, 'but can we talk about that tomorrow? I need to help Andy now.'

'This is what it leads to.'

'I'm sorting it out, okay?'

'You've been pushing me out of your life!' said Tony.

'What?' yelled Andy. 'I did everything for you!'

Cass tiptoed into the front garden with Florrie whimpering in her arms. 'Anna what's going on?'

'And now she's brought that baby out at night. That's it, I'm ringing up the police.'

Doris slammed her front door and Anna gripped her hands together, pretending to strangle her. 'Cass, just take Florrie inside, you can't help here. Tony's been sleeping with one of the students across the road.'

'You're joking!' said Cass, her eyes lighting up.

'Just put Florrie to bed and stay out of the way,' snapped Anna. 'You'll only make things worse out here.' Cass shrugged, and went back into the house, leaving the front door open.

Anna stared out into the street. Tony was clenching his fists in the middle of the road and Andy was standing with Ruby under the lamppost. She had her arms around him and was whispering something into his ear. Even in the streetlight, Anna could see that her cut-off jumper wasn't long enough to cover her lack of underwear. She glanced at Johnnie, who was coming out of the house with Ruby's dressing gown, and realised that Ruby was in no fit state to help tonight. Across the street Greg had appeared at his bedroom window, looking anxious and confused. Anna smiled at him, but he didn't see her. He was speaking to someone behind him, shaking his head. He turned away from the window and drew the curtains closed.

The three students were also awake, standing on their path. Anna ran over to them. 'What's the hell's going on?' the woman demanded. Her red hair formed perfect circles around her pale eyes. 'Is that Andrew Costello? He's supposed to be our letting agent. I thought we were being attacked by thugs, for God's sake. Mike nearly rang the police.'

Anna glanced at the lumpen youth lurking in the doorway. 'Well, you weren't,' she said, taking an instant dislike to her. 'So you can calm down and go back to bed.'

'I didn't know they were together,' said Will, pushing past

Anna. 'I thought he was straight. He told me he had a daughter.'

Tony started to laugh. 'See, Andy, even Will thought you were a breeder.'

Drunk and exhausted, Andy slumped against the lamppost. 'Do you hate me so much for having a family?'

'No, I loved you and they took you away from me.'

'They didn't,' cried Andy. 'How can you say that? What about Brighton?'

Ruby was staggering towards Tony with Johnnie hovering protectively behind her. 'Why don't you do us all a favour,' she said, stabbing him in the chest with her finger, 'and go back to your toy boy?'

'What? Before you get your fat hands on him you mean?'

'Dirty talk?' she said. 'How stimulating!' She slapped him across the face. Instantly, he slapped her back, hard, and Ruby stumbled sideways, her mouth bleeding. Before anyone could react, Johnnie charged at Tony, plunging into him and pushing him to the ground. Anna and Andy both rushed towards them, Anna looking helplessly on as Andy, shouting and pulling at them, tried to separate the two men. Eventually Johnnie was thrown back, panting on the asphalt, and Anna stood over him, blocking him, shouting at him to calm down. Ruby just watched them, in a drunken daze, wiping the blood off her face.

'If you ever hit her again,' Johnnie yelled, as Andy and Will dragged Tony up the street, 'you're dead!' Tony smiled, giving him the finger. He struggled out of Andy's grip and shoved him away, pulling Will back towards the house. Andy slumped on the road, watching them go.

'Forget it, Johnnie!' said Anna. 'It's Ruby you should be worrying about!' She walked over to Andy and held him tightly, kneeling behind him, leaning into his back. They were the only ones left in the street when the police car drove into the Close. 'Come on, Andy!' said Anna. 'We don't want any more trouble.'

'Speak for yourself!' Andy shrugged her off.

As the uniforms got out of the car, Doris appeared in her doorway, pointing gleefully. 'That's him, officers! He's the one. Shouting, swearing, fighting in the street.'

'It's nothing,' said Anna, trying to grab Andy's arm. 'A minor domestic. Too much to drink. We're going inside now.' She smiled apologetically. 'Come on, Andy!'

But he pulled away. 'You can all fuck off,' he yelled, running aimlessly up the street. 'I've had it with fucking everything.'

'Andy, no!' Anna watched him pick up one of the bins he'd sheltered behind nights before and throw it, scattering plastic packaging and scraps of food across the road. Both policemen ran over to him, grabbing his arms, and dragged him, struggling and defiant, into the car. Anna stared after his huddled shape in the back seat as he was driven away for a night in the cells.

Chapter 18

Hitting the Road

'Shirley, you silly girl.'

'Oh! It's you!'

'Of course it's me,' said Pearl, pushing through the front door and into Greg's hall. 'Who were you expecting this early? Another celebrity?' She glanced around at the magnolia walls, the bare low energy bulb hanging from the brown ceiling. 'It's not much to look at in here, is it, Shirley? No wonder you didn't want me round.' She walked up the hall. 'Well, let's get on with it.'

'What are you doing?' hissed Shirley.

'Getting your stuff,' said Pearl, as she headed up the stairs. 'You have packed, haven't you?' Shirley shrugged, staring sullenly at the cream and gold stair carpet. 'Oh, Shirley, you silly chump!' Pearl looked down at her and shook her head. 'You didn't really think you were stopping, did you?' She stood halfway up the stairs and pulled a roll of bin bags out of her breezeblock handbag. 'Well, it's lucky I brought these with me. Come on.'

'You can't go up there, Mum.'

'She's not here, is she?' Pearl thundered back down the stairs.

'Who?'

'Who? What do you mean "who?" Acorn! It's in all the papers, Shirley.' She rummaged in her bag, brought out a copy of the *Daily Express* and began flicking through. 'Here it is, listen to this. "Last week Acorn was more Ice-Pops than Eco-Pops. Now she's Eco-Poppins." I mean honestly! Where do they get that nonsense? "In a tearful doorstep scene Acorn was reunited with Coriander, the child she abandoned at birth. She now plans to live with ex-boyfriend Greg and daughter Cori in their very ordinary South London home." Look how they've brought out the stone cladding in the photo.' Shirley glanced at the small photo at the bottom of page twelve. Acorn, all teeth and hair, was standing on the doorstep with Coriander beaming in her arms. Behind her Greg could just be seen in the hall and to the left, peering through the bay window, was the shadow of Shirley. She burst into tears.

'Oh, Shirley,' said Pearl, putting her arms around her. 'It's all right, love. I'm here now, I've got Buzz outside in the Hottentots' van and we're taking you and your things back to the stable room.' Shirley cried harder.

When Pearl came struggling to the front door with a black bin bag in each hand and a pile more waiting to be thrown down the stairs, Buzz was still sitting in the van rolling a cigarette. He stared out of the passenger window, licking his Rizla paper, as Pearl shouted instructions from the doorstep. 'Come on, Buzz. I'm not paying you to sit on your arse all day in that van. You can see me humping in here.' He rolled the window down an inch – which was all it would go – and cupped his ear. 'You heard!' said Pearl, going back inside for more bin bags. Buzz left his skinny white cigarette on the dashboard, and cranked open the door. Gizmo's van was an ancient blue Bedford which Mutley, who fancied himself as a bit of a graffiti artist, had spray-painted in Gothic black letters

The Tooting Hottentots – Shit Happens. As the manager, Buzz was adding the tour dates and venues with a paintbrush on the back doors. He'd got five so far, counting the café.

'Is everything okay?' Greg was standing in his jeans at the top of the stairs next to the pile of bin bags. He watched Pearl walk back up the stairs towards him. 'Where's Shirley?'

'I've come to take her home,' said Pearl. 'Now that you've broken her heart.'

'Look, I feel shit about what's happened and everything . . . but now Acorn's come back, you know . . .' He glanced towards his bedroom door where Acorn was sleeping with Cori. He had moved out of the double bed and until Shirley left he was staying in Cori's room.

'Greg,' said Pearl, as she reached the landing. 'I think you've ploughed yourself a hard furrow with that one, but even as Shirley's mother, I think you're doing the right thing, for your daughter's sake. Blood's thicker than water, when all is said and done.'

'Thanks, Pearl.'

She took another two bin bags. 'Me and Buzz'll be in the van if you want to say goodbye to Shirley.'

Greg nodded, and knocked on the spare room door. When there was no answer he opened it gently. Shirley was sitting on the bare mattress with her back to him, staring out of the window.

'You okay?'

She shrugged.

'If there's anything I can do, you know, to help.'

'You can ask Acorn to leave us alone.' She spoke without looking at him.

'I can't do that, Shirley.'

'You mean you don't want to.' She turned to face him. He was still half behind the open door, holding the top with his left hand and leaning his shoulder against it. He shook his head.

'Please let me stay, Greg. I could look after you. And Cori.'

'It's too late for that, Shirley. Your mum's waiting for you downstairs in the van.'

'But you could tell her, Greg, tell her you want me to stay.'

Greg looked at the rug between them. 'Acorn's living here now, Shirley.'

'But I don't mind if Acorn stays over, Greg. I'll be nice to her, I promise. I'll stay in my room when she's here, just like I've done this week.'

'Be real, Shirley, it just wouldn't work.'

'We could make it work, Greg. I've thought about it. We could still be together when she's not here, and it would be our secret and we wouldn't tell anyone, not even Cori.'

'No, Shirley.'

'But we could . . . okay, I understand, we wouldn't even have to be together like that, not if you felt uncomfortable, but I could be here when she wasn't and we'd just be friends and then if—'

'Shirley, I've come to say goodbye. It's not going to happen.'

He left Shirley sitting on the bed and gestured helplessly at Pearl, who was waiting on the stairs.

Five minutes later, Pearl had Shirley out of the spare room, down the stairs and strapped into the front seat of the Hottentots' van. 'Right,' she said. 'We're off then. Back to the café.' Buzz opened the passenger door. 'You're in the back,' she said, without looking up. 'Just watch what you sit on. Shirley's got all sorts in those bags. Books, perfume, plates, the lot.'

'I'm sitting up front,' he said. 'Looking out for the van. Gizmo's a mate.'

Pearl leaned over, resting a hand on the gear lever. 'Buzz, what can I possibly do to this rust bucket that would make it look any worse? Anyway, I gave Gizmo a tenner to put me on his insurance for the day. So you don't have to worry.'

Buzz made a noise somewhere between a snort and a laugh, but he picked up his rollie and clambered across Shirley into the back of the van. Pearl could hear him mumbling, 'What fucking insurance?' as he settled himself among the bin bags, but she chose to ignore the implications.

'All right now, Shirley love?' she said. 'I'll soon have you home at the café.' Shirley stared out of the window at the damp stone-cladding, so Pearl turned on the ignition. She couldn't get the seat near enough to the pedals, because the sliding mechanism underneath had rusted, so to brake or change gear she had to stand up at a forty-five degree angle, hanging off the steering wheel for balance, and stamp on the appropriate pedal. This was easy enough for braking but when changing gear, Pearl had to support her entire body weight on one foot, whilst holding a moving gear stick in one hand and the steering wheel in the other. She explained all this to Shirley every time the procedure took place, which wasn't often as Pearl had already decided on her jack-of-all-gears. The van chugged, grunted and screamed most of the way back in second.

They ground to a halt in the side road that led to the back of the café. 'Okay, Buzz,' said Pearl, turning around, 'you can get out the back and unload. I want to talk to Shirley.'

'Can't open the doors from inside.'

'Well, use some brains and get out the front.'

Buzz climbed over their seats, smelling strongly of Shirley's lavender oil, and let himself out of the passenger door. When he had disappeared up the alley, taking a single bin bag, Shirley turned on Pearl, 'Come on then! Say it! I told you so! Why don't you just get it over with so I can get out of this stinking van?'

'Shirley, I don't want to say I told you so. I want to say that I understand how you feel.'

'Yeah, right,' said Shirley, picking gunge from the air vent.

'I don't know how you can have forgotten, Shirley, but three weeks ago my future disappeared like shit round a U-bend. My marriage was paraded as a sham in front of the Frinley town criers, and Gordon, the man I loved and had forgiven, was revealed as a total knob. I know what it is to feel hurt and betrayed by a man, Shirley, and I know what it is to love someone who never properly loved you back. We're in this together, you and me. The only difference is I want to be with you more than anyone else in the world and you'd rather be with anyone else but me.'

Pearl stared ahead at the steering wheel, and Shirley felt a pang of pity. 'I do want to be with you, Mum, it's just that—'

'It's all right, Shirley. You don't have to say anything. I just want to tell you a few things. They might not seem important to you, but I want to say them anyway. First off, I want you to know that as long I'm still alive—'

'Oh don't get all morbid, Mum!'

'As long as I'm alive, Shirley, you've always got a home. Not one you want maybe, and I'm sure I do everything wrong for you. But while I'm still on this earth, Shirley, you never have to be alone.'

'And secondly?'

'What?'

'You said that was the first thing.'

'Oh, Shirley, I worry about you, I really do.'

Chapter 19

Hallowe'en

Ruby stood on Greg's doorstep in her red basque and black silk cloak, plastic fangs curling over her lips. 'Trick or treat!'

'Oh, definitely treat.'

She stepped through the door and swished her cloak over his shoulders. 'Let me tell you, Greg baby, when I make tricks that is a treat.'

Greg laughed, embarrassed and edging away. 'Yeah, good costume, Ruby!'

'I'm a vamp.' She pulled out the fangs. 'It's the old story. Nice tits, shame about the teeth. But, then, I bet you say that to all the girls.' She grinned, ignoring Johnnie, who came in behind her. They stood, bunched in the narrow hallway. Ruby pointed at Greg.

'And why aren't you dressed up, you miserable sod? You were last year.'

'Um, it's Acorn, she takes Hallowe'en seriously, you know, as like a hallowed pagan festival.'

'You don't say! So it's just me and Cori dressed up, is it?'

'Just you, Ruby. Acorn doesn't agree with plastic masks and stuff—'

'Shame, she'd suit one.'

'—She's against trashing spirituality with commercialism, using Earth's resources and everything.'

'Frightful, isn't it,' said Ruby, putting her teeth in. 'So where is our famous Acorn the Activist?'

'Upstairs,' said Greg, walking to the kitchen. 'She's working on her poetry-reading with Cori.'

'Now you're really scaring me!' said Ruby, as she pushed open the door to the front room. Anna, Cass and Andy were sitting inside.

Johnnie followed Greg into the kitchen. 'Hey, Greg man, how's the bike going?'

'Almost finished, mate,' he said, opening the oven door. 'A bit of tuning and it'll be running like a dream.'

'You're a fucking star, Greg. How much do I owe you, man?'

'No worries!' He lifted a pot of potato out and turned down the heat. 'I got the parts from Bloggsie's yard, you know, 'cause he's a mate from school.'

'When you want a ride, Greg, she's yours. Is she in the shed?'

'I'll show you,' said Greg, throwing down the oven gloves and heading to the back door.

The bike shone in the half-light of Greg's shed. 'Jesus, man. Look at this.' Johnnie stroked the tank and straddled the bike. 'There's fucking hours of work here, Greg.' He flicked up the stand and sat on the saddle, rocking back and forth.

'I enjoyed it, mate. Gave me something to do, you know.'

'You've made me fucking smile again, thanks, man.'

Greg picked up a couple of spanners from the floor and slotted them into the row of nails hammered into the wood. 'You not smiling with Ruby then?' He kept his back to Johnnie. He could hear him rolling silently back and forward on the bike, but neither of them spoke. Greg wound the vice on his workbench closed.

'I don't know what to do about it,' said Johnnie.

'Ruby?'

'She's . . . I don't know.'

'I heard that spot of bother in the street the other week. Sorry I didn't, like, come down or anything, you know, with Acorn being here . . .'

'Yeah, don't worry about it, mate. Wasn't your problem. It wasn't our fucking problem, you know, but she's just like, out there, spoiling for a fight.'

'Seems all right now though.'

'She's not pissed yet.'

'Right!' Greg polished the headlight with his sleeve. 'Drinking a lot, is she?'

'All the fucking time, mate. I try and get her smoking some gear to calm her down, but she won't touch it. Any petrol in this?' Johnnie unscrewed the cap.

'Couple of litres maybe. Enough for a test.'

'I think she fucking hates me, Greg.'

'Who, Ruby? No way, mate! She loves you, Johnnie.'

'She's out of hand.'

'She always was.'

'No, I mean, she's . . . like the other night. She's, you know . . . I don't know what's going on in her head.'

'It'll get better, mate.'

'Will it?' He lifted his shirt and showed Greg the trace of a purple bruise on his chest. 'She's getting bad, Greg.'

'Shit!'

'She blames me for this stuff with her dad.' He studied the chrome around the petrol cap.

'What stuff? What's going on, Johnnie?'

Johnnie looked up and focused on Greg instead of the bike. 'It doesn't matter, mate. Stuff, you know, from Ruby's past.'

'Ruby'll be okay, Johnnie,' said Greg, hitting him on the shoulder. 'She always is.'

'Yeah,' said Johnnie, 'sure she will.' He got off the bike. 'But this is the best, Greg, you're a fucking hero. Can we take her out, up the street?'

Greg shrugged. 'You can, mate. I'd better get back. Acorn hasn't seen anyone here for years, you know, I don't want to leave her on her own for too long.'

'Oh, yeah, sorry, man. I didn't ask you, how's it going with you and her?'

Greg leant against the workbench. 'You know, I never thought she'd come back, and . . . here she is.'

'That's great, man.'

'I can't believe my luck, mate! I've thought about no one but her for six years.'

'Hey, come on. Forget the bike, let's go in. I want to meet your woman.'

Inside, Ruby was sitting with Anna, Cass and Andy in the front room, waiting for Acorn to come downstairs. Florrie was nestling asleep in Anna's arms.

Ruby drummed her fingers on the edge of the sofa. 'I don't think my smoking one tiny cigarette is going to give your baby emphysema.'

'No, Ruby.'

'Why don't you take her upstairs then?'

'I will. In a minute, when Acorn comes down,' said Anna. 'Can't you wait one minute, woman?'

'No, I'm dying here.'

'Well, go outside then. I'm dying not to bump into Acorn.'

'Ah, the great Acorn,' said Ruby, sticking a fang into the end of her unlit cigarette.

'Andy can't wait to meet her,' said Cass. 'It was only the promise of dinner with a Z- grade celeb that got him out of his flat at all. He hasn't been out since he escaped from Alcatraz.' She nudged Andy, 'Have you, Bird-man?'

'It was one night in Tooting nick, Cass.'

'At least they didn't charge you,' said Anna.

'Yippee do,' said Andy without enthusiasm. 'Doesn't that make my lonely life worth living!'

'Weren't the mugshots of Acorn in the paper fantastic,' said Ruby. 'Those teeth, that hair. I've always said the woman's half horse, half hippie.'

'Ruby!' said Anna.

'What?'

'Don't be mean.'

'What do you mean, don't be mean? It's the only reason I'm here.'

'For Greg's sake, Ruby, try to be nice, just for tonight. We're supposed to be welcoming Acorn back to Madrigal Close.'

'Yeah, and we all know why she's suddenly appeared out of the great blue yonder.'

'To save her career,' answered Andy.

'Of course, to save her career. She'll be off in less than six months. Probably with Cori in her bag.'

'Ruby, stop it! Greg might hear,' hissed Anna. 'Anyway, for all we know she might be for real. She might have wanted something bigger in her life.'

'My arse!'

'That's too big for anyone's life, sweetie,' said Andy.

Ruby threw her unlit cigarette at him. 'Don't tell me you believe all that shite about her finding herself.'

'No, but Greg believes her and I want him to be happy after all these years.'

The doorbell rang and Ruby pushed open the door next to her chair. She watched Acorn and Coriander come flying down the stairs in matching tassels and flounce, ready for the party. She closed it again and Anna lifted the curtain to see who it was. 'God, it's the new students.'

'What are they doing here?' said Andy, jumping up. 'I've got to go home.'

'No you haven't,' said Anna. 'You'll be fine.'

'But I can't face that Will! Not after what happened with Tony.'

'Sit down, it's too late! They're coming inside.'

Seconds later, Acorn stepped into the room with Coriander holding her hand. 'Hey, it's great to find you all in here. Come in, come in,' she said, gesturing for the three students to squeeze past her. 'We're friends old and new tonight. Why don't I do a few quick intros and then find Greg so we can really get our soirée going?'

She flicked her head back, narrowly missing Mike's eyes with her beads. He stepped back into the hall. 'Here are my newest friends, everybody. This is Lou, who's a fantastically talented painter, she's going to take the art-world by storm, and this is Will, he's a fantastically talented designer who's going to rock the fashion world. Aren't they gorgeous? They're twins, you know. And I'm going to take them under my wing, launch their careers. Lou's going to paint my portrait, for free. Can you believe that?'

Cass whispered in Anna's ear. 'I want to go home.'

'If you use recycled materials, honey,' Acorn was saying to Lou, 'we can do a feature about you on the show.'

Lou smiled, creasing the black kohl patterns around her temples.

'And Will's going to design a fantastic new outfit all from secondhand clothes and material. You, darling, will definitely be on the show. I want to use my access to the media to help other young artists. Now, who are the old friends we have here?' Acorn didn't introduce Mike standing behind her. 'So many faces from the past. Anna with her little baby I've heard so much about!' Acorn walked to the sofa and bent to kiss Anna's cheek. Anna covered Florrie's face and felt Acorn's beads thud onto her fingers. 'And, Cass, fancy you two staying together! And who's this?' said Acorn, pointing at Andy. 'Is this the donor of your baby seed, Anna?'

Anna blushed. 'This is Andy. And yes, he's Florrie's father.'

'Charmed,' said Andy to Acorn's back. She didn't notice. She had moved on.

'Ruby, larger than life, and twice as much fun. I thought

you would have moved on by now. But here you are. Same little house, same little street.'

Ruby smiled. 'I like to get my teeth into a place.'

'And you're so brave to choose Balham!'

'I'm always braced for a challenge.' Ruby sat back in her chair and Acorn turned to the door, glancing irritably at Mike, who shrank further into the hall. She linked arms with Lou. 'Well, darling, why don't we young ones find a seat around the table and begin our feast?'

She left the room with Lou in thrall and Mike following morosely behind. Will hovered in the doorway, only moving when Anna tried to squeeze past with Florrie in her arms. 'Right!' said Ruby, slamming her hands on the chair arms. Wisps of dust escaped from the worn fabric and drifted through her red fingernails. 'After that friendly welcome I'm going to smoke my fag outside.'

'Me too.' Andy leaped up to follow, avoiding Will's eye.

'Okay,' said Ruby, linking arms with him. 'I'm going out for a fag with a fag.'

'I'll come too,' said Will from the doorway. He led them into the hall and opened the front door. Andy and Will took a cigarette off Ruby and stood next to each other on the path. Will had an orange circle-print short dress on with matching flares underneath. He was shaking with cold. 'I didn't know you smoked?' he said to Andy.

'No,' said Andy. 'But then you didn't know I was gay either, did you?' His breath clouded the air between them. Will stepped back.

'It's just that when you said you had a daughter I didn't realise you meant a gay daughter.'

'Is she gay?' said Ruby offering them a light. 'Nobody told me.'

'It's in the genes,' said Andy.

'God forbid! The sins of the fathers passed down to the daughters.'

'Anyway,' said Will. He gave his unlit cigarette back to Ruby.

'I didn't really want this. I just wanted to say that I'm sorry about what happened!' He disappeared into the house.

'Wait!' said Andy, as Will shut the front door. 'It wasn't your fault, Will. I'm sorry I behaved like a sad old queen.'

Will pulled the door open, smiling with relief. 'You're not old, Andy!'

'Just a sad queen,' said Ruby, walking out into the road. 'But two out of three ain't bad.'

The dining table was made up of three tables, all different heights and shapes, pushed together and covered with different patterned Indian tablecloths. When Ruby and Andy came inside, everyone was already sitting down waiting for them. They squeezed behind the chairs to their places: Ruby next to Johnnie, Andy in between Anna and Cass.

'We're looking after you tonight,' said Cass, 'so you needn't worry about a thing.'

'And you're doing a fantastically talented job of it,' whispered Andy, pointing to the other side of the table with his knife. Cass looked up. Andy was sitting opposite Will.

Acorn was standing in the kitchen doorway wearing a see-through gypsy crop-top and tassled flares six inches longer than her legs. She coughed to get their attention. 'Hey, everyone,' she said when Cass and Andy stopped whispering and nudging each other. 'I think we should start the evening with a few words, but please don't expect too much from me. I'm pretty crap at speech-making, as all my friends here know.'

Ruby raised her eyebrows at Cass.

'It's so wonderful to see all you beautiful people gathered for our feast on this hallowed eve. And so I wanted to kick off the celebrations in my own inimitable style with a short poem from my forthcoming collection, *Time Gentlemen Please.* As you can see from the title, when it comes to my adult writing, I've lost none of my feminist bite. It's time for the men to listen to the needs of the planet.' Only Lou applauded. 'Thank you, darling. This little thing I'm about to read is from one of my riffs on the *The Waste Land*, a bit of sampling, you know. And if Toilets is listening, then I make no apologies to the Dead White Men.'

'What's she talking about?' said Ruby to no one in particular.

'Oh, sorry, Ruby, I thought everyone knew about Toilets. You must have missed some things on your life journey. Toilets – T.S. Eliot. It's an anagram, a little joke on the poetry scene.'

'Oh,' said Ruby, 'what a laugh you poets must have.' She turned her glass over and poured herself a drink.

Acorn smiled. 'Okay, here goes then, everyone. And by the way, this is a world première performance.'

She stood back and released Greg's brown beaded curtain from the hook on the side of the doorframe. It clattered across the doorway in front of her and she stepped further back, turning the fluorescent striplight off, and plunging the kitchen into darkness. Around the table the audience could still see her outline through the beads, leaning against the fridge. She began.

Is it time?
Does the yellow fog lick like a cat
At the typist doing her homework
Without knickers on?
The commuters are driving over London Bridge.
But the corpse you planted in Mylae
Will not soak up the CO_2.

The phallic twins have crumbled into dust –

I will show you
Fear in a handful of dust
Money in a breastful of milk
Fruitfulness in pesticides
That's neither mild nor mellow
But modified.
The fisher king has been—

Poisoned.

'Thank you.' Acorn parted the beads and stood, waiting for the applause. There was stunned silence.

'Wow!' Lou rose to her feet, 'That was fantastic, mind-blowing, Acorn.'

Greg smiled proudly with Cori sitting, half asleep, on his lap. Andy leant over to Cass. 'Was that brilliant or bollocks?'

Cass shrugged. 'No idea, just keep clapping.'

'I'm so glad you enjoyed my piece. I thought we could all have some fun with poetry tonight. I've written one of my famous "Eco-Pops" Scrap-Raps especially for my family to read after the feast.' She smiled at Greg and Cori.

Andy mouthed, 'Crap-Raps?'

'And I hope to encourage you all to explore your poetic creativity. I'm sure we'll all be writing poems to each other by the end of the evening.'

'God forbid!' said Ruby aloud, pouring herself another glass. Johnnie watched her.

'Well, perhaps not all of us,' said Acorn, pointedly. 'But now, let's give thanks to nature and feast on her fruits.'

The feast was a combination of vegetables of various hue and texture. The table was covered with pot after pot: vegetables puréed, roasted, souffléd and stuffed. Acorn directed Lou and Will to her favourite delicacies, and they shared stories about the virtues of caterers. When the dishes were finally cleared away, and the remains of the purées were drying to a crust on the plates, Acorn stood up. 'This hallowed e'en is when the past comes back to haunt us, and I'm glad to say I've come out of the past to haunt Greg—'

There was a knock on the door.

'Could someone get that? Anna, I think you're nearest, honey. Anyway, I'm going to start our little poetry-fest with some Scrap-Raps I've written especially for tonight, dedicated to Greg and Coriander, my two babes.' She unfolded a piece of paper she had placed under her plate. 'Okay, here goes then. A Scrap-Rap for the Goddess:

On Hallowe'en
The queen
Is seen
And Unseen

'And this is for Cori,

No hurry
No worry
No sorry
Just Cori

'And this one's for my man, Greg.

I ran
From my man
Now I span
Understan'?'

'I want to talk to Greg.' The voice from the hallway was loud and distinctly Shirley's.

Anna called after her, grabbing at her sleeve as Shirley pushed past. When she entered the room Greg stood up with Cori asleep in his arms. 'Shirley, what are you doing here?'

'I wanted to talk to you,' said Shirley, her face pink and blotchy from crying.

'This isn't a good time right now.'

Shirley looked around at the tables, at Andy and Cass, Johnnie and Ruby, Will, Lou and Mike, sitting with their empty plates in front of them. 'I see you're all here then. Nobody cared about me being pushed out. Nobody said this isn't fair to Shirley.'

'Of course not, honey,' said Acorn, sitting cross-legged on her chair. She had her back to Shirley and didn't bother to turn around. 'These people are Greg's friends.'

'Not like you then,' snapped Shirley.

'No,' said Acorn, pushing her chair back and turning around. 'Greg and I are clearly more than friends. We have a child—'

'You're not Greg's friend,' interrupted Shirley.

'Greg loves me,' said Acorn. 'And always has.' She stood up and put her arm on Greg's shoulder, smiling.

'You're only here because it was in the papers. You don't care about Greg. You don't even care about your own daughter.'

'That's enough,' said Greg. Cori was stirring in his arms. Anna slipped into the chair next to Andy, unnoticed.

Shirley pleaded into the embarrassed silence. 'But she doesn't love you, not like I do. I love you more than she ever will. Let me move in again, Greg, I'll show you how much I love you.'

'Listen,' said Greg, handing Cori to Acorn. 'I know you're upset and everything, Shirley, but please don't do this. It's not fair on anyone, it's not fair on you.'

'He means you're making a fool of yourself,' said Acorn behind him. 'You're trying to step into my life and nobody wants you here.'

'That's not true!' said Ruby, raising her glass to Shirley. 'I think little Shirley's got every right to be here. Good on you, Shirley.'

'This isn't the time, Shirley,' Greg said, ignoring Ruby. 'And you've been drinking. We'll talk in the morning.' He put his arm around her and led her into the hall.

'But she's only pretending to love you, Greg, I know it. She's only here for herself.'

'Actually,' said Acorn, stroking Cori's hair, and following them to the front door, 'I'm here for my lover and my daughter.'

Shirley started to sob.

'Okay, Shirley, you can't wander the streets like this.' Greg turned to Acorn. 'I'm calling her a cab, babe. She can wait in the front room. I'll sit with her for a while. You go back to the others.'

When Acorn returned to the table, Ruby lit a cigarette. 'You weren't very nice to Shirley, Acorn. What's wrong? Did she hit a raw nerve?'

'She was trying to ruin the evening, Ruby, for everybody.'

'She's a kid in love.'

Acorn sat down, wafting the smoke away from her face. 'Well, Greg's moved on. And the sooner she accepts it, the better for her.'

'Perhaps I should go and sit with Shirley,' said Anna, getting up, 'instead of Greg.'

Acorn smiled at her. 'Thank you, honey.'

Ruby watched her go. 'I'd say Greg's moved backwards not forwards.'

'Greg has done both, Ruby. He's connected the past and the present and found his future. '

'How poetic.'

'I think so.'

'But then, what do you know?' slurred Ruby. 'You think one photo-shoot with your daughter and it makes up for six years pissing about.'

There was a brief silence before Acorn spoke. 'Greg doesn't like smoking in the house. Can someone take this poison outside?'

'Come on, Ruby,' said Johnnie, taking the cigarette from her hand and crushing the lit end between his fingers. He pulled her up. 'Let's go. You can smoke outside.'

'Get off me,' Ruby broke away from his grasp, stepping back and knocking her wine glass off the table. It caught the edge of her chair and shattered, leaving shards of glass on the seat. 'I can smoke where I fucking want.'

Anna came back into the room with Greg behind her. 'What's going on? Are you okay, Ruby?'

Johnnie started to pick up the fragments of glass, but Greg stopped him. 'Forget that, mate, I'll do it later.'

'Come back with us, Ruby,' said Anna. 'The party's over.'

'The party never fucking was,' shouted Ruby. 'I know you're embarrassed, Anna, but don't get all pitying and uptight. Shirley's the only one here with the guts to tell the fucking truth. You all sit there not saying a fucking word to help her. Acorn came back here to save her shitty career, and we all know it.'

'I don't think that,' said Lou, staring straight at Ruby through the thick curls of her kohl-painted face. 'I think Acorn's fantastically brave, and frankly, you seem to be the fucking mess. Do you always get this drunk? Can't you control yourself at all?'

'Stay out of it, Lou,' Will grabbed his sister's hand.

'Let's take her home, Johnnie,' said Anna. 'Come on Cass, Andy, we're going.'

Andy glanced at Will as they both got up. 'At least you've met the neighbours.'

Will smiled. 'And you, again.'

'Come on, Ruby, everyone's leaving.' Johnnie reached towards Ruby and pulled her arm.

'Fuck off me!' she yelled, pushing him away. He stumbled, catching his hand on the broken glass and cutting his fingers.

'Okay,' he said, fumbling in his pocket, blood seeping into the denim. 'Forget it!' He threw a key onto the table. 'It's over, Ruby.'

She laughed. 'You're pathetic. With your little latch-key.'

'And you're a fucking drunk—'

He turned away and she grabbed his hair, tearing two of his dreadlocks with her fists. Johnnie's reaction was fast and final. He lashed out, striking Ruby in the face. She fell to the floor, her head slamming against the wall. Everyone was silent.

'Jesus! Ruby, I'm—'

'Just go!' yelled Cass, running around the table and pushing him away. 'Go!'

Johnnie staggered through the kitchen with Greg following

behind. Moments later a motorbike roared past the house and into the street.

Chapter 20

On the Rebound

'Thanks for coming,' said Shirley as Iain sat down at their table. He shrugged awkwardly. 'I got your number from the card you gave me and I thought we might be able to help each other. Do you want a drink?'

Iain nodded. 'Lager.'

'Right,' Shirley pushed back her chair, and walked as casually as possible to the counter. It was six o'clock and the café was half empty. A lone man in a suit was talking into his mobile and eating a plate of salad. A group of women were sharing the same pot of tea and arguing about yoga. Jasbinder was serving. 'Hi, Jaz, can I have two lagers?'

'Is this the new boyfriend Pearl was telling me about?' she said, pointing to Iain.

'God, no,' said Shirley. 'I only said that to Mum. You can put them on her tab, by the way, I'll sort it with her later.'

Jaz nodded and opened the fridge. 'Is your mum upstairs?'

'With Uncle Charlie,' said Shirley, grimacing.

Jaz gave her two bottles of Spanish lager. 'And you don't like him?'

'Well, you know,' drawled Shirley. 'He wears women's clothes!'

Jaz watched her coolly as she took the bottles off the counter and walked over to Iain. He was shuffling in his chair, sweating. Shirley put his drink in front of him. 'I suppose you want to know what this is all about.'

'Yeah, unless you just wanted a date with me.'

Shirley didn't smile as she sat down. 'It's about the Acorn story in *The Southside Student*. Everyone in college knows you sold it to the tabloids.'

Iain shifted uncomfortably, 'Yeah, that's journalism.'

'Who told you? Was it Rachel?'

'I never reveal my sources. So don't think—'

'I know it was her. She's always been jealous of me and Greg. You see, I'm his girlfriend, so I know all there is to know about Acorn. I was there when she came back for Cori. What do you think of that?'

Iain licked a drip of lager off the side of his bottle, dragging his tongue across the label. Shirley watched, repulsed. He smacked his lips. 'What do you want me to think?'

'That I can give you the inside story.'

'And what's in it for you? A 50/50 cut?'

'I'm not doing this for money.' Shirley leant forward and whispered. 'I want revenge. I want you to help me get revenge on Acorn.'

'Ah,' Iain, raised his eyebrow, a man of the world. 'Revenge.'

'Greg and I were really happy together until she came back,' blurted Shirley. 'I'm going to show Greg that she's a big fraud, pretending she loves him and everything after all these years, pretending to love Cori. I want him to kick that pretentious cow out.'

'Good story, that, "Acorn Rejected As Fraud".' He spelt it out in the air, and glanced at Shirley. 'I mean, obviously, the headline would sound better than that when I'd had time to think about it.'

'So you'll help me?'

'Well,' said Iain, leaning towards her over the table. 'That all depends on two things.'

'Which are?'

'Firstly, what do I have to do? I can't be involved in anything illegal, you know.'

'Well, I haven't thought it all through yet, but I want to get to Acorn's—'

'And secondly,' interrupted Iain, 'does this mean we're going to be friends?'

'Yeah,' Shirley shrugged, 'I suppose so.'

Iain grabbed her hand and licked it. 'I mean real friends.'

Shirley pulled away, rubbing her fingers on her trousers. 'You really are a sleazebag, aren't you?'

Iain shrugged. 'Revenge is a sleazy business, Shirley.'

'I'm not putting out for you, creep. So you can forget it.'

'I'm not asking you to.'

'You make me sick.' She folded her arms and sat back in her chair. 'Can't you just be nice for a change?'

'You don't get anywhere being nice, Shirley,' said Iain, copying her movements and leaning back in his chair. It was a little body language trick he'd learnt from his editor. 'You want to be nice, then send Acorn a good luck card. Send her a wedding present.' Shirley bit the side of her fingernail, not looking at him. 'Just watch Acorn take everything away from you. Acorn, the wonderful mother, it'll be all in the papers. You can watch the whole world lapping it up, she's a changed person, you've got to admire her, a TV star, everyone loves her. And all the time you'll know the truth. And only you. She doesn't even love him, she's got—'

'All right,' said Shirley. 'So will you help me?'

'I'll think about it,' said Iain. 'What are we having to eat? I trust this is all on you?'

'Maybe,' said Shirley. 'But if you're not going to help me, you'll have to pay yourself.'

'I've told you, Shirley. I will help, but on those two

conditions. It's you that has to make the decision. Are we going to be friends or not?'

Upstairs in the flat, Pearl had made a spaghetti bolognese. 'They'd kick me out of the café if they knew about this, you know. Spag Bol with real cow in it.' Pearl gave a plate to Charlene.

'You are wicked, Pearl.'

'Not half as much as I'd like to be.' She sat down next to Charlene on the sofa and balanced the plate on her knee. 'I wonder how Shirley's getting on with this new boyfriend.'

'Well, they've been down there for hours.'

'She needs some cheering up,' said Pearl, forking a ball of spaghetti into her mouth. 'Ever since that business with Acorn she's gone round like something the dog's peed on.'

'I'd say there's a girl right here needs some cheering up too,' said Charlene, putting her hand on Pearl's knee. 'Maybe you should follow Shirley's example. Get yourself a boyfriend.'

'Me? A boyfriend? Now I don't know whether to laugh or cry.' Pearl put her plate on the coffee table while she unscrewed the wine. 'Who's going to want me? I've got more baggage than a coach trip to France.' She put down the bottle and grabbed her stomach with both hands. 'And the spare tyres to match.'

'Don't put yourself down, love. You just need a pick-me-up.'

'Pick-me-up? Nobody could get me off the ground!'

Charlene poured the wine. 'That's not true, Pearl. You've got a lovely figure. Any man would go wild for you.'

'Oh, Lene,' said Pearl, swigging back the Lambrusco. 'I know you're only trying to help, but it's hopeless. I didn't meet anyone before I took Gordon back. Why should I meet anyone now?'

'You have met someone.'

'Who?'

'Me, Pearl.'

Pearl laughed. 'Well, I know I've met you, but I thought you meant boyfriends, you know—'

'I did.'

'Oh.'

'Don't you like me?'

'Of course I do, you daft sausage! But not like that. I couldn't. It wouldn't feel right.'

'Why not?'

'Well, I mean, the dresses, it's lesbianity, isn't it? And you're my friend. I know you've got a man's thingy and everything, but . . . Oh, I don't know what to think.'

'Would it be better if Charles was here, Pearl? I've brought a suit with me.'

'I don't know now. I'm all confused, Lene. I thought we were just friends.'

'And now I've gone and embarrassed you. I'm sorry, Pearl.'

'No, I'm flattered but . . . you're Gordon's . . . well, brother, aren't you? It doesn't seem right.'

'Oh yes,' said Charlene, with a twinkle in her eye. 'Just think how cross he'd be if he heard about it.'

Peal glanced at her. 'Cross? He'd be climbing the bloody walls! Pam would have to knock him down with a golf club!'

Charlene laughed. 'And we don't want to upset him, do we?'

Pearl smiled. 'Oh Lene, do you think we could? I . . . no, we can't.'

'We can. If you want to . . .'

'But the food's getting cold, just sitting there like that.'

'Never mind the food. I want to make love to you.' Charlene ripped off her wig.

'I don't know what to say.'

'Don't say anything, Pearl, just kiss me.'

'I've never kissed lipstick.' Charlene leant towards her and their mouths met. Pearl pulled away. 'That lip-gloss tastes just like Cointreau. Is it Chanel?'

'Clinique,' said Charlene, as they rolled over on the sofa. 'I've always wanted you, Pearl. You're all woman.'

'You too, Lene, I mean . . .'

'I'm a man underneath, Pearl. I'd like to show you how much of a man—'

They were interrupted by the front door swinging open and banging against the partition wall. Shirley had brought Iain up to the flat after he had insisted on seeing her bedroom in return for his involvement in the revenge. She had drunk more than she'd meant to, and told him she was planning to break into Greg's house and go through Acorn's things looking for evidence against her. After that he had held out for physical contact. Now she stood in the doorway staring at the sofa in disbelief.

'Oh my God!'

Charlene jumped up and grabbed for her wig. She and Pearl were smeared in the same red lipstick. They both smoothed their ruffled blouses.

'I don't believe this! How sick can you get?'

'Shirley,' said Pearl. 'Your Uncle Charlie was just—'

'Uncle Charlie?' said Iain, his eyes dancing with glee.

'Yeah,' slurred Shirley. 'This is my uncle! You thought I was a nice girl, Iain? From a nice ordinary family? Well, so did I. But now I know different. Let me tell you about my family, Iain,' she leant on his shoulder, and waved her finger in his face. 'My dad's been screwing around for years, and we've just found out that I've got twin brothers I never knew about. And then there's Uncle Charlie, who is not dead like I was told, but sitting on the sofa, wearing a dress and calling himself Charlene. And now to top it all, I find out my mother is a bloody lesbian.' She glared at Pearl. 'I'm taking Iain into my room and I do not want to be disturbed. EVER AGAIN!'

She grabbed Iain's hand and pulled him across the lounge, slamming the stable room door. 'God, I hate my family!'

'Fucking hell!' said Iain, leaning against the horsebox. 'And

I thought you were Miss Squeaky Knickers. You're the coolest chick I've ever met!'

Shirley narrowed her eyes. 'Are you taking the piss?'

'What? No way! What a family!'

'I hate them!'

Shirley sat on the bed, legs swinging out of the open side of the horsebox. She still hadn't got any other furniture in her room. All her clothes were folded in piles on the floor, but she couldn't bear to make the room seem more permanent. 'You're right! I am Miss Squeaky Knickers! If I wasn't, Greg would never have left me.'

'Shirley! What are you talking about?' Iain moved to face her. 'You're the hottest girl in college!'

'Do you think so?'

'I've always fancied you!'

'You fancy everyone.'

'You the most!'

'Really?'

'Yeah,' Iain sat next to her on the bed.

'Iain, I don't want to be nasty, or anything, but I think you should know I don't fancy you.'

'That doesn't matter.' He kicked his boots off and lay down. He had yellow nylon socks on.

'I don't want to hurt your feelings.'

'I understand.' He put his hands behind his head and threw Mr H off the pillow. 'You're not the first girl to tell me I repulse her.'

'I didn't say you repulse me.'

'You didn't have to. Did you design this bed?'

'God, no! I hate it! The most unsexy bed in the world. My mum did it with Uncle Charlie.'

'Ha, that figures! They want you to be a goody-two-shoes, while they go around like a load of perverts.'

'Yeah, that's right, perverts! That's what they are,' she yelled. 'Perverts!'

'So are you going to kiss me then?'

'What?'

'Do you want me to help you or not? You can close your eyes if you want.'

Shirley took a breath and leant forward. Close up Iain's face was pink and soft and his lips were chapped. She grimaced.

'Go on!'

She kissed him. It wasn't like kissing Greg. When she kissed Greg it mattered so much she was terrified of not being good enough, of not arousing him, of being ugly. With Iain it was payment for services rendered. She was by far the best-looking of the two of them, the more experienced, the confident one. His mouth was champing down on hers eagerly, desperately. She felt sorry for him. But more than that, she felt excited by her power over him. She felt aroused. She put her hand on his trousers to see what he would do. He whined. She pushed it further into his pocket and he whinnied. He was red in the face. She laughed and sat up over him. 'I think that's payment enough.'

'Shirley, please don't stop!'

'I've kept the deal.' His eyes pleaded with her. 'But maybe I could be nice to you.' She pulled her jumper off. 'If you said please.'

Iain nodded. 'Please, Shirley.'

'You promise you're going to help me expose Acorn?'

'I'll do anything.'

'Will you steal for me?' asked Shirley, unhooking her bra.

'Yes,' Iain nodded, panting. 'Whatever you want.'

'Okay,' said Shirley. 'But remember, I don't fancy you. At all. I'm just doing this out of charity.'

She allowed him to bring his sweaty head to her breasts. She was about to have the most exciting sexual experience of her life.

Chapter 21

Saying Goodbye

Pearl and Shirley watched from the back of the café as Gordon ushered Nick and Jack Smedley through the painted swirls on The Cosmic's door. The three of them stood awkwardly by the counter, the two boys zipped up to the chin in fur-lined parkas, Gordon stiff in a blue blazer and cream slacks. Anna smiled from behind the counter. 'Hi there, Gordon.'

'Hello,' said Gordon. He coughed. 'I'm meeting Pearl.' His fingers just touched the glass at the front of the counter as if making sure it was still there.

'She's sitting at the back of the café. I can take your order to the table if you want.'

'Right, thank you,' said Gordon, glancing to where Pearl was sitting with Shirley. The café was quiet. On the nearest table a middle-aged man was writing in a notebook, spooning mushroom risotto into his mouth without slowing his pen; further back a mother was feeding her toddler lentil soup, which he was flicking on the table, and two women were giggling over cappuccino. 'Well, boys, what would you like to drink?' The Smedley twins didn't look at their new father.

One shrugged, the other stared silently at the floor. 'They'll have two fizzy pops,' said Gordon. 'Whatever you've got.'

'And for you?'

He checked his watch. Six o'clock. 'A glass of house white. A large one,' he added, moving towards the back of the café. He paused several feet away from where his old family were sitting. 'Pearl, Shirley.' He stepped up to the table. 'How are you?'

Pearl was brusque. 'Fine, thank you, Gordon.'

He nodded, and dropped his gaze briefly to watch his hands slide over the chair-back in front of him before smiling at Shirley. 'And how are you, my love?'

Shirley shrugged. Under the table, Pearl nudged her with her foot. 'Fine.' Another nudge. 'Thank you . . . Dad.'

'I'm glad.' He let his gaze wander back to Pearl. She was rearranging the three yellow flowers crammed into the vase on the table. 'It's good to see you again, Pearl.'

'Is it?' She didn't look up.

'Well, anyway . . . here are the boys.' The twins had shuffled through the café behind him. 'Nick and Jack, you remember Pearl, and Shirley, your half-sister.' The boys stood unmoving, their faces mostly hidden by their oversized fake-fur hoods. 'Why don't you two sit down?' Gordon pulled two chairs out for the boys. They sat on them, obediently and silently.

'The fireworks should be fun tonight, boys,' said Pearl, trying to see into their hoods. 'They do a brilliant show on the common, don't they, Shirley?'

'Suppose so!'

'And it'll give you three a chance to get to know each other, now we've found out you're sister and brothers.' She paused to glance at Gordon. He shifted in his chair. 'It'll be fun, won't it, Shirley?' said Pearl, not taking her eyes off Gordon and gesturing for Shirley to speak. Shirley shrugged and bit at her fingernail. 'Well,' sighed Pearl after several seconds had passed in silence. 'Gordon. Are you all sorted for somewhere to stay?'

'Hotel in Clapham.'

'Nice?'

'Very pleasant.'

'That'll be nice then.' Pearl stared at the top of the shiny grey hoods, locked together and bobbing about like two seals. The silence stiffened. 'Well . . .' she said, 'how's Pam?'

'She's very well.'

'Good.'

Gordon drummed his right hand on the table. Over his shoulder, Pearl watched a young couple with a pushchair struggle through the café door. 'And Charles,' she said.

'Charles?'

'He's well.'

'Oh,' Gordon began drumming with both hands, his fingers automatically tapping the national anthem.

'Did you get the boys a drink, Gordon?'

'The girl there is bringing them over.'

'Right.'

'Her name's Anna,' said Shirley.

'Sorry?'

'Anna. The waitress.'

'Oh.'

'Why don't you take those boys to choose some dinner, Shirley?' said Pearl.

'Mum!'

The boys disappeared completely into their coats, their hands burrowing into their sleeves like startled rabbits.

'I don't want any arguments, Shirley. Help your brothers, please. You can all eat something while me and your father sort out his things up in the flat.'

Shirley stood up. 'All right. Come on then.' The two boys followed Shirley to the counter.

'Well,' said Pearl smoothing an imaginary tablecloth. 'I suppose this is it, Gordon. We've reached the end of the line.'

'Perhaps we could—'

'You go your way, I go mine.'

'Pearl, I—'

Shirley was back. 'Do you want a burrito?'

'A what?' said Gordon.

'Not for us, Shirley.' Pearl turned back to Gordon. 'We probably won't meet again until Shirley's wedding.'

'No way am I getting married!' blurted Shirley, turning back to the counter. 'Not after the mess you've made of it.'

'Well, there you are then, Gordon. What more is there for us to say?'

'Nothing,' mumbled Gordon.

'I've filed for divorce,' said Pearl. 'I should have done it months ago. I don't suppose you can object to adultery, given the circumstances.'

Gordon hung his head. 'No. Can we talk about this upstairs, Pearl?'

'Of course, I'm just letting you know. I want everything split down the middle. Except Shirley, of course. You can keep paying for her university until I get the money out of the house.'

'Pearl, I'm—'

'I hope you're not going to fight me over this, Gordon, I'll not be diddled over the house.'

'A white wine' said Anna, 'with a complimentary flapjack.'

'I'll have that,' said Pearl, taking the plate. 'You can bring your drink upstairs, Gordon. Put it all on the tab please, Anna.'

'No really, let me pay for it,' said Gordon.

'Don't worry, Gordon, you will.'

Anna went back to counter. Shirley had chosen burritos all round and Anna buzzed up to Cass in the kitchen. 'Three burritos, Cass. And will you ring Andy, see if Florrie's okay?'

The intercom crackled. 'If he needs us he'll ring here. Stop worrying.' Anna let go of the button. Shirley and the boys had gone back to the table. Anna folded the cloth in her hands and found jobs to do behind the counter. She rearranged the cakes, stirred the salad bowls, wiped the surfaces, served two new tables. It was the first shift she and Cass had worked together at the café. The first time Andy had looked after Florrie since splitting up with Tony.

Eventually Cass came down with the burritos. She served them herself and walked over to the counter. 'It's bloody quiet tonight.'

Anna took her apron off. 'Cass, do you think I could go back home? Just work a short shift tonight?'

'Stop worrying, Anna, Florrie's fine. And for all we know we could get twenty people in here in ten minutes.' The door opened. 'See, here they come.' Cass turned around. Ruby was standing at the door, her dark hair flat against her face, the black line of her split lip vivid against her red lipstick. 'Hey, Ruby, are you okay?' Cass offered her a stool by the counter. 'I didn't think you were coming out tonight.'

Ruby shrugged. 'I changed my mind. I wanted to see you.'

'Well, it's great to see you,' said Anna. 'Shall I get you a cup of coffee or something?'

'I'll have a bottle of house red, Anna, to share with you two.'

'Have something to eat with it, Ruby. What would you like? Cass could make you something special. Have you had anything today?'

Ruby smiled. 'Just get some glasses, Anna.' Anna glanced at Cass and reached for a bottle of Merlot. 'I called into your house just now,' said Ruby.

'Did you see Andy? Is Florrie okay?'

'She's fine. They're watching "Teletubbies".'

'See!' said Cass. 'I told you there's nothing to worry about.'

Ruby arranged the glasses on top of the counter and took the open bottle from Anna. 'Let's have a toast. To Florrie.' She poured large measures and they clinked glasses and drank. 'Please, God, she has a happy life.' Ruby drank again. 'And to your family. Back together as friends.' She finished her drink and poured herself another. Anna was about to say something, but Cass checked her. They watched Ruby staring into her wine, fingering the scab on her lip.

'You all right, Ruby?'

'I had a cuddle with Florrie. Told her what a lucky girl she was.'

'You're so good with her,' said Anna, taking the bottle off the counter, out of Ruby's reach. 'She loves you.'

'Yeah,' Ruby smiled, not looking up. 'I told her what I'd learned about life.'

'Blimey, bet that was an eye-opener for her,' said Cass. 'Let's hope her first words don't shock the Health Visitor.'

'And was Andy okay?' Anna asked.

'Anna's worried,' interrupted Cass, 'because the doctor's put him on valium. He's spaced out of his face. I've told him, he just needs a new man in his life.'

Anna frowned and shook her head at Cass. Nobody had heard from Johnnie since Hallowe'en. Ruby put her hand across Anna's. She had scratched her red nail varnish into ragged doodles. 'It's okay, Anna. You don't need to protect me. I know Johnnie's not coming back. I don't want him to. I'm over that now.'

'I know, I just didn't want you to feel—'

'Upset? I'm fine, really.'

'You know what we need,' said Cass, 'a girls' day out. Loads of shopping, slap-up meal, bit of a dance. What do you reckon, Ruby?'

'Another time,' she said standing up. 'I'm not really up for it now. Listen, I'm going home. Too exciting here for me. You two finish the wine.' She turned to go.

'Bye, Ruby. Take care of yourself tonight.'

Ruby looked back. 'Give me a hug,' she said, her arms reaching out to them. She held Cass tightly.

'It'll get better, Ruby,' said Anna, wrapping her arms around her. 'You chill out tonight.'

'Yeah, I will.'

'And if you're at home tomorrow, I'll bring Florrie round and we can shake, rattle and roll.'

'That sounds splendid fun, darling,' said Ruby. 'But sadly, I'm going to have to miss it. I won't be around tomorrow.'

'Ruby,' called Shirley as Ruby reached the door, but Ruby didn't hear her. She left without looking back. Shirley sat down again and picked up her burrito. 'That's my friend, Ruby,' she said to the boys. 'It was thanks to me that she got together with her boyfriend, Johnnie, he's a great friend of mine too. You see, I usually have these fantastic firework parties, you know, much better than the common, and everyone gets off with someone wonderful around the bonfire. It's so romantic.'

'Who did you get off with?' asked one of the twins, the first words he'd spoken to her.

'It's not the same for me,' said Shirley. 'I'm the hostess.'

'No one then,' said the other twin.

'Actually,' said Shirley, biting into her burrito. 'His name was Iain and I'm still seeing him.'

'Everything you came with is in that suitcase,' said Pearl, standing on the exact patch of carpet where Gordon had once knelt. 'And in those bags are the things you bought when you were living here. I don't want you saying I've had anything that's yours.' Gordon walked towards the sofa, put his wine on the coffee table, and picked up a plastic bag. He looked inside. A pair of jeans, some T-shirts, wrap-around sunglasses. He dropped it and picked up another. A bomber jacket.

'I won't be needing these, Pearl.'

'Well, I don't want them,' said Pearl moving to the kitchenette and pouring herself a scotch. 'I thought you liked them.'

'I did, I mean . . .' he dropped the bag. 'I won't be wearing them now.'

'Now that you're back in Frinley.'

'Yes.'

'I don't suppose Pam likes you in a T-shirt.'

'No. You know Pam, she's a collar and tie sort of woman.'

'Collar and lead more like,' said Pearl, not realising how right she was.

'Anyway,' said Gordon. 'I think it's better if I just leave those clothes behind.'

'Like you're leaving me!'

'Pearl,' he moved toward her. 'You know how much I wanted . . .'

'What?' Pearl put her hand on her hip. 'What did you want, Gordon?'

'You, Pearl! And this!' He gestured to the things around him, the flat, the café, the London rooftops beyond the window. 'This other life.'

'Too late for that now!'

'I know . . . and . . . I'm sorry.'

'Are you?'

Gordon nodded. 'Oh yes.'

'And what exactly are you sorry for, Gordon?' said Pearl, pulling out one of the dining chairs and perching on the edge. 'For lying to me for twenty years? For being caught with your pants down? Or because now you're having to pay for it?'

'Do you want the truth, Pearl?' asked Gordon sinking back on the sofa. 'I'm sorry for everything. That I lied, that I was caught. But most of all I'm sorry that we had a new start and it was snatched away.'

'But you're not sorry you're with Pam?'

'I'd rather be with you, Pearl.'

'Tough, you should have kept your pants on.' Gordon nodded. 'Well, I suppose you'd better get downstairs. Those boys will be waiting. You'll get the solicitor's letter soon enough.' Gordon picked up his suitcase and walked to the door. Pearl didn't speak until his hand was on the latch. 'You know what I don't understand, Gordon. How you ever thought you'd get away with it! Did you really think you could move in here and leave all those years of betrayal behind?'

Gordon put the case down. 'No.' He turned around to face her. 'But you'd done it, hadn't you, Pearl? Escaped. Left us all behind in Frinley.'

'I made a new life for myself, Gordon. It hasn't been easy for me, moving here, all these new people.'

'But you've done it. You're still here. Living in Bohemia.'

'No thanks to you!'

'No, but then maybe that's the difference between us. I was never going to fit in here, was I? The Cosmic Café! For God's sake, who was I trying to fool?'

'You've been fooling everyone for years.'

'I've been fooling myself.'

'I won't argue with that.'

'And I was fooling myself to think I was going to be a New Man. I've learned my lesson, Pearl. Frinley's where I belong. On the golf course. Not here. Not wearing jeans and sunglasses. I think we both knew that really.'

'I thought you could do it.'

'So did I. But then there's no fool like an old fool.'

Pearl watched him pick up his suitcase and leave without saying goodbye. She stood on the landing watching him as he walked down the stairs, hoping for a glimpse of his grey hair curling up at the back of his neck. She didn't go back into the flat until long after she'd heard the café door open and close two stories below. Not until Gordon and his children were out in the cold, watching fireworks.

Chapter 22

Fireworks

Ruby stared at the tablets in her hand, the valium she'd got from Andy and four strips of paracetamol. It was probably enough. She hoped so. She put them on the table next to the vodka and lit a cigarette. The bruise on her lip was tender, but she pressed the filter against it and let the smoke curl around her tongue before dragging it down. Anna had bought her a book, years before, *How to Give Up Smoking the Easy Way*. It had said to do this, to inhale slowly. Ruby held her hand over the smoke, and watched it spill around her palm, threading through her fingers. She remembered laughing at Anna, as she stood on the rug, reading that book aloud. Now Ruby, imagine this is your last ever cigarette, taste it in your mouth, feel the smoke in your lungs. Ruby looked at the cigarette in her hand. Here she was, doing it for real. Her last ever cigarette. Anna's voice echoed in her mind. It says here that if you really want to quit, Ruby, it's not difficult at all. And when you faced the facts, it was true. It was, as they had said all along, not hard to give up.

She put the cigarette in the ashtray, carefully squeezing it into a groove in the glass. Outside she could hear the fireworks exploding, sizzling and sinking in the sky, leaving red shimmers above the rooftops. She twisted the top off the vodka. Should she get ice, a slice? Do it properly? Or just pour it down her throat? She poured it into the glass, keeping the bottle balanced on the rim until it was full. The notes were already written, one for Johnnie, one for Anna and Cass. The apologies given, the excuses made. There wasn't much to say in the end. But she wanted them to know what little there was. She was tired. Tired of the memories. Tired of being wrenched by guilt and anger. Tired of screwing up. That's what she was leaving behind, not them. Her will was waiting for them at Stokes, Coffin and Hand, her father's solicitors. She couldn't resist that final bitter irony.

She picked up the glass and the cigarette. One last drag. The vodka burnt her lip. Then the tablets. She looked at them, white and innocent in her palm. She had always thought that she'd do this with more style, more drama. Diving into the Thames off London Bridge, throwing herself in front of a train at Waterloo Station. Playing to the audience right to the end. But when it came down to it, she wasn't so different. Just alone in her front room with a handful of pills. She put a valium onto her tongue and drank it down. And then another. A paracetamol. Another.

The phone rang. Ruby closed her fist around the pills and sat motionless on the sofa. The ansaphone clicked onto its usual *Cabaret* impression: 'Put down the mobile, the fax and the phone, this woman is out to play. Life is a Cabaret my friend. Leave a message and I'll ring back if I like you.' She smiled grimly. Not this time. It was Anna.

'Hi, Ruby, it's me. Don't worry about picking up. It's just that it's dead quiet and I thought I'd ring to see if you were okay. If you fancy a drink or something next week, bit of a chat, you know, just give me a ring. Okay, hope you're chilling out and everything. Bye.'

The phone clicked into silence. Ruby opened her hand.

There were nine tablets sweating in her palm. She tipped them into her mouth and gulped down most of the vodka. It was too much. She retched, coughing up the tablets into her lap. Vodka dripped down her nose, bile rose in her throat. She lit another cigarette to take the taste away and picked the valium off the wet creases in her skirt. One at a time, she put them back into her mouth, sipping the vodka. He skirt was sodden against her legs so she stood up and let it slide to the ground. In a few hours nobody would be worrying about her fat thighs.

She sat in her knickers finishing off her cigarette, and slowly working her way through the pills on the table. She didn't want to be sick. Perhaps that was enough. When could she just lie down? She was starting to feel woozy. The phone clicked again, but now she was only half listening. Anna's voice filled the room.

'Ruby, I've just realised that today's your year anniversary with Johnnie. Why didn't you say? No wonder you're feeling a bit low. Why don't I come round after work? What do you reckon? If you're up for it, give me a ring at the café, and I'll steal us a bottle of wine. Okay, bye.'

'Hi, it's me again, Anna. If you're there can you pick up the phone. I'll hang on here until you get to the phone . . .'

'Hi, I'm here.'

'I was getting worried then. Is everything okay?'

'It's all fine, sweetie, Florrie's all snuggled up asleep, and I'm just about to put my feet up with a plateful of pasta.'

'Thanks, Andy. I thought I was going to get away early, we were so quiet before, but now the bloody café's packed, so it's going to be a late shift.'

'Honestly, sweetie, don't worry. We're all happy bunnies here.'

'Good.'

'And if you find me slouched on the sofa when you get back, don't tell anyone about the dribble.'

'Your secret's safe with me.'

'Listen, Anna, I've got to go, there's someone at the door.'

Andy put the phone down and glanced at his hair in the hall mirror. Not bad. He scrunched a handful at the front and teased a couple of spikes into place before opening the door. It was Doris.

'Oh my God,' said Andy, his hand over his beating heart. A firework burst in the sky behind her, framing her head with a green halo. 'What do you want?'

'Where's Anna?' said Doris, one lace-up shoe on the threshold.

'She's not here,' said Andy. 'She's working.'

'And where's that baby?'

'Asleep.' Doris was trying to look past him into the hall. 'Sorry, Mrs . . . um, Karloff, whatever your name is, what is it you want exactly?'

'Why are you here?'

'Well, not that it's any of your business, but I'm babysitting.'

'Why aren't you still in prison?'

'Right, I'm shutting the door now.' Over Doris's shoulder Andy could see Will coming out of his house. A white spray screeched through the sky. 'If you want Anna, call tomorrow.' He shut the door in her face and went back to the front room. He waited a few seconds, ready for the bell to ring again. It didn't so he sat down in front of his pasta. Then it rang.

'For fuck's sake.' Andy dropped his fork, and stomped to the door, yelling. 'I've told you, Anna's not here.' He opened it. 'Oh . . . it's you.'

'Hi,' said Will. 'Have I come at a bad time?'

'Um, no,' said Andy, looking over the garden wall. 'Sorry, I thought you were that weird old bag from next door.'

'Well, I'm not.'

'No. Sorry, I mean, Anna and Cass aren't in. I'm just here babysitting.'

'I know. I saw you just now at the door. That's why I came over. To say hello.'

'Oh . . . I see . . . well, hello! Do you want to come in?'

'Thanks.' Will wiped his feet.

'You've got trousers on.'

Will looked at his legs. He was wearing lime green flared cords. 'Pardon?'

'It's the first time I've seen you with trousers on, as the faggot said to the bishop. Oh God, what do I sound like? Just ignore me, sweetie, I'm having a bad year. Do you want a glass of wine or something?'

'Thanks.'

Andy showed Will into Anna and Cass's sitting room. His massive plate of pasta squatted on the coffee table like a reproach.

'I didn't realise you were eating.'

'Would you like some? I don't normally eat enough to feed a small village, by the way.'

'Are you sure?'

'About you or the village?'

'About me.'

'Absolutely. I'll get you a plate.'

'Okay, Ruby. It's me again. You haven't rung back, so I know you don't fancy a drink tonight, but would you do me a favour and just pick up the phone because I'm beginning to get a bit worried about you. You know what I'm like. I know I'm being a complete pain in the arse, as usual, but just pick up the phone to make me feel better. Unless you're asleep. Or with someone? Is Johnnie back? Okay – just ignore me, I'm being pathetic. I won't bother you again, I promise.'

'Andy, it's me . . . Can you pick up? . . . Okay, you're probably with Florrie, I hope she's okay. But do me a favour, Andy, just look out the window to see if Johnnie's bike's outside Ruby's. She's not answering the phone, so we were sort of wondering, since it's their anniversary, if he's come back—'

'Hi, Anna.'

'How's Florrie?'

'She's fine, not a peep.'

'And you've got the monitor on?'

'Yes, yes.' He covered the mouthpiece. 'And I've got someone here. We're having a meal.'

'Not Tony?'

'Of course, not Tony!'

'Oh good, you had me worried then. Who is it?'

'Will, the guy from across the road.'

'OOOOOooooo.'

'And you can stop that, Cilla.'

'He's gorgeous!'

'I know,' Andy whispered into the phone. 'And I'm about fifteen years too old for him.'

'Bollocks. I thought he fancied you the other night.'

'Did you? You never said. Do you think he does? Really?'

'Definitely.'

'But, I don't know, Anna. It doesn't feel right. I mean, don't you think it's a bit weird? After everything that happened with him and Tony.'

'Maybe it was all meant to be, Tony would go for Will, but really it was you and Will who were destined for each other.'

'Very romantic, sweetie! But it's only been two and a half weeks since that whole police business. I'm not even beginning to get over Tony. Oh, I don't know, I'm just a big mess. And these tablets make me make me feel like I'm flopping about all over the place.'

'I'm sure Will could help you there.'

'Ha, ha! That's not what I meant!'

'Well, he's there and ripe for the plucking.'

'And, as you say, he is gorgeous!'

'So what are you doing chatting to me? Get off the phone. Get back in there. Me and Cass will stay at the café as late as possible. Oh, Andy, there is one thing, before you go. Will you just look out the window for me?'

'Hold on, sweetie!' Andy took the phone to the door and looked out. 'His bike's not there, Anna.'

Ruby was drifting, dreaming. There were voices, noises, colours outside the window. She smiled, her eyes closed, sinking into the cushions under her head. The vague sense of Anna's voice filled the room, but the words were meaningless.

'Ruby, can you hear me? I'm on a break so we can talk for a while if you want. Ruby, would you pick up the phone? I'm worried about you now. Ruby, I don't even care if you are asleep and I'm being stupid and waking you up. Just please pick up the phone.'

'I thought Ruby might be here.'

'She was,' said Anna. 'She went home hours ago.'

Johnnie sat on a stool by the counter, the same stool Ruby had sat on earlier that night. 'I tried her there. She wouldn't open the door.'

'Do you blame her?'

'No.'

Anna smiled over Johnnie's shoulder at two middle-aged dykes leaving the café. 'Ruby loves you, Johnnie. But what you did . . . I don't know what you expect.' She walked away and left Johnnie alone at the counter while she cleared the empty table. He watched her for a while, but she ignored him. He stood up to go. 'When you see Ruby, just tell her I was looking for her, okay?'

'Okay!' Anna listened to him leave, pushing her cloth over the worn wood of table six. The café door opened again and this time she looked up. A group of student types were bunching around the counter. Through the window, she could see Johnnie walking across Balham High Street towards his bike. She glanced at the busy tables, at the crowded counter, and left the café. Stepping out onto the pavement, she called over to him. 'Johnnie, wait!' The lights had changed and the street had filled with traffic. She called again, but Johnnie had his helmet on. He kicked the bike into life, and pushed it out into the traffic. 'Johnnie,' yelled Anna, waving her cloth, 'Johnnie!'

Steering the bike into the flow of cars he roared away from her. Anna watched him race towards Clapham and put her cloth down. She went back into the café. There were customers to serve.

She took the new orders – three lasagnas, two nachos and a salad – and buzzed them up to Cass, speaking slowly into the intercom on the wall. 'Oh, and, Cass, Johnnie was here and I didn't even tell him.'

'Tell him what?' said a voice behind her. Anna turned around, switching off the intercom. Johnnie was back, standing at the counter. 'I saw you in my mirror. You were calling me back.'

'I'm worried about Ruby, Johnnie. I think you should go back there, now.'

'She doesn't want to see me, Anna.'

'Make her tell you that. Make her open the door.'

'I'm not making her do anything. I hate myself for what happened, okay? I'm not about to force her to see me.'

'But you've got to.'

'Forget it, Anna.' He walked out of the café and Anna followed him onto the street, calling after him. 'Johnnie, why don't you ring her?'

'I have, okay? She's not answering.'

'Can I use your phone?' He shrugged, unzipping his leather jacket, and threw his phone to Anna. It connected to the ansaphone. 'Ruby, I know Johnnie's not there because he's here, so will you pick up the phone?' She shouted above the noise of the traffic and the teenagers letting off rockets in Safeways car park. 'He wants to talk to you but you wouldn't answer. You can hear I'm worried, Ruby. I know you weren't going anywhere tonight so why won't you pick up the phone? Ruby, I get off in two hours and if you don't pick up this phone I'm coming round whether you want me or not.' She hung up and looked at Johnnie. 'Do you think she was in?'

'The lights were on.'

She dialled again. A thirty-something suit opened the café door. 'Excuse me, are you serving or what? I'm waiting to order here.'

'Well, you'll have to wait a bit longer,' said Anna, the phone to her ear. 'I'm dealing with a personal emergency here.'

'You should be dealing with your customers!' He barged past Anna as she waited for the ansaphone message to finish. 'Okay, Ruby, listen to me. I'm going to keep bugging you until you pick up the phone! Ruby! Answer this fucking phone, Ruby! RUBY!' Passersby walked around her as she screamed into the phone, but Ruby didn't answer. Anna hung up. 'I'm scared, Johnnie. I think she might have done something stupid.'

'Hey, what's going on?' Lou ran across Madrigal Close towards the biker kicking Ruby's front door. She stopped in the middle of the street. 'Stop! I'm calling the police.'

'Johnnie!' screamed Anna, running into view. 'She's on the sofa in the back room.'

They disappeared around the side of the house and Lou followed. She looked through the rear window as Johnnie and Anna tried the back door. Ruby was lying on her side, a vodka bottle and plastic pill cases on the table in front of the sofa. There was vomit on the carpet. 'Oh, my God!' She fumbled in her bag and found her mobile to ring the ambulance.

Johnnie picked up a metal chair from Ruby's patio and threw it at the back door. It cracked the glass but didn't shatter it. He picked it up again and smashed the legs against the door until the glass gave way. Then he stood on the chair and climbed through the ragged gaps, his biking gloves protecting his hands. Once inside, he threw Anna the key and ran to Ruby. Lou watched through the window as he lifted her up in his arms and dragged her to her feet. Anna was fumbling with the keys, crying. She dropped them, and stood on the chair. 'No!' Lou ran over to her. 'For God's sake, don't be stupid. If you try to get through that way you'll cut yourself up.' She picked up Ruby's keys, opened the door and rushed inside.

'Stop it,' she said to Johnnie. 'Put her down. You have to leave them. Listen to me. I know about overdoses. Put her back on the sofa. I've seen this all before. Please!' She pushed past Johnnie to get to Ruby. 'We have to see if she's breathing.' She got her face powder compact out of her bag and held it over Ruby's face. The mirror misted faintly. 'She's alive.' She felt her wrist. 'But her pulse isn't good. Look on the floor. See if there are any pills down there. The paramedics will need to know what she's taken.' She glanced over the table. 'This is just paracetamol.' She picked up a smaller tablet. 'But this is something else. Tranquilliser probably. Was she on tranqs?'

Johnnie looked to Anna, who was standing in the doorway, hands over her mouth, tears welling in her eyes. He shook his head. 'Well, it doesn't matter. She could have gotten them off the street. I'll take them and wait for the ambulance outside.' She took Anna's arm as she left the room. 'Come on, Anna, I'll make you some tea in the kitchen.' Anna allowed herself to be led away, glancing back at Johnnie as he knelt over Ruby and sobbed. Behind them, vivid through the dark sash windows, silver fireworks exploded across the sky.

Chapter 23

Framed

'Honey, you look gorgeous. The cameras will love you.' Acorn stepped into the hall. 'Lou, this is Mina, my make-up girl.'

Mina, who in spite of anti-oxidising, free-radical beating, wrinkle-lifting foundation looked a good fifty, didn't smile. 'You'll need some powder on those kohl patterns,' she said.

'Now,' said Acorn, 'we'll need the biggest room in the house.'

'Upstairs,' said Lou, leading the way. Will had cleared out his bedroom for Lou's big artistic break, painting Acorn's portrait for the 'Eco-Pops' gallery. All the furniture except the tatty '30s wardrobe, which was too heavy to move, had been piled into Lou's small studio at the back of the house. And Lou, who had been trawling through skips and scouring municipal dumps for anything that might be useful for the portrait, had stored all her finds neatly in a corner of the room. 'Will's bedroom's the biggest, but the light's no good.'

'No matter, honey,' said Acorn. 'I'm after that impoverished artist feel.' Lou opened the door. Will's room had been painted dark brown, orange and cream, but the damp still showed through where the roof was leaking in the corner above the wardrobe.

'Perfect,' said Acorn, walking to the damp corner. 'I'll stand here. Now, have you got the materials we agreed?' Lou pulled on a lumpy dustsheet and revealed an array of old paint tins, glue tubes, wood, clothes, curtains, and plastic objects. Acorn looked at them with distaste. 'And you think you can do something with that? Remember, experimental's good, but it's got to be flattering.'

'Hello!' A voice called from downstairs.

'That's Shaun, the cameraman. Wait there.' Acorn stood on the landing. 'Is Tracey with you, Shaun?'

'She's in the van.'

Acorn went trotting down the stairs, shouting up instructions as she went. 'Mina, don't touch those black swirls. I want Lou to keep that look.'

Mina opened the toolbox.

'Who's Tracey?' asked Lou, looking out of the window into the street. There were two white vans parked outside the house.

'Director/producer,' said Mina, reaching for the make-up remover. 'They all slime like slugs whenever she's around.'

When Acorn came back up with Tracey, Shaun and Mina had already rearranged the room, the lights and Lou's face. Lou looked at herself in Mina's mirror, new swirls, same design (from cheekbones to ears and eyebrows to temples) perfectly finished. She smiled. 'You're good, Mina.'

Mina nodded without smiling.

'Tracey, this is Lou, our young artist, isn't she gorgeous?'

'Charming,' growled Tracey, extending her hand. She was wearing black leather trousers and an unflattering purple shirt that rouched where it was tucked in at the waist. Her brown hair was cut exactly like Lou's elderly father's in his pre-war school photo: shaved at the sides, two inches long on top and greased into a centre parting.

Lou took her hand and shook it, gently. It wasn't hard to see how to get on with Tracey. Lou glanced at Acorn with interest. She avoided her gaze.

'Are you ready for us, Lou?' asked Tracey.

Lou smiled. 'I think, Tracey, you're what I've been waiting for.' Behind Tracey, Will was leaning sleepily against the bedroom doorframe, watching. He'd just got out of Lou's bed and was wearing her dressing gown. He mouthed 'Slut!' Lou turned away.

'Okay,' said Tracey. 'Are we going for three parts? I think three. And what were we giving it, one twenty each? Let's make it one eighty. Lou, I'm giving you nine minutes to strut your sexy stuff.' She winked, reminding Lou of their village butcher back in Rutland, who always gave her mother extra steak. 'So it's materials and backgrounds today, structure and collage part two, finishing and unveiling in three. Okay with you, Acorn, darling?'

'Perfect, Tracey.'

'Right, you two sort out the chat. We'll start filming in thirty. I'll be in the van.'

She passed Will on the way out. 'Who are you? The lover?'

'The twin.'

Tracey didn't break her stride. 'Better and better.'

Will walked into his emptied bedroom. 'Does Tracey smoke cigars?'

Acorn looked up. 'No, why?'

'Final touch, you know. Just thought she would.'

Lou didn't look at him. 'Will, I need this time with Acorn.'

'Don't get nervous, darling, I'll go in five.' He smiled. 'I just wanted to wish you luck and see how you are after last night.'

'I'm fine.'

'Did she pull through?'

'I don't know.'

'What's happened, honey?' asked Acorn.

'Ruby took an overdose,' said Will.

'Really? Last night? That's so weird because I've been dreaming about her falling off a cliff. But then she reeked negativity, didn't you think?'

Will shrugged. 'She drinks.' He glanced at Lou, 'They're all like that.'

'For someone like me though, honey, she was a really polluting presence, so for me,' Acorn pressed her hands to her breasts, 'the world is better without her.'

'She might not be dead,' said Lou sharply. 'She was still alive when the ambulance came.'

'God, did you hear it?' said Will.

'I've been at my city flat, honey. I can't stay too many nights here, even for my darling Coriander. It's the air. I suffocate if I stay too long south of the river.'

'It was v. exciting. I was just about to make a move on Andy and all hell broke loose. The guy who hit her was there on his bike and Anna from across the road went in the ambulance. But Lou was the star of the show.'

'Were you?'

'No!'

'You were. She rang the ambulance, did all the stuff, sorted them all out.'

'It's not as if we haven't been through it before, Will.'

'Yes, but that's with Mummy, it's different with a stranger. If Ruby's still alive, it's thanks to you, Lou,' said Will, looking out of the window. Shirley was hovering on the opposite side of the road. 'Mind you, when Mummy took that overdose last year she was back home next morning. Perhaps Ruby didn't make it.'

'Will, can we please get on! We've got to rehearse for the show. I've got to start painting.'

'We can't do it now, Shirley.'

'Why not?'

'There are people here,' said Iain, pulling his woollen hat further down his face. 'We'll be seen.'

Shirley pulled the hat off his head and threw it to the ground. 'If you don't want to help me, Iain, just go home. And we'll pretend the other night didn't happen.'

They were standing opposite two white vans parked in the road outside Greg's house.

'They look like workmen,' said Shirley, looking at Tracey. 'Probably on a break. We'll wait them out.'

Iain picked his hat up. 'They're not workmen. They're TV. Look.'

Shaun came out of the house with a camera over his shoulder. 'Tracey, Acorn's asking for you upstairs.'

'But that's my old house. What are they doing there?'

'I don't know,' said Iain. 'But I think we should come back tomorrow.'

'Wait!' said Shirley grabbing his sleeve. 'Don't you see? This is perfect. If that bitch is filming next door we can keep an eye on her.' Greg's old van was not by the side of his house, so Shirley knew that he must be out on a carpentry job. And Coriander would be at school. Acorn was the only danger, and now they knew exactly where she was. 'If she comes out, or Greg comes home, just ring the bell and tell them you're a fortune-teller. I'll sneak out the back and hide in the shed until it's safe. It's not even as if I'm breaking in,' said Shirley, waving a key in Iain's face. 'After all, I never gave it back.'

'This is stupid, Shirley, you're bound to get caught. And what if they see me hanging around and ask me what I'm doing?'

'They're filming. Say you want Acorn's autograph or some-thing. Come on, Iain, you're the journalist, don't be such a baby.' She pulled up the drooping zip on his jeans. Why was it that men like Iain could never quite fasten their trousers? Did he think a sagging fly was a turn-on? Like an off-the-shoulder dress? She took pity on him. 'Remember, there'll be a reward if you help me.'

Shirley looked across the road to make sure no one was sitting in the vans, and then slipped up the path to Greg's house. The key was like melting butter in her hand and her stomach felt like a walnut rolling up her throat. But she wasn't going to back down now. She glanced at Iain wandering up the pavement and opened the door. Inside, the air was musty and the familiar smell smothered her resolve. She had to be quick. She tiptoed up the stairs to the bedrooms. She didn't know exactly what she was looking for. Just something that would show Greg what Acorn was really like. A diary, letters, photos. She opened Greg's bedroom. It looked the same as it had when she was sleeping there. Same yellow sheets, same jeans and socks thrown over the chair in the corner. Shirley opened the wardrobe, the chest of drawers. Some boringly plain knickers, a tarty bra, and a small parcel of lavender. Peeping out of the window, she could see Iain, pacing up and down on the pavement, eyes fixed on the house next door.

In Coriander's room there was a framed photo of Acorn with Ant and Dec, and several snapshots of Acorn, Greg and Cori childishly pressed together in a large clip frame. The spare room was just as she'd left it, even the newspaper cuttings that she chewed in despair and spat onto the floor were still there, dried onto the boards. She went downstairs, glancing in the front room, tiptoeing through to the dining room. There were two small bags on the table. Shirley unzipped the larger one. Clothes. She rifled though, hoping for the crackle of paper, expecting any minute to hear the doorbell, but there was nothing. The other bag was full of toiletries, all herbal and animal free. She pushed it away and felt something hard. There was a pocket inside. She opened the bag again, feeling along the material at the side until she found a concealed zip. Inside was a set of keys, a purse, some letters, a diary. Shirley held the keys in the palm of her hand. Acorn's flat. That's where she would find what she was looking for. She scribbled down Acorn's address from one of the envelopes: Church Street, Stoke Newington, and opened the diary.

Leafing through, it was impossible to decipher, with strings of initials and shapes under various dates. Shirley looked up the October day Acorn had turned up in Greg's life. It was marked $C+$ P^*. What did that mean? Cori, perhaps, and . . . what? There was no mention of a G for Greg, not until Hallowe'en, which said $C+$ $G+\square\square\square$. Shirley puzzled over it, flicking through the stars and squares in November, looking for more references to Greg. In December, several pages had been completely scored through and *EP Lapland* written across them. Shirley flipped over them to Christmas Day. It just said *Mxxx*. The weeks before were full of $C+P^*$ or $C+$ *get* P^*. But what did it mean? Presents perhaps? Get presents for Cori. But Acorn hadn't brought her a present when she turned up in October. She'd brought the paparazzi. Shirley flicked back through the pages, C always had P^* after it. Then Shirley thumped her fist on the table. The press, photographers, papers. Acorn was using Coriander for publicity. She turned back to the scored pages. Did they mean that 'Eco–Pops' would be in Lapland? That Acorn would be out of the country? Shirley tossed the keys in her hand. That could be her chance. All she needed to do was copy the keys before Acorn got back, and persuade Iain to do one more stint as a lookout.

'My name's Ruby Gold and I'm an alcoholic.'

'Well done, Ruby,' said Maureen, the group's counsellor. 'And since this is your first time with us in the group, perhaps you could just tell us a little bit about what got you to this particular place in your journey.'

'You mean apart from the train.'

Maureen smiled patiently.

'And all those lovely flavoured vodkas.'

'Yes, apart from that.'

'Well, I suppose you must want me to say that I had a pretty good stab at killing myself.'

'You stabbed yourself?' asked the suicidal alcoholic on the plastic chair next to her.

'Pardon?'

'Did you stab yourself? Me too. Wayne, Exeter.' Wayne lifted his T-shirt to show her the livid scar across his abdomen.

Ruby was impressed. 'Wow, that's pretty cool, Wayne.'

'Ruby, I think this is a good time to tell you the rules of the group,' said Maureen, still smiling, but thinly. 'This is the

Building Up Self-Esteem for Self-Harmers group, or BUSES
for short. And the first rule of being on the BUSES is—'

'No mooning?'

'—is not praising self-inflicted injury.'

Ruby nodded. 'I get it. Not big and not clever. So, Wayne,
how did you do that?'

'Bowie knife.' Wayne mimicked the action of slicing his own
abdomen. 'I wanted my bitch girlfriend to find me in a fucking
bloodbath.'

'And did she?'

'Naw, Grunge went off his fucking head. Had to lock him
in the fucking kitchen and call a fucking ambulance.'

'Grunge?'

'My dog. Thought he was going to eat my fucking guts
before I'd fucking died.' Ruby laughed. 'It's not fucking funny.'

'No. So was Grunge put down?'

Wayne's eyes widened. 'No, he fucking wasn't. He's a
fucking pedigree. He's with my nan.' Wayne pulled his T-shirt
down and turned away from Ruby to face Denise, thirty-three
with arms criss-crossed like graph paper. 'Sick cow.'

Ruby smiled. She was beginning to enjoy herself.

Maureen coughed. 'If we could get back to welcoming
Ruby.'

Ruby looked around at the others. Richard, on the other
side of the circle, in his mid-fifties and a cardigan, smiled
shyly at Ruby. He looked so naïve she almost wondered if he
wasn't in the wrong room, bluffing drug addiction and suicidal
tendencies because he was too embarrassed to admit he should
be in Beginners Spanish. Except there weren't any other
options here. No woodwork or ballroom dancing, certainly no
wine tasting. The whole place was a remote residential retreat
for people like her who had finally stopped clinging to the arse
of society: the addicts and the drunks. Private payers, following
in the footsteps of the fat and famous, and the funded, those
whose social workers had squeezed the tit of local government
for so long that a single drop of the milk of human kindness

had finally come their way. Ruby wondered where Richard fitted.

Next to Richard there was Norman from Bromley, also older and permanently on the verge of tears. He avoided Ruby's gaze, leaning into his lap to hide his face. In the forty years since leaving school, Norman had never unpinned the scrawled 'Kick Me' sign from the back of his jumper. Ruby was amazed that he'd lived this long. The others in the circle of chairs were of less interest to her. There were the inevitable thin white men, all in their early twenties, angry and twitching, in withdrawal. She had been through many men like that before she met Johnnie: them sponging off her, her using them for sex. And she was tired of them. Even suicidal she deserved better than that. And then there were the women. Five of them including Denise, all of them either terrified or belligerent.

'Could you tell us about trying to kill yourself, Ruby?'

'Well, it was nothing like as exciting as being eaten by my own dog.'

'I'm sure it was meaningful to you, Ruby.'

'I just took a few pills and was sick on the carpet.'

'And you survived.'

'Obviously.'

'And how do you feel about that?'

Ruby shrugged. 'Surprised.'

'You didn't expect to live?'

'I wasn't taking those tablets for a headache, Maureen.'

'I mean you weren't expecting to be found.'

'No.'

'And would you like to tell the group why you wanted to die, Ruby?'

Ruby looked around, at Wayne, still ignoring her for insulting his deranged dog, at Denise scratching her scarred forearms, Norman discreetly wiping his eyes with the cuff of his jacket. 'Because living was too painful.'

'Do you still feel that way, Ruby?'

'Yes.' Why would she have changed her mind? After a week

with the monastic order of the twelve steps, a week of one-to-one therapy with Jeremy, she still wished she had died. Not enough to try again, not right now. But enough to remember the disappointment she felt when she opened her eyes and saw Anna's anxious smiling face, when she felt Johnnie's smooth hand holding hers.

'And what makes living so painful, Ruby?'

Ruby looked at the faces around her, some looking at her intently, waiting for the answers, some staring at the floor, at their scars, at their knees. 'Memory,' she said. 'Horror, guilt, rage.' She had become good at key words in her sessions with Jeremy. She now knew, thanks to Jeremy, that repressed anger was the toxic waste of her emotional life, that tears would water her soul, and that each day was a new beginning.

'Thank you, Ruby,' said Maureen. 'Everyone has a different answer to that question. But all of us have to accept ourselves and our pasts to move into our futures.'

'So how do you feel?' Johnnie sat on a stone bench at the side of a gravel path in the grounds of the retreat, his helmet by his side. 'Or are you sick of being asked that?'

'If I am, you're the only one who's realised.' Ruby walked in circles on the grass in front of him.

'You're looking good, Ruby.'

'So are you.' She smiled and they settled into silence. 'I suppose you're going to ask why I did it?'

'No.'

She nodded and walked away over the grass. He picked up his helmet and followed.

'How was the bike on these country roads?'

Johnnie shrugged. 'It'd be cool in summer.'

'I'll remember that next time.'

He smiled. 'You do that.'

They walked as far as a hollow in the lawn where the frost hadn't melted and the grass was crisp and pale underfoot.

Ruby looked back to the house and its backdrop of tall, skeletal trees.

Johnnie followed her gaze. 'It's a beautiful place.'

'Yeah,' said Ruby, turning away. 'Your typical loony bin. Looks like heaven, feels like hell.'

Johnnie walked backwards, still looking at the house. 'What are the others here like?'

Ruby shrugged. 'You know, saddos, weirdos, losers. And that's just the staff.'

He smiled and took her hand. They walked together across the grass and back to the gravel path that led to the car park. 'I'm waiting for you, Ruby.'

'I know.'

'I'm still living at the house, but if you want me out, I'll just go.'

She shook her head. 'No, I need someone there to stop Doris looting it.'

They stopped at the bench and sat down. Johnnie put his arm around her and she leant on his shoulder. He stroked her hair. 'It'll get better, Ruby.'

'Don't tell me, "Every day is a new beginning".'

'Something like that.'

'How about "Pain is the root of knowledge"?'

'Too depressing.'

' "Only those who dare truly live"?'

'Now that I like.'

'Me too. I'll make it my mantra.'

He nodded to the house. 'So who feeds you all this new-age stuff?'

'My counsellor, Jeremy. He's the freakish offspring of Oscar Wilde and Patience Strong.' She glanced at Johnnie. He was just looking at her, smiling.

'I love you, Ruby.'

As the sun went down behind the house, he was still holding her in his arms on the cold stone bench, hoping that all their words and kisses would make her want to live.

Chapter 25

Mamma Mia

'What are you looking so pleased with yourself about, Shirley?' The back door of the café banged open as Pearl and Charlene came down from the flat. Shirley, sitting at the far corner table with Iain, closed her denim bag and put it out of sight on her lap.

'Nothing! We're trying to have a private conversation, if you don't mind.'

'Well, don't mind us. We're off out now. So what do you think then, you two?' Pearl opened her coat and spun around. She was wearing a cream jumpsuit with a brown crocheted waistcoat. 'Show them, Lene.'

Charlene's blond wig was crammed into a white woolly hat. She had on knee-high white boots and, when she undid her coat, a short white belted dress.

'Bet you can't guess where we're going,' said Pearl.

'The loony bin,' said Shirley. Iain snickered.

'The Abba musical! We've been looking forward to *Mamma Mia* for weeks, haven't we, Lene?'

'Eons.'

'You know, Iain, me and Lene loved Abba from the moment we saw them on Eurovision. They used to call me the Dancing Queen in Frinley. Did you know that, Shirley?' Shirley stared at her mother, stony-faced. 'I suppose you were probably too young to remember.'

'Thank God!' Iain whispered, smirking.

'We'll be off now then. Oh, Lene, hold on. Let me just do something with your eye shadow.' Pearl smudged her finger across the iridescent blue line under Charlene's eyebrow. 'You're all lopsided.' She reached into her bag for a tissue, licked it and rubbed it across Charlene's eyelid. 'That's better. Shirley, does that look better to you?'

'Perfect, very flattering, Uncle Charles.'

'Oh, I can see you're in a mood, Shirley. Come on, Lene. Let's leave these young things to be cool and sulky while we oldies go and have a good time.'

As soon as the café door was shut, Shirley opened her bag. 'You wouldn't believe how many of these little video cassette things there are in Acorn's flat, Iain. She's got a whole wall of them, and they're all marked up with exact dates. And I reckon that 'M' character in her diary's definitely her boyfriend. There's photos of him everywhere, and shaving foam in the bathroom.' She fumbled in her bag. 'Look, I got this one, 19 October 2001. That's the day when she came back. What do you think's on it?'

'Don't know,' Iain shrugged. 'Video diary?'

'Well, I want you to find out.' Shirley shook several more cassettes out of her bag.

'Me?' said Iain.

'You can make me a tape from these in the college editing suite tonight.'

'No way!'

'You told me you could use the editing suite any time you wanted. 24/7.'

'I can.'

'So! What's the problem? Acorn's coming back from

Lapland in two days. I want to get these back on her shelf tomorrow and have a look at her PC while I'm there.'

'I won't do it.'

'Why not?'

'Duh, let me think. Oh, yes, because I'll get caught with stolen tapes.'

'Not if you're careful.'

'Not if I don't do it.'

'I thought we were in this together.'

'No one will touch a story from stolen tapes. There's nothing in it for me.'

'Iain, you can't back out. I need you.' She glanced at his pink face. 'Anyway you've had lots out of this already.'

'Yeah, breaking and entering. Twice.'

Shirley held up one of the cassettes. 'Doesn't it make you feel excited, being a criminal?'

'No!'

'You know, sort of powerful that you've taken something that's not yours? Like, dangerous?'

Iain shook his head. 'Not when there's nothing in it for me. It makes me feel like a mug.'

'It makes me feel dangerous, Iain. What if I came to the editing suite with you? What if we locked the door so there was just the two of us? Would you do it then?' Shirley licked her lips, slowly drawing her tongue around her mouth.

'You said you weren't doing that any more, after last time.'

'I say that after every time.'

'There's no lock on the editing suite.'

'Oh.'

'But, your mum's out.'

Shirley smiled. 'We could play in the stable room. What do you say?'

Iain nodded.

'But what's in it for me?' said Shirley. 'What will you do for me, Iain?'

'The tape,' he mumbled.

'Say it again,' said Shirley, cupping his face in her hand and kissing him.

'The tape,' he said. 'I'll do the tape.'

She smiled and led him to the horsebox.

'I wish I'd put my ordinary shoes on, Lene, I'm not like you. I can't walk in these heels.'

'Hold on to me, Pearl, I don't mind.'

Pearl took Charlene's arm and they turned off Balham High Street into Bedford Hill. The rain had left a damp film on the pavements and the concrete glistened under the streetlights. A woman carrying her week's groceries pushed past them, Safeways' bags clinking against her swollen calves. 'You know,' said Pearl, watching the woman's bent back as she hurried up the street, 'I don't think I've ever been to Soho.'

'Well, your eyes are going to be opened tonight, my girl.' Charlene slowed up, surveying the display of wigs in a shop window.

'Eyes opened, legs closed. Story of our lives, hey, Lene!'

'If only it was the other way around!' They laughed and Pearl leant her head against Charlene's shoulder.

'Of course,' said Charlene, gently kissing Pearl's head. 'It could be different.'

Pearl pulled away. 'Don't, Lene. I told you last time. It wouldn't be fair on Shirley if I started up with another man now, especially not with you.'

'Because of this?' Charlene gestured to her reflection in the shop window.

'Well, I don't think that helps. But you being Gordon's brother is enough to upset her. You saw how moody she was tonight. She's a very sensitive girl, Shirley. She knows nothing of life.'

'Unlike that crowd.' Charlene pointed to the reflection of a crowd of teens and pre-teens walking up Hildreth Street behind them. Pearl turned around.

'Oh, they shouldn't be drinking at their age.'

'Let's get going, Pearl, we don't want to attract their attention.'

'Attract their attention! They don't want to attract mine more like. Frinley may be many things, but at least you didn't have gangs of kids drinking and mouthing off in the streets.'

'Pearl,' said Charlene, 'Let's just walk to the station. We don't want to miss the show.'

Pearl took her arm. 'I would never have let Shirley out drinking at their age. Half of them are just children.' A chorus of laughter sounded from across the street and Pearl looked over. One of the older boys, wearing a grey hood over his face, pointed at them and pretended to be sick. She looked away. 'It's not right, Lene. At least the boys have got hats on. Those girls must be freezing to death in those little skirts.'

'Just keep walking, Pearl. Ignore them.' Behind them the gang were crossing the street, swinging bottles and cans, a few of the girls stumbling and leaning into each other, the older boys leading the way. Pearl could hear them heckling and jostling behind them. They were focusing their attention on Charlene.

'He looks like your mummy, Ducca.

'He looks better than Ducca's fucking mother.'

'Fuck off.' An assault of laughter.

'Just keep going, darling,' whispered Charlene. 'They'll leave us alone at the station.'

Three boys started walking beside them on the road, matching their stride, imitating their nervous steps. Pearl clung onto Charlene's arm, trying not to look at the boys inches away from her, marching along the yellow lines. A few of the girls ran in front of them and blocked the pavement ahead, shouting obscenities. Charlene turned Pearl towards the road, looking for a gap in the traffic. 'Let's cross.'

'Don't push so hard, Lene,' said Pearl. 'They're only children for all their filth.' A lorry hurtled past them, splashing water up their legs. 'And now look at my costume!' Pearl stepped back and her bag was yanked off her shoulder. 'What the . . .? Give that back.' Pearl turned on one of the smaller girls, she guessed her to be about twelve, who was waving the sequined gold bag above her head. Pearl moved towards her with her hand outstretched. 'All right, you've had your fun. You've made yourself feel big. Now give me that back.' The girl threw the bag to her friends and Pearl swivelled around as it sailed over her head, scattering tissues and coins onto the pavement. She faced the others jeering behind her. 'Do I have to call the police?'

'Give the lady her purse back!' yelled Charles's voice. Pearl turned back in surprise. Charlene had gone now.

'You going to make us, faggot?' It was the boy Pearl had first seen. He slouched towards them, his eyes almost hidden by his hood, swinging a bottle at his side.

'If you're the leader of this rabble, then tell them to give the lady her bag,' said Charles. Pearl reached for his hand and wrapped her fingers around his palm.

'Come on, then!' the boy said, taking a final swig from his bottle and smashing it into a lamppost. 'Let's see what you can do, you fucking faggot.' He held up the jagged glass neck, slicing the air in front of him. 'What, scared I'll cut your tits off?' The others laughed, moving forward, circling around them. Pearl glanced at Charles. She felt sick with fear.

'Let us go!' he said. 'We're not doing you any harm.'

'Yeah, you are! Making me look at your faggot face,' said the boy. He lunged forward with the broken bottle and Charles, moving sideways to protect Pearl, caught his heel against a drain and fell twisting to the ground. The boy stood over him, laughing, and kicked him hard in the face with his soft trainers. 'Freak!' he screamed. 'Let's teach this fucking faggot to stay off the streets!'

Pearl sobbed as girls and boys surged forward, faces smeared with hate, pushing against each other to kick out and trample on a stranger. She screamed at them to stop, pulling the smaller ones away, begging the people on the other side of the street to help her. She could just see Charles, curled and silent, on the ground. Then she heard shouting. Two men in army jackets were running towards them, swearing and threatening. The children stopped kicking and ran one after another into Sistova Road as the men chased after them.

Pearl knelt on the pavement, bending over Charles. His clothes were filthy, his white hat pulled and hanging off the back of his head. 'Oh, my love,' she said, placing her hand gently on his shoulder. He turned his head slowly and stiffly towards her, grimacing with pain, trying to smile. His face was grey with dirt and shock, blood spreading over the blue shadow on his right eye. 'Charles, my love, what have they done to you?'

'I'm all right,' he said, moving his arm carefully and squeezing her hand. He was shaking as he moved his fingers to his face to feel his teeth. 'Just a little bruised. They were only children, weren't they?'

Pearl looked up to see the two men jogging towards them. She waved, calling out thanks, but stopped when she saw their faces, their embarrassment. They stopped a few feet away and stared down at Charles, at the blond curls sticking to the blood and make-up, at the skirt pushed up over his stockings. And they laughed. Pearl cradled Charles's head, shielding him from the humiliation, as she eased the grips from his hair and removed the matted wig. His grey hair was flat and sweaty underneath. 'Oh, my love,' she said, helping him to sit up on the cold damp pavement. 'Can you stand?'

Slowly Charles raised himself to his feet, leaning heavily on Pearl for support, and limping by her side, he struggled the three hundred yards back to the café.

'I'm sorry I've let you down, Pearl. I'll replace the money you've lost. It's such a shame about your lovely bag.'

'You'll do no such thing,' said Pearl, her arm around his bruised ribs. 'And never mind about the bag.'

'I'm sorry you were frightened, though.'

'Frightened?' Pearl shifted his weight against her shoulder.

'I've never been so scared in all my life, Charles. I thought they were going to kill you.'

'They just wanted to rough me up a bit.'

'Has this happened before?'

'Once or twice.'

'Oh, Charles, why do you do it?'

'I won't hide who I am, Pearl. Not any more. I'd rather get beaten up than hide Charlene away like a guilty secret.'

'Well, you're a fool, then.'

'Maybe, but at least I'm not a coward.' Charles leant against the shop fronts as they struggled down the High Street, slow and self-conscious, ignoring the curiosity of passersby. He let go of Pearl's arm as they approached the café. 'I'm sorry about tonight, Pearl. I should never have let you go out with Charlene.'

Pearl turned to face him, and held his grazed and dirty hands in hers. 'I went out with Charlene because she makes me laugh and she's my best friend. And I'm walking back with you, Charles Gates, because you're the bravest, and most extraordinary man I've ever loved.' And she reached up to kiss him, in the middle of Balham High Street, for the whole world to see.

Chapter 26

From the Horse's Mouth

Shirley turned the corner of Madrigal Close and saw Greg sitting by himself on the stone-clad wall outside his house. She stopped on the edge of the pavement and pulled the strap of her denim bag further over her shoulder, her breath making fuzzy clouds in the cold December air. Sliding her left hand across her bag, she undid the zip and fingered the padded envelope inside. All the letters she had printed from Acorn's PC were in that envelope, together with the video Iain had made from Acorn's tapes. Greg would soon know all about Acorn's other life, about her boyfriend Milo, her plans for Cori, her secret videoing. Shirley felt the laughter exploding in her throat as she thought of Acorn being exposed. 'Hi Greg!' Her voice sounded high and breathless.

Greg looked up, rubbing his hands together and blowing on his fingers. 'Shirley, hi! What brings you here?'

Shirley stepped towards him, smiling, her hand clutching the envelope as she crossed the street. 'I came to see you. But why are you sitting out here? It's freezing.'

'Oh, right. Acorn needs the house for a while. She's got a

photographer taking pictures of her and Cori. I'd thought I'd just stay clear until they need me.'

Inside, Acorn was engaged in a photo shoot for the post-Christmas edition of *HIYA!* magazine. To celebrate the New Year, *HIYA!* wanted heart-warming stories of love and rec-onciliation, and Acorn and Coriander, newly reunited as mother and daughter, were the main feature. Ricky, the photog-rapher, had snapped them doing the washing-up, giggling together on the bed, and finally hugging by the living Christmas tree. When Ricky was happy, Acorn sent him and Cori to make coffee, and settled down on the sofa to be interviewed. Tyler pressed the button on her machine with a bronzed fingernail. 'Acorn, first, thank you for inviting us to your daughter's home. It's a wonderful story, you two being together again after so many years. I think the first question has to be, how did it feel when you saw her again?'

'Well, Tyler,' Acorn pulled the lacy sections of her gypsy skirt across her legs, 'Coriander was just a little baby when I was called out to the world, and she was a beautiful six-year-old when I returned from my weary travels. So my first feeling when I saw her was overwhelming joy, like feeling the light on your face after years in darkness. I was allowing myself the joy of being a mother again.'

'That's lovely, Acorn. But I suppose the question our readers will want to ask is why you never came back before?'

'I think I was in denial, Tyler. That's why when other people despise the media for intruding into their life, I will always be grateful. It was as if the press gave me permission to say, "Yes, I am a mother, I want to be with my child".'

'That's wonderful.'

'And, of course, honey, as soon as I admitted those feelings, out came all the maternal heartache I'd been repressing for so long. I just *had* to be with my daughter. You know, Tyler,' said Acorn, looping her beads behind her ears and moving closer, 'I think what I've been through is probably a more extreme version of what so many women suffer. Other women have their work, I have my vocation. I also had a baby. I couldn't see how to bring them together. And so, like many other women out there, I cruelly denied myself the family I deserved.'

'I'm sure our readers will be moved to read that, Acorn. And what about Coriander? How has she reacted to you coming back?'

'Well, you can see for yourself, can't you? We adore each other. In fact she wrote me this little poem just the other day. Here,' she passed Tyler a piece of paper from the table beside them. 'I've typed you a copy. You can use it in the article if you like.'

Tyler scanned the page. 'This is lovely, Acorn. She's obviously overjoyed that you're back. And it's so clever, so sophisticated for a six-year-old.'

Acorn smiled proudly. 'She takes after me.'

Shirley looked over Greg's shoulder into the house. She could see the back of Acorn's head on the sofa and the head and shoulders of a blond woman sitting next to her. 'It's for a magazine,' said Greg. 'I think Cori's dead chuffed, having all these photos done. She thinks she's famous.'

'Aren't you in the photos?'

'No way!' said Greg. 'I don't want to be in some woman's magazine.'

'Of course you don't! Greg, I've got something for you.' Shirley pulled the bag off her shoulder and gave him the envelope.

'Oh, Shirley, I can't accept a present from you.'

'It's not a Christmas present. Well, it is in a way, I suppose, but not really.'

Greg tore open the package and pulled out the tape. 'I haven't got anything for you yet.'

'I thought you had a right to know, Greg, she's just making a fool of you.'

Greg stared at the unmarked cassette. 'Shirley, what is this stuff?'

'It's what she's doing, Greg. Look!' Shirley took the envelope out of his hand and pulled out the bundle of papers. She held them up to his face. 'These are letters about her production company, Nature's Child. They've sold their first show and it's all about Cori. And these are her other ideas, look, 'That's My Dad', a game show to find sperm donors. How sick is that? There's loads more there. And this,' she snatched the tape out of his hand. 'This is what she's been taping. Everything's on here, Greg, right from that first day when she did that stupid poem on the stairs. She's filmed you the whole time she's been here.' Greg stared at her, his eyes clouding. 'I'm sorry, Greg. I know it must be a shock to find out the truth about her.'

He turned and stared at the house. Acorn was just visible sitting on the sofa. 'Where did you get it?' His jaw was clenched, his voice tight.

'Greg, I—'

He turned fiercely and gripped Shirley's elbow. 'Where did you get it? Where did this stuff come from?'

Shirley hesitated, his knuckles were white where he held her. 'They're . . . they're from Acorn's flat. She's got all these recordings. Shelves of them. You're hurting me, Greg.'

He glanced at his hand on her arm and let her go, pushing her away from him. 'Her flat?' He stood up. 'What do you know about her flat?'

'Does it matter?' Shirley backed away and stumbled over the curb. 'I did it for you, Greg.' She held out the letters and tape. 'They're for you.'

'For me? Jesus, Shirley!' Greg sat back on the wall, rubbing his fist against the stubble on his chin. 'What did you do? Break in?'

Shirley shrugged and mumbled at the ground. 'I just borrowed some stuff.'

'My God, you did break in!'

'Don't you see what she's doing? Acorn's using you, Greg, it's all in here.'

He stared at her, breathing hard. For a moment Shirley thought he might cry, or hit her. She stood awkwardly, watching him, not daring to speak. Then she put the papers on the pavement in front of her with the video on top. 'I'm sorry, Greg.' She stepped back, her empty bag clutched in her fist.

'Are you?'

'Of course! I love you, Greg.'

He shook his head. 'I don't believe this.'

'I'm still here for you, Greg, and when she's gone—'

'What?'

'—I can move back in.'

'Jesus, Shirley. You think I'd take you back after this?'

'I did it for you.'

'Well, I don't fucking want it.' He lunged forward, kicking the pile of evidence. 'Any of it.' He kicked again and the video skidded into the middle of the road, the papers scattering as the wind caught them.

'But—'

'I thought you were a nice girl, Shirley.'

'I am!'

'Oh no, you're warped.'

'You don't understand.'

'I understand plenty. Now get out of here before Acorn sees you.'

He turned his back on her, striding back up the path to his front door. As he disappeared into the house, Shirley yelled after him, 'Her boyfriend's called Milo.'

Chapter 27

The Gift Bunny

'Andy, at last.'

'Sorry I'm late, sweetie, got held up at work.'

'The Karloffs are expecting us any minute,' said Anna, looking past him into the street.

'I know, I know, the dreaded Christmas drinks.'

Anna wasn't listening. She pushed Andy away from the door and tiptoed up the cold tiled path in her Rudolph socks. 'That's strange. It's still dark.' She stood at the gate, staring at the Karloffs' house. Clumps of wire were hanging down from the two huge frames perched on the roof. It was Santa and the Gift Bunny, silhouetted against the evening gloom. 'Boris should have turned them on by now,' she said, looking back to Andy. He was standing in the doorway, gazing at Ruby's house. She tiptoed back and put her arm around him. 'Ruby's okay now, Andy. You have to stop blaming yourself.'

He shrugged. 'So you keep telling me, sweetie.'

'She could have got those pills from anywhere.'

'But she didn't, did she? She got them from me.' He went

into the house and Anna followed, glancing back at the unlit snowman in the Karloffs' concrete front garden. 'Do you think there's something wrong next door?'

Andy took off his coat and hung it on the overflowing pegs in the hall. 'Perhaps they decided against the Hammer House of Christmas look this year.'

'Then why put them up?'

'Don't ask me. Maybe Boris took a tumble with the Gift Bunny.'

'Nah!' Anna shut the front door. 'Cass has been watching him up there for days. She says the old bugger climbs like Spiderman.'

'Come on, Andy,' shouted Cass from the sitting room. 'There's a present here for you.'

'A Chrimbo pressie for me?' He peeped around the door. Cass was sitting with Florrie on her lap, an elaborate silver and orange parcel on the coffee table in front of her. He bounced over to the sofa and sat on the cushions next to her. 'Girls, it's fabulous. But I thought we were waiting for the day.'

'It's not from us,' said Cass. 'It's from an admirer.'

Andy gasped. 'Who?'

'Not telling.'

'An admirer!' He fingered the silver ribbons curling over the orange paper. 'How exciting! I wonder who it is.'

'Put him out of his misery, Cass.'

'Do I have to?'

'Yes,' said Anna, kneeling on the rug in front of them.

'Okay, it's from Doris.'

'What!' Andy shrieked.

'I think she's taken a fancy to you,' said Cass. 'Inviting you to Christmas drinks and everything.'

'Oh no! You're joking!'

Anna laughed. 'It's from Will, Andy.'

'Oh my God!' Andy slapped Cass on the arm. 'You bitch-face cow! My nerves are in shreds.' She fell back on the sofa, laughing.

Anna picked up the present and shook it gently. 'He brought it round this afternoon.'

'Really? I haven't even seen him since firework night.'

'That's because you've become a bloody hermit,' said Cass, 'hiding away in your flat all month.'

'Excuse me, Cass, sweetie, but getting arrested, rejected, and nearly murdering your best friend doesn't tend to get the party juices flowing.'

'Will will.'

'What?'

'Get your juices flowing.'

'Don't even say it, Cass! I'm such an old mess, he probably thinks I'm a charity case. I bet this present is really an OAP hamper full of tinned pineapple and corned beef. '

'I think he's got a crush on you,' said Anna.

'Well, come on! Open it!' Cass said, nudging him. 'If it cost more than twenty quid, he definitely likes you.'

'You're so superficial, woman,' said Andy. He pulled at the bow then stopped with the ribbon dropping from his fingers. 'But there's all that history with Tony.'

'But Andy,' said Anna, leaning towards him, 'didn't we all agree that if Will had known—'

Cass drowned her out, grabbing Andy's head in both hands and rocking it from side to side. 'Move on, move on, move on.' When she let him go, he re-arranged his hair and smiled. 'Remember, anything over fifty quid and it's love,' she said, helping him tear off the paper.

Andy opened the box inside. 'Oh, sweet Jesus!' he said, his hands over his mouth. 'Look at this, girls.' He lifted out a dark green silk shirt, jewelled all the way down the front edges in red, silver and black. 'It's the most beautiful thing I've ever seen.'

Anna examined the edging. 'He can't have made this himself, can he?'

'Either that or he's spent £800 at Yves Saint Laurent,' said Cass, holding one of the sleeves in her fingers. 'Try it on.'

Andy stripped off his jumper, and slid the shirt over his skin.

'It feels fantastic. What do I look like?'

'Dead sexy,' said Cass. 'That boy must be fucking talented because even I fancy you in that.'

Andy pouted at her.

'But look at the fit,' said Anna. 'It's perfect.'

Cass raised her eyebrows. 'He's certainly had his eye on you.'

'Look! There's something else in here,' said Anna, reaching into the box. She pulled out a tiny dress, made from the same green silk with jewelled velvet trim around the bottom. 'Oh, my God, look at this, Andy. He's made a matching dress for Florrie.' She leant across him to take Florrie from Cass and held the dress up against her. 'Let's put it on.'

Andy looked at his daughter dressed up in her new finery and bit his lip. 'She's beautiful,' he said. 'I think I'm in love again!' Tears were dribbling down his cheeks.

Cass laughed. 'Look at the state of you, you great pansy.'

'You should tell Will how you feel,' said Anna.

Andy watched Florrie as she played with the edge of her new dress. 'I'm too shy. It's all so romantic.'

'You have to,' said Anna. 'He's leaving today to go home for Christmas.'

'Right,' said Cass, standing up. 'If you don't get your coat on and get over there now I'll make you come to the Karloffs with us.'

Andy stood on Will's doorstep, preparing himself to ring the bell, wondering what he was going to say. Across the road Anna and Cass were staring at him out of their window and he waved them away, pointing at the Karloffs. He could see Doris's blurred shape hovering behind her frosted glass door. Suddenly Will's door burst open and there stood Lou, grappling with a large wrapped canvas. Her short, sharp hair was now purple and her face was decorated with matching spirals. 'Fuck,' she said, as a layer of bubble plastic came loose and caught on the door.

'Hi!' said Andy.

She looked up. 'Oh, hi! Didn't see you there. Do you want Will?' Before Andy could speak she turned around and yelled into the house. 'Will! He's here. I told you he would be.'

Andy grinned nervously. 'Am I so predictable?'

'Yeah.' She didn't smile. 'Will! Come on!' she shouted, picking up the canvas and lurching past Andy onto the path. 'He'll be an age,' she said. 'He's having a clothes crisis.'

'Oh,' said Andy. 'Shall I wait inside then?'

'If you want.' Lou shrugged and put the canvas on the gravel path, leaning it up against the wall.

Andy stepped into the hall, not sure whether to close the front door. He wiped his feet on the mat and smiled at Lou. In the garden opposite, Boris was fiddling with the wires draped around the down-pipe. 'The present was fabulous.'

'I know.'

Someone thundered down the stairs but it was only Mike. Andy pointed at the bubble plastic. 'So what've you got in there, Lou?'

'A painting.'

Andy nodded, resisting his urge to slam the door in her face. 'Of anything in particular?'

She pondered. 'It's Acorn. I've done it for "Eco-Pops" out of recycled stuff, you know, collage.'

'Fabulous!' Andy looked into the house to see if Will was coming. There was no sign of him. Over the road, Boris disappeared behind the frosted glass door.

'Yeah, she wants to show it to Greg before it goes to the studio.'

'So are you taking it to her?' he asked hopefully.

'She's picking it up.' They both stood there looking at the painting. Andy could just make out some flesh-pink lumps under the plastic. 'She wants to do a presentation at this drinks party. Here she comes.'

Acorn and Cori were clattering out of the house next door, giggling and holding hands. They had their fingers against their lips. 'It's a surprise!' said Cori, glancing back at Greg. He was behind them, standing in the doorway, watching Acorn as she ran down the path and over to Lou.

'Oh no, Lou honey, you've wrapped it,' said Acorn, peering down at the picture on the path. 'Darling man!' she said, walking into the house and seizing Andy's arm. 'Would you be a love and help Lou take all this stuff off it. I don't want my moment ruined by reams of . . .' she waved her other arm in the air, 'of voluminous plastic.'

'Mummy's made a picture,' shouted Cori. She'd seen Anna and Cass emerging from their house on their way to the Karloffs' Christmas do. They waved at her and she danced across the empty road. 'I'm in it too. She's giving it to Daddy.'

'That's wonderful,' said Anna, glancing at Greg. He was staring at Lou and Andy as they moved the canvas around, peeling off layers of bubble plastic and parcel tape.

'Mummy says it's fantastically talented,' said Coriander, holding Anna's hand. 'She says it shows her inner warmth.'

Lou twisted the frame to release the final layer of wrapping and even in the streetlight, the theme of the portrait became horribly clear. The picture was a 3D montage, a mixture of painting and collage. It showed Acorn standing with a baby at her breast, her body made of sculptured and painted driftwood, the baby a bisected plastic doll glued into place. Birds and insects, made of feathers and leaves, were flying over her beatific head, and animals of all sorts, some of them bits of stuffed toys, were gathered at her feet. In children's plastic letters the words 'Mother Nature' were spelt across the egg-box frame.

'Don't look, Daddy,' yelled Cori as the frame was revealed. But Greg had seen it.

'Anna, Cass!' Acorn called across the road, 'I know it's a

cheat now we've all had a glimpse, but when I present this to Greg in that little house later, will you just pretend it's a huge surprise?' She smiled broadly, teeth protruding.

Greg was walking towards her. 'There won't be any presentation.' His voice sounded like rough-sawn wood.

'Don't spoil it, Greg,' said Acorn, winding her beaded hair around her finger and turning towards Lou. 'You've been terrific, darling, you really have. I love the look you've given me.'

Greg stared down at the exposed picture leaning against the wall. 'Is this really how you see yourself?' He picked up the canvas. 'Some kind of Earth Mother?'

'It's what I represent,' said Acorn. 'Lou has perfectly captured how my public sees me.'

He frowned, examining the picture. Anna watched him tense and she bent down to speak to Cori. 'Would you like to come inside with me and see Florrie's new party dress? It's ever so pretty.' She led her into the house. Greg watched them go.

'And what about me and Cori?' He put the picture down at his feet. 'Are we just part of the image?'

'Of course not, honey.'

Across the road, light poured out from sitting-room window. Cori was standing with Anna and Cass, stroking Florrie's head. Greg stared at them, his back set against Acorn. 'So why aren't you staying with us for Christmas?'

'I've explained all that, Greg.' She rolled her eyes at Lou. 'I'm in the media rat race now. My time's not my own.'

'You're spending Christmas with Milo.'

'What? What are you talking–?'

'I know all about you, Acorn. I know about the secret filming, I know about your boyfriend.'

'Greg—'

'I know you're a selfish lying bitch—'

Acorn appealed to Andy and Lou. 'You're witnesses to this verbal abuse.'

'–and I want you out of our life!'

'You can't do that!'

'Oh yes I can. I put up with you for Cori's sake. But you're not here for her. You're here for yourself.' He picked up the picture and threw it high over the overgrown hedge. 'So you can fuck off!'

The bulky canvas hit the road with a scraping thud and Acorn's face hardened. 'I'm the one who gave birth! Coriander's mine.'

'Fuck off, Acorn.'

'You'll be hearing from my lawyers.' She barged past him into the road with Lou following. 'I'm taking her away from you, Greg.'

'Jesus Christ, you're a bitch.' Greg stared at her as if he were seeing her for the first time. 'But you're not the only one with lawyers, Acorn. You see, I've taken advice, and no court in the land will give you custody.'

'You're forgetting, Gregory, I'm famous now! I've got powerful friends.'

'No, you've got nothing. You're a sad, shallow cow. I'm the one with friends.'

Lou picked up the damaged canvas. 'Come on, darling, I'll get you a drink.' She guided Acorn towards the house, carrying the flattened portrait, dangling feathers, twigs, and torn egg-cartons, in her arms. Greg watched them go, then crumpled against the wall, his head in his hands.

'You were fantastic,' said Andy, leaning against the gate next to him and putting his hand on Greg's shoulder. 'I was really proud of you.' Greg didn't answer. 'I never knew you could be so macho, sweetie.'

'And what am I going to tell Cori?'

'Whatever makes her happy. Cori's a lucky girl, Greg, to have a dad like you. You make me realise what it's all about.'

He grimaced. 'Yeah, a load of grief.'

'No, a load of growing up,' said Andy. 'And when I get to be a Big Daddy I want to be just like you.' The jangling sound of hand-bells echoed across the street from the Karloffs' house.

'Why don't you forget about drinks with Doris and go to Anna and Cass's for a while? Celebrate Christmas with your real family.'

Will appeared, breathless and flushed, in the doorway. 'Sorry I've been so long, Andy, I had to change. I thought Lou was looking after you.' He saw Greg leaning against the wall. 'Oh, is something going on?'

Greg stood up. 'I'm just leaving.'

'I didn't mean to interrupt.'

'No problem,' Greg hugged Andy before sauntering over the road to Anna's.

'I thought I heard voices,' said Will, watching him go, 'but I was listening to *Hunky Dory* and—'

'You're into David Bowie?' asked Andy, walking towards him.

'He's my god. Why, don't you like him?'

'Does the Pope like choirboys? When I was eight, sweetie, Ziggy Stardust changed my life.' Andy smiled. 'But then that was in 1972, before you were born.'

'I was born out of time,' said Will. 'I should have been there with you.' He blushed and looked down to Andy's feet on the mat. 'I mean for the music.'

Andy coughed. 'Anyway, I just came round to thank you for this fabulous shirt.'

'You like it?'

'Like it? It's the most beautiful thing I've ever worn.'

'I was worried it was too much, you know.'

'It is, far too much. I can't accept it, Will.'

'But you have to. I made it for you, Andy, and you wear it perfectly. I won't take it back.'

'Then you'll have to accept a present from me in return.' Andy leant against the open door and reached for Will's hand. His short green nails shimmered against the fairy lights strung up in the hall. 'Will you come to Paris with me?'

'What?' Will's face shone as he stared down at his own fingers in Andy's palm.

Andy looked into his eyes. 'New Year in Paris, sweetie, just the two of us. What do you say?'

Will nodded, smiling. He wrapped his arms around Andy's neck and they kissed for the very first time. Behind them, on the Karloffs' roof, the Gift Bunny exploded in a shower of glass and golden sparks.

Chapter 28

Christmas at the Café

'We're closed,' yelled Pearl at whoever was banging on the café door behind her. She eased back in her chair, pushing herself away from the table. Most of the other café workers were still eating, talking with mouths full of food, waving their cutlery against the noise. Pearl undid her trouser button. She had only had the pâté starter and a couple of champagne toasts and already her new velvet flares were pinching. 'I knew I was too old for hipsters,' she said, lifting herself off the seat and trying to hitch them over her buttocks.

'Darling, you look eighteen,' said Charlene, leaning over to kiss her on the cheek. 'Especially with all that tinsel down your cleavage.'

'Oh yes, that's me all over, Lene, size eighteen and itchy tits.'

Charlene laughed, topping up their glasses. 'You think that's bad. I swear, this is the last time I'm making myself tinsel tits for Christmas.'

Pearl winked as she took her glass. 'We could give each other a scratch later.'

In the next seat along, trapped between Dee and Charlene, Shirley sneered into her soup. Pearl pointed across the table. 'What's that face for, Shirley? I hope you're not going to be a misery today. You could always have spent Christmas with Pam and your father.'

'Maybe I should've!' mumbled Shirley, keeping her head down, avoiding Greg sitting opposite.

'Oh, cheer up!' said Pearl, gesturing around the cluttered table. 'Look, we're all smiling, even Buzz has got his hat on.' Shirley glanced at Buzz on the other side of Dee, and he tapped his head, winking at her with his good eye. There was another knock at the door.

'Right comrades,' said Buzz, adjusting his paper crown. 'I can hear people wanting to join us and I'm going to let them in.' He stood up and blinked, swaying slightly. 'Let everyone share this good feel.'

'Dead right, Buzz,' said Cass, slapping him on the back as he got to his feet. 'Let them in. Come on, Andy, Anna, budge up you two, we'll get some more chairs.'

'I'm budging,' he said. 'Just watch the shirt.' He brushed Cass's fingerprints off his green silk sleeve.

Anna shifted her chair closer to Greg's. 'I told you not to wear the shirt Will made.' Florrie was on her lap banging two spoons on the table. 'It's bound to get crap down it.'

'Give him Florrie's bib,' said Cass from the end of the table. 'You know what he's like for dribbling.'

Andy faked a smile. 'Very droll, sweetie.'

Buzz was a little shaky on his feet after the champagne cocktails. He put his hand on Dee's shoulder to steady himself and she tutted loudly, rolling her eyes at Cass. 'You love him really,' said Cass, shifting her chair. 'Doesn't she, Buzz?'

'Yeah,' said Buzz, lunging forward and wrapping both arms around Dee's neck. He nuzzled his face into her cropped black frizzy hair.

'Off!' she yelled, raising her hand and slapping his head,

partially flattening his grey mohican. He moved away, chuckling, and hovered behind her chair.

'What d'you put in his cocktail?' Dee demanded.

Cass shrugged, shaking her head. 'Champagne?'

Without looking behind her, Dee pushed Buzz further back. 'Never do it again.'

The knocking at the door got louder and more urgent. 'What if there's a nutter out there?' Shirley said, staring at her mother, and ignoring Buzz loitering behind her. 'We could all be murdered.'

'Oh, aren't you Christmassy, Shirley,' said Pearl.

Buzz grabbed the back of her chair and grinned down at her, tilting his head to one side. She dropped her eyes, but not before noticing that most of his back teeth were missing on one side. 'Where's your fucking bourgeois Christmas spirit?' he said, rocking her chair from side to side, scraping it across the wooden floor, and walking it away from the table. When they'd travelled several feet, he let go and smiled at the others. Coriander giggled, and Shirley yanked her chair back to its place. 'I just don't want strangers,' she said, not looking at anyone and muttering under her breath. 'There's enough strange people here already.' Buzz tousled her hair and zig-zagged towards the door.

'I don't mind if they're strange,' said Andy, 'but can we just check they've washed recently. I don't want to gag on my egg-nog.'

Cass laughed. 'You're all heart, Ebenezer.'

'I don't care what they smell like,' said Pearl at the other end of the table, 'as long as you don't expect me to look after them. I've waited on strangers all year, I'm not doing it today.'

Buzz twisted the Yale and opened the door. 'Come in, comrades,' he drawled, 'and join our non-denominational winter feast.' Two people walked into the café, holding hands.

'Ruby!' Anna jumped up, Florrie in her arms, 'Ruby! You're back!'

Ruby smiled. 'We thought we'd join the festivities!'

'You look fantastic!' said Anna, pushing her way around the table. Ruby held out her arms and they hugged with Florrie squeezed between them, laughing and pulling Ruby's hair. Cass joined them, kissing Ruby on the cheek, wrapping her arms around the three of them.

Ruby looked around the table. Johnnie had already sat down next to Greg with Cori on his lap. 'Andy,' she called. 'Come here, darling.'

'Oh Ruby, I'm so sorry, sweetie.' He stumbled out of his chair and Ruby reached out to him as he edged around the table. 'I'm so sorry.'

Ruby put her arms around him. 'Darling, you've got nothing to be sorry for.'

'But if it wasn't for me being so stupid and—'

'You wanted to help me.'

'I know, but—'

'Listen, darling.' She held him by the shoulders and pushed him to arm's length. 'I want you to listen to me. I should never have asked you for those tablets. It was me who was wrong. Will you forgive me, Andy?'

'Oh Ruby!' A sob burst from his throat and he wiped his eyes with the back of his hand. 'I'm such a girl.' Ruby pulled him towards her and he crumpled against her shoulder.

Standing behind him, Anna smiled. 'He's a little emotional,' she said. 'He's in love again.'

Ruby looked over to Johnnie. 'Me too.'

'Now can anyone manage more pudding?' said Pearl, standing up with the plate in her hand. Her velvet hipsters were gaping wide at the open zip. 'Ruby, have you had enough?' Ruby nodded, passing her cigarettes around the table. Johnnie and Greg were sharing a joint with Buzz. 'Anyone?' Dee and Cass were behind the counter making coffee, Florrie was asleep on a cushion in a quiet corner of the café. 'Well in that case, I'll finish the crumbs.' She tipped the plate until the last solid

chunk of Christmas pudding slid into her bowl. 'It's a shame
to waste it.'

When Cass and Dee brought the coffees to the table, Ruby
took Anna's and squeezed onto the piano stool next to her.
Cori was sitting at a nearby table colouring a Christmas poster
with felt-tip pens. 'It's wonderful to see you, Ruby,' said Anna,
putting the cups on top of the piano. Ruby stared at the keys
and began to pick out the tune of 'Jingle Bells' with one finger.
'That was the first Christmas dinner I've eaten in over twenty
years.'

'I know,' said Anna, watching her finger prod out the hesi-
tant tune. 'How do you feel?'

'Fucking stuffed!'

Anna smiled. 'I meant emotionally.'

'Of course you did, darling,' said Ruby. She stopped playing
and put her arm around her. 'You know, Anna, I think you're
the best friend I've ever had. Not the most wild, I'll grant
you, but the best.'

'Thank you, Ruby. I love you too.'

Ruby looked away, smiling, and slapped her hands against
her thighs. 'And emotionally? I feel good. I've enjoyed myself.'

'I'm glad. You've really achieved something today, Ruby.'

'I know.' Ruby smiled. 'I got through that entire vegan
dinner without farting once. All we need now is the hokey-
cokey and my Christmas will be complete.'

'I'm up for it,' said Anna.

'I wasn't serious, darling.'

'You want me to be wild. I'll be wild!' She stood up. 'We
want to do the hokey-cokey, who's up for it?'

'Nobody,' shouted Johnnie, laughing with Greg.

'Come on, you lot. It's Christmas,' she said. 'Cass, you'll
join in!'

Cass was drinking coffee with Andy. 'With the hokey-cokey?
You're bloody joking.'

Ruby chuckled and sat back on the piano stool. 'Go for it,
tiger.'

Anna walked over to Coriander, and began colouring a pink shiny bauble on the partly-green Christmas tree. 'Cori, I bet you want to do some dancing. Shall me and you get everyone dancing?' Cori nodded and ran over to her dad. 'Greg,' said Anna. 'You've always been a good mover.'

'I don't think so.'

'Come on, Daddy!' Coriander tickled him off his chair. 'We're all dancing.'

'Look, Cass,' said Anna, 'Greg's joining in.'

'No, I'm not.'

'He will if you do. Please, Cass, do it for me. Do it for Cori.'

Cass sighed and drained her cup. 'All right, all right, if it will make you happy.'

'Hooray! Who else?'

Cass grabbed Andy's arm. 'Andy's up for it.'

'No way, sweetie,' he said, as Cass yanked him up from his chair. 'And mind the shirt.'

'Me and Lene are in.' Pearl leant back in her chair and forced her zip up. She pushed herself up without bending in the middle. 'What about you, Shirley?'

'I'm not making a fool of myself.'

'That's what you say. We'll leave you with Buzz, shall we? I don't suppose he'll grab you now he's asleep.' Buzz was slouched over the table, snoring softly, a half-smoked rollie quivering on his lower lip.

Pearl and Charlene stood together in the space Anna and Ruby had cleared for the dancing. Behind them, Greg had Coriander in his arms and was leaning against a table talking to Johnnie. Cass and Andy were sitting down again. 'Shouldn't we all make a circle?' Pearl asked looking around. 'Come on, Cass, you can hold hands with me.' Cass heaved herself up, pulling Andy with her and they joined up with Pearl. The four of them stood in the empty space. 'Let's be having you then!' said Pearl to the rest of them. Andy felt someone pinch his bum. It was Ruby. She took his hand in hers, holding

Anna's on the other side. Greg and Johnnie ambled into the circle, Cori taking Charlene's hand and smiling up at her, puzzling.

'Are you a girl?'

'Only sometimes, my love.'

'Oh,' she swung their arms together. 'I'm always a girl.'

'Well, now we're all up here like lemons,' said Pearl looking around the circle. 'I can't remember how it starts.'

'You put your left foot in,' said Andy. 'And please don't ask me how I know.'

Ruby squeezed his hand. 'In, out, in, out, shake it all about. I know you've been there, darling.'

'And hope to be back soon, sweetie.'

'I should think we've all been there, been sick, washed the T-shirt,' said Pearl loudly.

'Come on then,' said Anna, 'left foot, everyone. And you've all got to sing.' Cori put her foot on top of Charlene's outsize stiletto and they all droned under Pearl's more enthusiastic falsetto. 'You put your left foot in, your left foot out.' Charlene jiggled Cori's foot until she giggled and stepped off.

'Louder!' Anna shouted. 'In, out, in, out, you shake it all about,' Ruby winked at Johnnie as he wobbled on one leg; Andy hung onto Cass. 'You do the hokey-cokey and you turn around,' Charlene grabbed Pearl around the waist, lifted her arm, and spun her around. Greg bumped bums with Cori, and Anna danced over to where Florrie was just waking up.

'That's what it all about!'